OBLIQUITY

SPECULATIVE FICTION FROM THE PACIFIC NORTHWEST

*S*ince 1999, members of the Science Fiction Writing Co-operative have shared their passion for speculative fiction. Ann Lovejoy, Northwest gardener and writer, and Paul Hanson, manager of Eagle Harbor Book Company, founded the supportive group where, under the aegis of science fiction, writers of all sorts hone their skills in fantasy, hard science, horror, and slipstream fiction, myth, mystery, and magical realism.

OBLIQUITY

TUESDAY NIGHT PUBLISHING
SCIENCE FICTION WRITING CO-OPERATIVE
Eagle Harbor Book Company
Bainbridge Island, Washington USA

OBLIQUITY

TUESDAY NIGHT PUBLISHING, SCIENCE FICTION WRITING CO-OPERATIVE, 157 Winslow Way East, Bainbridge Island, WA 98110

First Edition: January, 2006

Acknowledgments

We owe special thanks to Kathleen Alcalá, Brian Herbert, Ann Lovejoy, Tamara Kaye Sellman, and Douglas Heinlein for their help and participation in the production of this book.

This project is supported, in part, by the City of Bainbridge Island Arts and Humanities Fund, administered by the Bainbridge Island Arts and Humanities Council.

STORIES

LODESTONE
An Orphan's Tale

PAUL HANSON

My first memory is not of the faces of loving parents looking down upon me in my crib, nor of a comfortable home seen from child's eyes. No, my first clear memory is simply of a cup. It is a simple metal cup with filigree knot work purfling the lower half and, carved into the surface of the upper half, an intricate letter C. I have spent long hours staring at this cup, tracing the maze of knots and whorls, the interweaving always leading my eye on a new path. Since I was only called Guillard, the C held no significance to me as yet beyond my wondering at its meaning.

This cup was my sole possession in a home where such luxuries were not commonplace: an orphanage in the town of Bayonne, a prosperous village on the coast. At the mention of the word "orphanage," readers at this point may shake their heads and tut their tongues, expecting a tale of woe or abuse at the hands of my wardens. However, considering my circumstances, I could not have hoped for a more pleasant home. We were all well cared for and amply fed. Our caretakers took our welfare to heart. Being sufficiently funded, they were neither greedy nor stingy. More so, they were anxious to educate these many youths left in their care.

Our appointed teacher, Master Bart as we were expected to address him, had a most unorthodox method of teaching—although we had never known any other so it seemed perfectly right and fitting. Sometimes it was remedial, sometimes advanced, but it always consisted of a steady if rather haphazard progression through the alphabet. He would decide upon a particular theme and gather us in the great room in the left wing of the orphanage where we arranged ourselves at the three long, ink-stained oak tables running the width of the room. Planting himself grandly erect behind the podium, he would grasp its edges tightly and in his eucalyptus voice state quite plainly the subject for the day's lesson. After a dramatic pause, he would turn from the podium, write the word with an extravagant flourish upon the chalkboard and accompany it with a quick sketch that, as likely as not, barely resembled the subject at all. He was a captivating storyteller who rolled his R's thrillingly and we relished his long and eloquent, if rather pointless, relation of anecdotes, tall tales, fables, and Bible verses. The length of each lesson was subjective, depending solely upon the depth of his knowledge on a particular subject.

I was always most anxious for the arrival of the letter C to our lesson and would listen rapturously to every word, awaiting a clue to the possible meaning of the letter cut into my cup. It seemed that my mood for many days was dependent upon whatever subject Master Bart chose for the letter. After the fifteen minutes on Cantaloupe, I was disappointed and vaguely despondent. Chess filled my head with dreams of castles and kings and with fantasies of a grand heritage while Cauliflower left me listless and dull. I was nearly unbearable for the week Master Bart discussed Camelot. I was chivalrous to the girls and challenged all others to duels and jousts. My fellows humored me for we all harbored dreams of a royal parentage that would reclaim us one day.

Although we were afforded a grand view of the sea through tall windows at the front of the classroom, the most interesting feature lined its other three walls. Glass-fronted shelves stretched up to the ceiling, filled with a grand miscellany of the wondrous, plain, and strange that Master Bart would use to augment his lessons. Although we marveled at the contents within, wondering at their origins even more than we wondered at our own, we were very nearly always surprised by whatever curiosity he would pull from the shelves. Ofttimes Master Bart would suddenly remember a story for his lesson and, launching into a lengthy preamble, would walk around the periphery of the room, roll the ladder along its rail, unlock the cabinet with an ornate key secured by a thin gold chain to his waistcoat, retrieve some curio, and return to his place at the podium without interrupting his tale.

One day, as Master Bart was lecturing on Charon under the topic of Greek mythos and he had reached the point in his story about coins on dead men's eyes, his face took on that brief faraway look of remembrance and he made his way around the room to one of the cabinets. Whatever it was he sought must have been tucked in the back of the shelf because he had to remove a few things before he found it. The first was a squat, pear-shaped ceramic jug with a wax seal over the mouth, the second a book that he had to hand down to one of the boys seated near the base of the ladder. The boy very nearly collapsed under its weight and we sniggered at his plight. Seeing the third item, my ears filled with a rushing sound that drowned out all else Master Bart said.

I recognized at once the doll Master Bart pulled forth to make way for his true goal. I had seen it many times before while peering at it through the glass. Not a young girl's doll with porcelain skin and a frilly dress. Rather, it was stocky and the skin glowed a reddish-brown hue of burnished mahogany. Beady black eyes glinted beneath a bald sloping forehead. A wide lipless mouth underlined an atavistic face whose lack of expression implied veiled malice. Dressed simply in a ragged blue poncho that reached down to knobby feet, it held its arms out from its body, hands pointing out in different directions.

Because I had never seen it outside the case, I had never seen its back. Now, as our queer professor groped for whatever still lay just beyond his reach, I could see on the doll's back, embroidered onto the poncho right above Master Bart's hand where he gripped it, the selfsame intricate letter C surrounded by filigree and knot work, identical to the one on my own dear cup. Although the remainder of the lesson was a haze to my eyes and a blur to my ears, I learned later that Master Bart was watching my face intently all the while. In the meantime, my thoughts spun around the image of the C discovered in that most unusual place.

That night, as those around me dreamed, sleep eluded me. Although it may be more accurate to say that I eluded sleep. I yearned to find my way back to that doll and see the mark again, for now doubt assailed me and I wondered if it was some trick of the light or my imagination that caused me to see that which was not there.

Not a soul crossed my path on my winding journey to the huge double doors sealing off the classroom. I slipped in and crept straight to the cabinet where the ladder remained from Master Bart's rummaging that afternoon. Starlight and moonlight lit my way, streaming in through the wall of windows overlooking the glistening sea. Up seven steps, I reached the level of my destination. I don't know how I expected to open the cabinet. Master Bart always relocked the doors when he was done with the lesson and had returned the contents to their home. He made a dramatic point of pulling out the key, turning it in its lock and pulling on the door to check its fastness. Maybe I just hoped to more closely look over the doll undisturbed.

I spied the doll, staring implacably at me through the glass. Moonlight glinted in black eyes nestled under an overhanging brow. I pulled on the handle of the cabinet door. Nothing happened, of course. I twisted the handle and pulled again. The door swung open on well-oiled hinges and a smell, antique and exotic, wafted out. I checked myself, tense with a mixed sense of anticipation and foreboding. Time held its breath. Silver-lined clouds hung like frozen phantoms in the night sky. Waves beat upon the shore below. The large clock ticked in the main hall and its gears clunked preceding the chiming of the hour. Midnight announced itself within the walls of the orphanage. Time had not stopped after all.

Reaching for the doll, I found myself in the same predicament as Master Bart. I had to first pull out the bottle and cumbersome book to reach it. I grasped the fat and unwieldy bottle with both hands, sloshing the liquid within. A small part of me wondered at its contents. I gingerly situated it on a rung above my head. Next from the cabinet came the book. Pages bulged from between its worn leather covers, threatening to spill out. Once again, both my hands gripped tightly as I struggled under its weight, setting it on the step below the jug.

Finally, my goal unobstructed, I was able to attain the cause of my disobedience. I stretched my hand out for the doll and grasped it around its body under its outstretched arms. Pulling it out, I must have leaned against the book for it teetered and fell to the floor with a loud whump. Pages burst forth from their bounds as if they had been held there under a great pressure. Now, freed, papers flew about like doves released at a coronation.

I stared at the sudden disarray, aghast at the potentially alarm-raising racket. After long moments of held breath, straining to hear any other sounds, I heard none. I returned my attention to the doll where it sat momentarily forgotten in my hand. Clutching it to my breast, I climbed down the ladder, picking my way among the papers, and sat down to examine my prize.

With its face, I was already familiar. I turned it around and examined the letter on its back, comparing it to the cup I had brought with me. Assuredly, it was identical. Just below the stitching, though, was a surprise. A small gold key protruded from the doll's back. I turned it a little and waited. A series of clicks emanated from within the doll's body. I could feel it coming to life within my hands. After a few moments, its mouth began working open and closed as if chewing and a raspy voice came forth.

"Your father has gone in search . . ."

I dropped the doll in surprise and stared at it, dumbfounded. But my shock at hearing the doll speak was quickly overshadowed by the realization that it must be speaking to me. It had not yet finished its message. I snatched it up, turned the key once more, and waited.

The voice came forth as if from a far distance, " . . . of the island of Salidas. . . "

I fumbled frantically at the key and turned it many times until it would turn no more. Its thin lips worked themselves up and spoke, " . . . near the Isle of Mé, where no two maps agree."

The mouth stopped moving. I waited. Turning the key again had no effect. It was wound as far as it would go. I feared breaking my little messenger so ceased my efforts. I looked to the rest of his body for any other clues he might hold. I lifted the poncho he wore, his sole garment. Seared into his back was the same crest as on his clothing and my cup. The front revealed only a potbelly that reminded me of Headmaster Poincaré. We rarely saw him and rarer still heard him speak. He ruled through a combination of a reputation of noble parentage and stern, yet fair discipline. Recalling him, I suddenly remembered that, if caught, no matter how caring my wardens, I would be punished severely.

I scurried around, picking up the pages that had hidden themselves in the shadows around the base of the ladder. Gathering them together on the table, I intended to return them to the book in some semblance of neatness. On the table, the pages swam in a pool of moonlight that revealed them to be a series of maps. A feeling came over me that I was somehow being led down a path from which I could not turn. I riffled through the pages, now heedless of punishment, searching for any mention of the islands of Mé or Salidas.

On most of the maps, I noticed the same image of a hand pointing up to the letter N. I did not yet understand the significance of this symbol—remember, please, my subjective experience, for Master Bart had not yet explored the points of a compass, as rudimentary to an education as this may seem. However this hand did remind me of the doll's hands. His right hand pointed upwards and his left hand extended straight out. Up and right. Spreading the topmost map out with my hands, I searched for my village, Bayonne. The ragged coastline met the sea, dotted with rocks and outcroppings. I spied familiar shapes in the irregular lines: silhouettes of monsters with squinty eyes, bulbous noses and toothless, gaping mouths. Bayonne leapt to my eye, my sprawling town nestled very small in the map.

Knowing that your life is a small piece of such a large world is far different than feeling it. I felt it now in my soul and the weight of that insignificance sank into my being. Self pity rose against me unbidden. I resented my life, my lack of parentage, my inconsequential existence, and was overwhelmed by the size of the task before me. How could I hope to find my way in such a large world?

I half-heartedly followed the coastline up. Well-known towns turned to half-familiar ones and became foreign. The coast slanted to the right, my finger followed. Up and right. It led inland. But how could an island lie on dry land? After a bit, a thought occurred to me: what if I turned the doll around to face the map? Now it directed left and up. My finger traced a new path: left and up.

Within a blank expanse of ocean sat a cluster of islands. But neither of the ones I was searching for. I found another map and tried again. And another, forgetting where I was and that I might be caught any moment. Then, finally, there it was: the island of Mé. Now that I had finally found it, it seemed so obvious. How could I have not seen it before? I searched back on the other maps. Yes, there it was . . . and there. I just had not seen it. But this was not my goal. I searched near Mé for the island of Salidas. Clusters of islands dotted the maps with their random shapes and jagged coastlines, confusing to an uninitiated map reader. And there were many around Mé. I peered at the surrounding islands but could not find the one. I flipped to another map, momentarily panicked. Again I could not find it. I stopped, willing my breathing to slow. The island must be there near Mé, the doll had clearly said so. I peered closer at the map spread out under my outstretched hands, pausing my eyes over each shape. There was an island below Mé, nearly a quarter the size of Mé, oblong, but with no name. I looked back upon the previous map. It was not below Mé . . . but there it was, off to the left. Suddenly giddy, I went to each map and found the unnamed island. There, to the right. Further to the right and above, but smaller. On another, it was not there at all. That must be Salidas. *Where no two maps agree.* The doll was unmistaken. But how was I to find an island that was never in the same place twice? Then I determined that if all these mapmakers had found it, then so could I.

I rolled up any of the maps I could find that depicted both Mé and the floating island of Salidas along with one showing

Bayonne. My path was chosen. I decided to leave the orphanage that night. Stuffing the remaining sheaves into the book, I intended to return it to the shelf from whence it came when a rough voice pierced the silence. "Take the jug. A sip will shorten the journey."

You may imagine my startled reaction, sure that I had just been discovered by some night watch wandering the halls. But the doll's lips again slowed to a halt. Was this how it would be then, my small messenger dispensing advice to guide me on my path? So be it. I retrieved the brown bottle from its perch where, until the doll's words, it sat forgotten. If not for his timely message, I might well have knocked it off while climbing the ladder with the unwieldy book. I eyed the little creature and wondered what inner intelligence was at work behind his implacable expression.

Sure that I would be discovered if I risked returning to my bed for any of my belongings, I crept the halls and rooms of the downstairs, availing myself of clothing and any items I might need on my journey. The kitchen provided me with provisions, and I slipped out the scullery door, wending my way through reeds and rushes, over drift logs, and down to the rock-and-sand beach. Thus like a thief I snuck forth from the only home I had ever known.

I halted and looked back. The orphanage towered with steep-pitched roofs broken up by many angled gables suggesting secret rooms. It both beckoned and beguiled. I felt that I knew no more of its contents than any other passerby. There it stood, magical, mysterious, the windows shining silver with reflected moonlight . . . all save one pushed out, revealing the dark within. Perhaps through some trick of the moonlight I thought I spied the twin glint of Master Bart's round spectacles looking out upon me from the shadows. But, before I could wonder further or look closer, I became aware of a small scuttling that grew louder.

Looking down, I saw that the beach had come alive around my feet. Up and down the strand, the rocks had become animated and were flowing down from the rushes and the scrub grass, around the rocks and drift logs, parting around my feet planted in the sand, down into the ocean where the waves swallowed them.

Crabs. They were thousands of tiny crabs. Their blue bodies glinted, making their sideways pilgrimage to the sea. We shared the same journey. Turning on my heel, I made my way up the shore, my feet wading across their current.

It was not long before I left the crabs behind and my only companion was the moon which had, by now, climbed high into the sky. I began my journey up the strand with great vigor, the excitement of my goal driving my legs over the occasional rock and limb. Waves whumped rhythmically against the rocks that responded with a long hiss. Whump, hsssssssss. Whump, hsssssssss. Large rocks challenged my balance whilst small ones sucked at my feet. Washed-up, decaying strands of kelp slipped and tangled and beach flies burst forth, angry at the disturbance. My satchel thumped against my side, drawing heavy on my shoulder.

The lateness of the hour and my tedious journey quickly overcame my initial enthusiasm and youthful vigor and, sooner than I expected, I found that I required rest. I sought a suitable spot and settled my back against a large tree trunk washed high up the beach. I couldn't help but think, as I unslung my heavy satchel upon the ground next to me, that my steps would be much lighter without this burdensome weight to carry. I began to reconsider some of the things I had, in my haste to pack, stuffed into the bag.

By far, the heaviest was the ceramic jug. But the doll had said specifically to bring the bottle so I could not very well leave it behind. *A sip will shorten the journey.* I wondered at that as I pulled it forth from its confines and picked at the wax seal. The cork exposed, I pulled at it firmly, yet gently so as not to break it. It came forth with a low, echoing pop that reverberated within the bottle. It smelled vaguely of licorice. Lifting the unwieldy jug to my lips, I took a small sip. It tasted of licorice as well, but also of other things musky and herbal. Its congealed gooiness burned its way down my throat.

A part of me feared poison as warmth settled in my stomach then radiated throughout my body. Then the fatigue was pushed from my limbs. I felt immediately refreshed. I stood, again foisting the satchel which now felt much lighter and set off anew, my stride long and my tread light.

Very soon, the tingly heat spread to my head and I felt and heard the slow steady beat of my heart, rush-thumping in time with my steps. The pulsing of the waves faded into the background. Rocks whispered their response. Smell faded. Vision blurred. Awareness dimmed. My world shrank to the slow beating of my heart and a voice. . . .

Days and nights passed as one, images fleeted as if all was a waking dream. A voice, my only constant companion, guided the way. A whisper half-heard, advice heeded without question, steering my feet on their path: *Wade . . . climb . . . run . . . slow . . . crawl . . . duck . . . hide . . . row . . . row.* This dream-walk was briefly interrupted only when the elixir wore off at untold intervals and a ravenous hunger overtook me. Thankful for the foodstuffs I had plundered from the kitchens, I filled my belly to satiation. Another sip, another interlude of journeying, insensible save for the doll's voice, simple instructions made audible in my head by some magic held within the elixir.

The small boat I was in halted with a grinding crunch and I was thrown to the floor, abruptly awakened. I had thieved this boat as instructed by the doll, which I had come to name Tagor, while under the influence of the potion. Rising from the boat, I wondered what obstacle had interrupted my journey and pushed my hair back out of my eyes. It had grown surprisingly long on my journey and I wondered absently how long I had been gone. Time slipped by unaccounted as if in a dream. The boat had run aground atop a shallow outcropping of an island that otherwise rose sharply from the water. Rough barnacles crumbled under my boots as I stepped ashore. From where I stood, these barnacles completely covered the island save for a few spaces where the rock underneath was exposed, smooth and shiny, black as onyx. I considered climbing the sheer face as some of the barnacles seemed large enough to support my weight, but decided that there was really nothing I needed on such a barren island. The face curved away in all directions obscuring much of it, but it appeared to be naught but desolate rock. Besides, I was consumed by hunger. My body's fuel had been depleted by my exertions while under the potion's spell. It seemed to provide for everything but sustenance. Hunger gnawed at my belly, demanding attention.

As I tore into a hunk of salted pork, I vaguely wondered if I was close to the Isle of Mé or Salidas but was sure that Tagor would have said something if I was nearing my destination or steering off course. I pulled him out of the satchel and looked into his eyes. Nothing. I consulted some of my maps but could find no indication as to my location that would help. Soon, my hunger sated, I pushed off, took a sip, and resumed rowing. Clouds gathered overhead and a few drops of rain splashed my face.

Creaking, swaying, the smell of stale brine, burning lanterns. My eyes opened to a wood-beamed ceiling a few feet from my face. I was aboard a ship, in a bunk. My belongings lay folded in a pile on a stool next to me. A startled yelp from the other side of my bed drew my attention to a boy no older than myself seated on the floor in the corner. He leapt to his feet and darted out the door.

I could hear his shoes thumping on the planks, running away. Then a heavier tread approached and a short, swarthy man let himself into my chamber. "Well little Coudray, you are awake at last, huh? The crew had wagers as to when you'd awaken . . . and if." Why did he call me this, I wondered. His words were curiously accented and he smiled a not unkindly grin although his eyes held no mirth. He pulled another stool over to my bedside. "I can tell from your face that you are curious how I know your name, huh? Well, that is a story. One's whose ending you will shed light upon. But first . . . here . . . you must eat, huh?"

I'd not noticed the boy had returned with a plank of food. My stomach churned and I devoured the fish stew, forgetting all of my manners and slurping down the steaming gobbets of white fish. The soup dripped down my chin unheeded. I nearly broke my teeth on the bread provided, so my host took the liberty of dropping it into the remaining broth to soften it up. It took a goodly while before it had soaked up enough to be edible and then I found it filling and quite tasty. Satiated, I wiped my mouth on the back of my hand and regarded my benefactor. He was still smiling, the edge of a gold tooth gleaming at the corner of his mouth, though still the humor did not reach his eyes.

"You remind me of your father when he first came aboard. He was much famished like you, huh?" He had a curious manner of speaking in which his sentences turned up at the end as if in question even when they were not. "What is it about your family that leads its men into the ocean so ill-prepared, huh?"

I must have gaped at him again, for he chuckled and continued, pleased with himself, "Yes, I know your father, Doctor Coudray. I pulled him from the sea same as you. Though his boat was more suited for the ocean than yours. Even though its mast was broken and he was much running low on food and water. But despite your meager supplies and simple rowboat, you've done well, huh? But it is good that we crossed your path. Your boat was nearly filled with water but still you were unaware." He chuckled. "You pulled on the oars as if devils rode your wake. Where is it you were going anyway, huh?"

My brain was awhirl. Could it be that he did know my father? Was I really named . . . what . . . Coudray? I ignored his query and answered instead with some of my own. "You know my father? Is he here on this ship? May I see him?"

"Hold, little man . . . hold." He clamped a hand on my shoulder, his hand rough and his grip strong. He saw me wince and eased his grasp on me. "Your father's not here. He's not been here for a while, huh? In truth, I've been looking for him since he . . . since he left this ship many months ago. As I said, Doctor Coudray came to me two years ago, like you have now, in much need of rescue. I fed him, nursed him back to health and, after learning of his . . . ah . . . skills, employed him as this ship's physician. He and I shared a friendship. He told me that when I found him, he was in the midst of searching for his wife and that he had left behind an infant son. If that was you, he must've left you long ago, huh? What are you? Ten? Twelve?"

"Ten," I said. "People say I'm tall for my age."

"Yes, yes. Ten, you say? Then he left you at least seven years before I found him? It must be important for him to leave you for so long, huh? Yes . . . very important, I think." He looked away and rubbed his chin, considering for a moment. Then, "Where was I? Oh, yes. He stayed in my employ for much time as we traded up and down the coast and among southern islands. His skills were very useful to us. All was well. Business was good. Then, not long ago, I noticed a change in his behavior . . . his withdrawing. But I paid it little mind." He waved his hand as if shooing away a fly. "He was a man prone to . . . ah . . . taciturn moods and we had become used to his solitary habits, huh?

"Then one morning, the watch raised the alarm. We found one of our lifeboats gone and our doctor with it. Too late, I recalled our position and its being close to where we rescued him. You see, that was the first time we had passed here since then, our . . . contracts having carried us on other routes. If our shipment had not been in danger of spoilage, I would have changed course and searched for him right then. Alas, I could not until our contracts were filled, huh? Now, having done, I've sailed us back here in search of the doctor . . . your father. We've been sailing these waters for many weeks with no sign. And now, instead of him, we've found his son, huh? What providence!" He clapped his hands and laughed a short, barking laugh then leaned back in his chair, squinting at me and raising an eyebrow. "So tell me . . . why *are* you out here . . . and why all on your own?"

"How do you know I am his son?"

His eyes narrowed. "This is two times you have answered me question for question. I hope there will not be a third, huh? I will answer yours, though. And then perhaps . . . you will answer some of mine, huh?" He paused and waited for my response. He looked prepared to wait me out as long as needed. I nodded meekly. "Very good then . . . I knew you by the crest on your cup. He had the same crest on a ring he wore—reversed, though, for use as a seal. You are little Guillard, huh? But not so little any more I see."

He chuckled a little to himself. An evil little laugh, I thought.

But for the first time, disbelief turned to real hope. The meaning of the C was clear: Coudray. My name was Guillard Coudray. This man indeed knew my father. But I did not trust him. His manner set me ill at ease. Before he could ask his question, I groaned and held my stomach.

"What? What's wrong, boy? Huh?" He leapt to his feet.

Waves of nausea passed over me, at least as far as he could tell. I gave all the signs, so much so that I almost believed it myself. Exercising one of my boyhood talents, I feigned illness. The Captain cuffed the boy who had delivered the meal. "Did you bring him bad soup, huh? Good food . . . I say good food, don't I?" He rushed to the door. "Watch him! Make sure he's not too bad off, huh?" On his way out, I heard him grumble, "After all, we've no doctor to help him. Where's that drunk of a cook, huh?"

The boy watched me, fear in his eyes. "Do ye need somethin'? Water? Bucket? The fish weren't bad, I swear it. I've ate some myself and I en't sick!"

Taking a chance, I halted my ruse. "I'm not sick," I said. I felt bad for the boy for taking the brunt for my performance. I added, "I'm sorry he hit you."

Momentary anger and confusion clouded his face, and then it broke into a mischievous grin. "Smart, you." He tapped a finger to his temple. "Captain, he's a hard man. Yer right to put him off. He din't tell ye everything."

"I had a feeling."

He looked at me sideways. "Is the doctor really yer father?"

"I don't know . . . maybe. It sounds like he could be."

He paused, considering, then nodded curtly as if deciding the matter. "It sure sounds like he is. Listen, I've been on this ship most of me life. I hear things. Captain and the doctor did talk sometimes like he said. But they weren't friends. Captain di Guigno doesn't have friends." He shook his head ruefully. "But he sure pried at the doctor to get him to talk. Mostly yer father was quiet though—like he knew some secret—and it made Captain edgy." He looked down at the floor, digging at the planks with his toe. "I liked him. He treated me decent. He looked at me funny sometimes though . . . kind of sad like . . . I dunno." He shrugged and looked up, his brows knitted. "Captain, he worked at him a long while to get at his secrets. Gettin' him drunk worked best, I guess. They'd laugh and laugh, then t'would go all hushed and they'd talk real quiet. He was lookin' for yer mother all right. But he was also lookin' for an island that din't exist but that sinks big ships. A black island."

My sharp intake of breath interrupted him. Alarmed, he asked, "What? What did I say?"

"I think I know this island. I think I've been there."

"Ye have? How do ye know? Captain wants to find this island. He thinks there's great treasure there . . . or great magic. He figures if yer father wants it so bad, it must be worth a lot. He sees what yer father can do and wants what he has . . . wants what he wants."

"What did you mean 'what my father can do'? The captain mentioned his skills, too, like they were special."

He nodded sagely. "They were. He was more'n just a regular doctor. He made potions that no one'd heard of before: Cures for sea sickness, they made the crew work faster and longer without sleep, kept 'em happy and smiling. He made machines, too. They stitched up cuts, set bones. He made one for navigation. The doctor called it a homin' compass. Captain named it his 'little friend.' Once we visited a place, we could always find our way back. It would point the direction to show the way. Even another ship! I dunno how it worked but the captain loved that one most, I think. Captain wanted other potions and machines that the doctor could make but wouldn't. I heard him say he'd help him find his wife in return but he still refused. He found ways to keep the doctor aboard so he could get more from him. . . I don't really know how, I don't understand such things." He shrugged. "Then right before the doctor disappeared, I heard 'em arguin' about somethin'. I couldn't hear it well. But then a few nights later, he was gone and Captain was mad . . . very mad . . . he had the watch whipped and a couple of others for good measure." He rubbed his backside absently. "Since the doctor took his potions and machines with him, they still suffer. He took Captain's little friend, too. He din't like that sneaky trick."

Captain di Guigno's heavy tread approached once again. I gave the cabin boy a meaningful look, mouthed a quick 'thank you,' and rolled over on my side, feigning sleep and clutching my belly once again. He burst through the door and I could hear the barely restrained fury in his hushed voice hissing through clenched teeth.

"Well, how is he, huh? Emile says the food weren't bad. So why's he sick?"

"He din't sick up but he did go back sleepin'. I think he's not recovered yet. Maybe he woke up too soon, eh?" I imagined the boy's wide eyes blinking innocently up at the Captain and almost smiled.

"Hmmm . . . maybe . . . anyways, get you to the galley and clean up, huh? There's a mess in there now."

Both of them departed and I was finally left alone to gather my thoughts. I had to escape. This much I knew. Captain di Guigno was a dangerous man and my father fled him for good reason. But I wondered at Tagor's silence. I pulled him out of the satchel and looked him over closely. Then I remembered the key. I remembered that I had not turned it since the beginning of my journey. It turned many times, just like the first time.

Out came the familiar raspy voice, "Row . . . row. . . . Your father is here, your journey is done . . . go back . . . turn around . . . bail . . . bail."

His voice ground to a stop. So he had wound down and was now catching up on all that he could not say before. I had reached my father? How did I miss him? Perhaps he was on the island of Salidas at the same time as myself but we could not see each other. I cursed myself and my stupidity. Now Tagor seemed to have no counsel on my current predicament. I had to get off this ship. I tried to think of some way to enlist the cabin boy to my cause. He seemed amenable up to now and sympathetic to my plight. Perhaps he would be willing to commit further. I considered bribes, cajolery or even tempting him with joining me on my escape since he seemed to suffer under the captain's cruel hand. Fortunately, all of my belongings were with me in the cabin. All but the food which had most likely spoiled anyway and . . . searching my satchel . . . the maps. Thankfully the captain had overlooked the jug. I hurriedly dressed and was just about to venture forth when the door creaked open. I braced myself. It was only the cabin boy. He did not look surprised.

"I thought ye might be leaving, so I brought ye this." He pulled out a bag from under his shirt and handed it to me. Looking inside, I saw more provisions than I had packed when I first set out. "And this." He pulled out a piece of parchment. "The doctor wrote letters and I delivered them for him whenever we put in at port. This was the last. I never got a chance to deliver it." He handed it to me. It was a letter addressed to Monsieur Bartholomé Dionne in Bayonne, and sealed with blood red wax imprinted with the letter C.

Despite the danger of discovery, I could not wait. My hands shook as I broke the seal and unfolded the letter. My eyes drank in the flowing words penned by my father's hand.

My Dear Friend,

I apologize for the delay in this letter reaching you. We have been at sea for many months now and Captain di Guigno will not allow us to go ashore at port. He is a driven man and I do not know how to prevent him from this course he has set. We are nearing the waters where my dear Hannah disappeared so long ago and fear besets me. I am so close to my goal but I have tried to warn the captain that a ship of this size will surely perish as others before it but he'll not listen. I grasp the pattern, I trust my conclusions: The risk is too great. The crew has no say in the matter as most of them work in a stupor under the influence of my potions. I would not have them exploited in this manner but the captain threatens to beat them otherwise. As I have refused to treat abused or tortured sailors for him any longer, I must give in to him. But I have resolved to leave this ship at the earliest opportunity and will continue my pursuit on my own. The captain will be wrathful, I am certain, but I cannot have this ship endangered or her crew maltreated by my presence any longer. I will seize what medicines and inventions I can and hope that I am not discovered.

 I hope that Guillard is well. I think of him daily and am reminded of him when I look upon this ship's cabin boy. He is the one who has seen to it that my previous letters were delivered to you. Although a bit rough, he is of fine character and I often wonder what sort of young man Guillard is growing into under your fine care and tutelage. I trust that the considerable sum I left with you is still sufficient payment for his continued residence at the orphanage. I know that you do not completely agree with what I have done but am hopeful that in honor of our friendship and the memory of my dear Hannah, you remain true to my wishes. If I fail and do not return, I would rather Guillard not know of my imprudence. If I am successful, we will all be together as we should have been. Know that I continue to carry the lodestone that will draw you to me should I become lost. Remember, it is linked to the doll. Keep it secure. It will be your guide.

 I remain your indebted friend,
 Doctor Vivien Coudray

 I read the letter again. His hand penned those words that I held in my hands. This was the closest I had yet come to him.

Many questions were answered but not all. Looking up from the page to the cabin boy through eyes blurred with tears, I said, "Thank you . . . thank you so much." The words were thick in my throat. "The captain will beat you for this, won't he?"

He ignored my tears. "For the letter? He won't know. For the food and yer escapin'?" He shrugged resignedly. "Not too bad. No worse'n usual . . . and not as bad as ye if ye stay."

"What about my boat?"

"It's tied alongside the ship. It's been bailed and is sea-sound."

"What about the captain . . . the crew?"

"I'll take care of the crew. Captain's in his quarters, poring over yer maps. I hope ye din't need 'em."

I shrugged. "They helped me once but no longer. I'm sure they'll be no help to him."

He shrugged in return. "Captain's got salt; he may guess more than ye credit him. But no use to it now. He's got 'em. Ye don't. And ye have to get off this ship. Ready?"

I paused, considering. "Do you want to come with me?"

"Naah." He smiled a wry grin. "Here's the closest I've ever come to havin' a home . . . fer worse or better. Nah, I'll stay. Thanks though." I didn't understand his decision. But he had to choose his own path just as I had long ago. He turned and I followed his rolling gait out the door.

I know now that there was no possibility of escape without his help and guidance. I'm sure I would have chanced upon some crew member if not for his intimate familiarity with the layout of the ship and the crew's whereabouts. Just before venturing forth onto the deck, he instructed in me the quickest route to my boat. Then, with no more than a farewell wink, he disappeared up through the hatch. The cool night breeze dispelled a bit of the below-deck stench that clouded my nostrils. I waited, concealed, as he distracted the crew with some clever ruse that I could not see although I heard their laughter, imagining him acting the clumsy fool.

I peeked out, fearful of hidden eyes. I had begun my journey long ago in the light of the full moon and now it was but a sliver, providing me with a cloak of darkness. I scurried across the deck, slipped over the rail and monkeyed down the rope to where my boat awaited. The oarlocks I bound with cloth to quiet, then pulled at the oars as quickly as I dared, the anchored ship dwindling.

Sure that I was indeed far enough from the ship, I ceased rowing and pulled Tagor out. I resolved to freshen his winding upon each awakening from my trance. I would not repeat my mistake. I returned him securely to the satchel across my shoulder, sipped the journeying elixir which was nearly half gone, and resumed my quest. As the comforting delirium overtook me, I thought of all the boy had done for me, no doubt at great expense to himself. I realized with a start that I had never even learned his name.

"*Awaken. . . .Awaken. . . .Danger behind, danger below.*" Tagor's gravelly voice in my head pierced the haze, leading me back to a premature semi-consciousness. Turning my head around sluggishly, I searched for the danger of which he spoke. Drugged delirium still clouded my senses. My slowly beating heart roared in my ears in time with waves breaking on the hull of a ship bearing down upon me. I could only grasp fragments of what occurred next . . . Captain di Guigno's bellowing laughter and wordless shout . . . a plume of water spewed forth from the ocean's surface . . . a swell lifted up my boat like a toy . . . the captain's face gawped at me, triumph changed to shock . . . his ship's hull splintered with a bone-shattering crunch . . . shouts turned to screams . . . the mast cracked with a thunder clap . . . sails billowed down toward me, blotting out the sun, the sky . . . day to night, covered and smothered . . . capsized . . . pushed down, dragged down into the sea . . . silence . . . as deep as the grave.

Weightless, I floated. Beams of lights danced down into the cold depths of the blue world. I saw others floating, suspended like myself. Like macabre puppets slowly wheeling. Everything had turned so calm so quickly. Was it a dream? Was I dead? Were we all dead?

Tagor's voice in my head again, "*Danger approaches. Your father approaches . . . .*"

A shadow grew as it advanced through the gloom, the

indistinct shape slowly resolving itself: a monster … a creature … a whale, its monstrous bulk graceful in the water. A cloud of debris surrounded it: barnacles breaking loose, crumbling free of its hide with every massive flex of its fins, every bend of its body. A low rumble I felt more than heard coursed through my head, my bowels, my bones as the leviathan neared. It was a growl … a moan … a final roar muffled by the water before my end. I found myself too stunned to swim, to fight. The end seemed inevitable. Spreading my arms, I resigned myself to fate.

Impact. Pushed back, the remaining air rushed from my lungs, barnacle shards cut my face, ripped my clothes. But it was almost … gentle. Then … air … my lungs drank it in greedily. I rolled onto my back insensible and basked in the sun's warmth.

I came to my senses at last, though still feeling the effects of the potion. I lay atop the immense beast; its black body glistened and heaved with life below me. A rush of water and air plumed from its blowhole as if held under a great pressure. Another burst forth, showering me. I rolled over. An arm's length away, the great blowhole contracted. There, next to the maw, scarred onto the creature's black hide, was my father's seal, but reversed and raised as if it had been pushed out from within the beast. The selfsame C—first my legacy, then my guide, and finally my salvation.

"Son," said a new voice in my head. Deep. Soothing. Yet it seemed to come from a great distance. "You found me? How did you … ? The doll … Bartholomé gave you the doll."

"No. I took it. Master Bart didn't know. Father? Is that you? Where … ?"

"I am here. I am a part of Salidas now. We both are … though Hannah's voice is silent. My potions have made this possible. I hoped only for answers but Salidas surprised me . . . . I should have been safe." His voice began to fade and I strained my ears to hear. But the voice was in my head and it did no good. "But now we can be together … as we should have been long ago … and all this time. But the decision is yours. Do you … wish it … ?"

Fading further, the voice trailed off to nothing. The elixir had finally run its course and the last traces of the spell were gone. I opened my satchel frantically, searching for the bottle. But, alas, I found only broken shards that fell between my fingers.

I splayed my hands over the black hide, feeling the life pulsing, emanating from within its great bulk. My parents' spirits lived in this beast . . . as could mine . . . ? A deep moan reverberated. How could I choose this path? How could I not? Another moan . . .

I had to choose.

"No. I do not wish it."

Pregnant silence filled the air.

A long groan of sadness welled up from deep within it. Then the creature turned and swam toward the horizon, carrying me away from the setting sun.

We traveled long then and, to fill the silence, I recounted my journey since seeing the doll in Master Bart's hand. That done, I chronicled my life: stories, anecdotes, wandering tales with no direction. At some point, it occurred to me that my ramblings resembled Master Bart's lessons and realized that in the absence of my parents, he had been as near a father as I had ever known. All the while, we glided through the water swifter and smoother than any ship. At some point, sleep overtook me—my first real sleep in a very long time—and pulled me into oblivion, a fathomless darkness with no stars, no moon, no voice.

They found me on the beach, battered, exhausted, and in sore need of care. Back in the orphanage, they tended my wounds. Some were very deep and the scars still remain. Master Bart visited my bedside every day, his role of teacher temporarily abandoned along with his theatrics. He revealed his relationship with my parents and his role in sparking my journey. A bit I knew, some I had already suspected. I was surprised to learn that he had left the cabinet unlocked after seeing my look of recognition in the classroom, but his intent was merely to prompt questions, not to incite my departure. During my recovery, he narrated stories about my parents whom he had known long before my birth and we speculated as to what motivation drove my father to so obsessively search for my mother at the expense of all else. But his mind was his own. As was his path.

I was back where I began, though I was not the same as I was when I left. Besides my scars, I carry no other tangible evidence of my journey—as if it were all a dream that began with my first sip of the potion. Tagor survived, but his voice has been silent since his last words: *Your father approaches.* Perhaps whatever intelligence my father imbued him with has run out or perhaps he is merely broken. In either case, I have not the means to enchant or repair him. The maps sank with the ship and all her crew including, to my great regret, the nameless cabin boy. I continue to seek out maps for newly discovered islands not previously marked by cartographers. These maps are my best method of tracing his route, his never-ending journey. While explorers and mapmakers all have different names for these islands that appear and disappear from map to map, I have only one.

ISLAND OF DREAMS, ISLAND OF FEARS

KALEENA FRAGA

Miguel strides slowly down the silvery white Sri Lankan beach, gazing out at the calm, sparkling water, pale jade in the glow of the golden sun. The dark red sand, normally covered with its blanket of liquid blue, is now exposed to the world, sending startling colors of orange and yellow onto the beach. It is an unusually low tide; the water seems miles away. The nakedness of the coast draws many of the locals, and now the dark-skinned Sri Lankans are everywhere, picking up fish that have been caught on land, and examining the exotic shells. Miguel nudges a bunch of dark magenta seaweed with his foot. Never in the States has he seen anything like this. From the looks on the Sri Lankans' faces, they haven't either.

Miguel starts down toward the water, through the throngs of people clustered about the vibrant beach. He wonders how far it really goes out. Some curious young children are at the water's edge, shrieking with delight as they splash each other and crawl about in the wet sand. The sound of voices stabs the morning air; men shout animatedly to each other in tongues that Miguel doesn't understand. Women call anxiously to their children, and the children laugh as they squirm from their mothers' arms. Miguel watches the scene with a thoughtful look in his dark eyes. His father would have enjoyed such a sight, being from Sri Lanka himself, but Miguel is sure both his parents are still at the hotel.

He frowns as he thinks of them. His mother would have liked to never leave California, but his father had been promising his Uncle Yee a visit for years. Yee, a Hindu extremist, is considered insane even by his fellow Sri Lankans. But Miguel's father was good to his word, and here they are. Miguel dreads meeting his uncle, one of the main reasons he had left the hotel to walk the beach. Miguel is part Hindu, but his mother's Christian beliefs have been taught to him too, and he doesn't want to listen to Uncle Yee's mad rants.

He stops at the edge of the water and tests the temperature with his hand. It isn't warm or cold, but somewhere between, almost like bathwater. He gazes out at the children as they splash around and rolls up his pants. He wades in a bit, surprised at how very far he can go. The water is so shallow. Miguel squints at the sea. As far as he can see is ocean, and sitting on the ocean are little fishing boats, the Sri Lankan men making their livings. They wait so patiently. Miguel's father once told him that the fishermen will wait all day for a catch since it is all they have to live on.

Miguel turns and looks back up at the beach. The land seems so far away, miles away, although he knows it could only be a couple hundred feet. He pauses a moment and takes in the landscape.

It's odd, he realizes suddenly, that it's so quiet. There are human voices, but usually the screech of a seagull or a seal's sad song would linger in the air. It is strange that today only human voices can be heard. Miguel takes four more steps out into the water, and then freezes. Some deep instinct, hidden by centuries of civilized living, explodes in his chest and fear rockets violently throughout his body. He takes a sharp breath and looks frantically about. But he can't see anything to be afraid of. Around him, Sri Lanka seems peaceful.

Then he hears it.

It is a dull murmur at first, a near whisper in his ear. But the murmur strengthens to a roar, a roar full of such rage that he wheels to see what is happening. And then he sees. . . the fishermen's boats out on the water are gone, and now, racing toward him is the biggest wave he has ever seen. In a split second, the water had leapt toward the sky, and now it is roaring toward the beach. It looks like a picture from a surfing magazine, except the only thing surfing this wave is fear.

He gives a strangled shout as his brain freezes with horror. He stumbles backwards. He turns and races toward the beach. The others hear his shout, see the waves, and human screams shatter the calm that had settled on the Sri Lankan shore. The water at his ankles slows him down, and the mud sucks at his feet. Tears of horror are forming in his eyes, blinding him and, although he urges himself to go faster, he knows there is no way he can outrun this wave.

I'm going to die . . . I'm going to die . . . I'm going to die. The thought screams in his head, and yet he pushes himself on, faster and faster. His feet touch the solid sand, and he thinks for a second, as his heart pounds and he gulps in air, maybe he will make it.

But even as he considers the glorious idea of living, the wave crashes over his head with the force of a giant fist and pulls him backward into its dark jaws. He kicks furiously against the ocean he has loved and admired. But this beauty has turned into a beast, a ferocious, deadly beast. He has no way to fight it. The frigid darkness is all about him, and his grasping fingers find nothing but merciless water.

Miguel wakes with a groan, turns over and vomits. He is on a beach and beneath his salt-soaked body, the sand is warm. He coughs violently and raises his head. His thoughts are a jumble. The pale white sand gleams beneath his fingers and he scoops it up with one hand. He sits up and looks out at the water. It is dark blue and so still that it seems solid. Where is he? It may be a Sri Lankan coast, he thinks doubtfully. But the landscape, although amazingly similar to that of Sri Lanka, is totally different. Rockier, maybe, and it's colder. Not in the sense of the temperature, but in the general feeling of the place. Colder. Much colder. He picks at what is left of his shirt. The bottoms of his jeans have been ripped off, and his shoes are gone. He tries to stand up, and nearly topples over as his legs shake precariously beneath him. The very motion makes him a bit dizzy, and he blinks his eyes to regain his head.

"Hello?" he calls weakly into the silence. There is no answer. He realizes if there is someone here, they may not speak English. They might speak Sinhala or Tamil, Sri Lanka's official languages. Miguel knows a few phrases of this tongue, but his pronunciation isn't good, as he had proved at a restaurant, ordering a Coke and getting a smoked pig. That had been just yesterday. Or had it? How many days has he lain on this beach? He frowns and takes a few experimental steps forward. There is no pain. He flexes his fingers. They are all there and none of them hurt. He takes another step forward and grimaces. There is a pounding pain in the small of his back, but already it seems to fade, so he ignores it.

"Hello?" he calls again. If there are any people here, then one would think they would answer to the sound of another voice regardless of its language. Or maybe—wherever this is—he is alone. He sits down.

A tsunami.

That's what happened. He remembers it clearly now, the monstrous wave screaming in his head and pulling him away from the beach. It had taken his breath and his shoes. He shakes his head, stunned he is still alive. He had lost consciousness under the water; he could still remember that half-sob that had been a breath. He looks out at the water. It is so still.

A tsunami.

So what has happened to his parents? To Uncle Yee? Their hotel is a good forty-minute walk from the beach. It's possible that they had survived. Miguel couldn't imagine that it had killed them. No, their hotel is too far inland to have been affected by that wave. Depending of course, he thinks grimly, on the force and accuracy of the tsunami. In the depths of his mind, where he keeps his school life, Miguel remembers his science teacher telling them about tsunamis. But the thought is like an oiled weight in his hand, and before he can really grasp it, it slips away.

There is a vibrating sensation next to his leg, and he jumps to his feet, expecting to see some sort of snake or lizard. But the beach is still devoid of any life. He puts a hesitant hand in his pocket and slowly retracts his cell phone.

For a moment he just stares at it, listens to its weak ring. He is past shock that it has survived the water. He glances around, wondering if anyone is watching him, and flips the phone open.

"Hello?" There is a long silence on the other end. His brow furrows and he is about to hang up when he hears a faint voice. He still can't make out any words, so he places the phone closer to his ear.

"You see this, Miguel? This is a trombone. You see? It is your instrument. Understand?" Incredulous, Miguel hears his own voice respond.

"Yes, Ms. Burns."

"Good. You see . . . this? This is music. And you see that on my wall? That is a clock. A clock, Miguel. Combine these three things, trombone, music and clock, and you've got yourself practice time. I'm going to have to fail you if you don't practice Miguel, and no one wants to fail *band*."

He snaps the cell phone closed and shoves it back in his pocket. His fingers linger a moment on the cool plastic and then he shakes his head and runs both hands through his hair. He remembers that conversation with Ms. Burns. It had been years ago, when he first picked up the trombone at his father's urgings. A memory . . . it must have been a memory. But then who was on the phone? He dimly wonders if he is going insane.

He thinks he should be frightened, confused, certainly, but he isn't. He's almost calm. Maybe it's because his brain still refuses to believe that any of this has happened. The strange call fades from his mind, and he begins to move down the beach, toward a huge black rock that juts into the sky. He pauses as he reaches it. He stares up at its magnificence and then places his palm to its surface.

He swears as it cuts him and snatches his hand away. The cut is a thin one, and only a drop of blood appears on his palm.

He shakes his hand, pondering what he should do now, when he hears a faint voice.

Cautiously, he steps from behind the rock. A man sits on the beach, a wide-brimmed hat covering disheveled brown hair. His wide gray eyes stare blankly at the sea from beneath thick brown brows. The man is shivering uncontrollably and wraps long, skinny arms about his slender form.

"Que? Que aconteceu? Onde estou eu? Eu estou . . .assim frio assim frio assim frio . . .o que está acontecendo?" Miguel doesn't recognize the language. It sounds something like Spanish, but he doesn't think it is Sri Lankan.

"Excuse me," Miguel calls softly and takes a step toward the man. "I don't speak—" The man's head swivels to face him, and the panicked features relax. With a soft sigh, the man falls limply to the ground. Miguel stares a moment as horror and revulsion flash across his features. Unable to stay still and unsure what he can do for the man, Miguel turns and walks quickly away.

He nearly runs into a girl who has just stepped from the woods. Woods that Miguel hasn't even noticed until now.

"Don't be afraid," she says with a smile.

"Afraid?" he echoes doubtfully. "What is there to be afraid of?" She blinks oily black eyes at him, and Miguel is convinced she is a native of Sri Lanka.

"Where are we?" he asks, taking a step toward her. She doesn't move, but her eyes regard him with caution.

"I couldn't say," she says lightly. "Not in a way we would both understand." She isn't speaking English, Miguel realizes with a start. And yet . . .yet he can understand everything she is saying.

"The tsunami," says Miguel quickly, and looks fearfully back at the water as if expecting the wave to come and swallow him up again.

"Is dead," the girl whispers, "until next time."

"Next time?" he repeats fearfully. "There will be a next time?" She watches him sadly and he falls to his knees. "Please," he whispers, "answer me." She kneels next to him and places warm fingers on his chin.

"Not in your lifetime. Someday. Long from now. No worries, no worries." She smiles at him and touches his hair with long brown fingers. Then, quiet as a ghost, she gets to her feet and glides back into the woods. Miguel does not make a move to follow her as he kneels there and clenches the pearly sand with his fingers.

"I'm not afraid," he calls. But there is no response. He doesn't expect one.

He *isn't* afraid. Shocked, certainly, and maybe a little confused. Thoughts pour clearly through his mind: concern for his parents and uncle and wonderment at what happened. He wonders if back home in California his friends are watching the news and worrying if he is all right. Surely such a wave must have made the headlines. His best friend, Jacob, would be chewing furiously at his fingers and yelling, "Sri Lanka, Sri Lanka! That's where Miguel is!" And then Jacob's new dog, Sunny, would bark with excitement and jump about until someone put her in her crate. Even as he is thinking this, Miguel hears barking.

A black dog races toward him, its pink tongue lolling from dark lips. Its loud woofs are like music in the solemn air. Miguel is surprised to hear laughter from his own mouth. All his wonderments, concerns and fears melt like ice cream and, feeling nine again, Miguel chases after the dog. His laughter and the dog's barking fill the once quiet air.

Allan Hardy moves through the lines of bodies as he walks slowly toward Timothy Potts, the other Englishman on the trip. People from all nations have hurried to volunteer to help these poor people. On the plane ride to Sri Lanka, Allan had shared an aisle with a woman from the States and a man from Germany. They'd both been in London for holiday but had left for Sri Lanka as soon as they heard the news of the tsunami. Neither had much medical background, but they were eager to help in any way they could.

Tim is on the ground, turning over a body that had been face down in the sand.

"God, it's a kid, Allan."

Allan squats next to Tim and looks down. A boy, maybe fourteen . . . fifteen, perhaps, lies on the beach, his dark brown eyes open in a look of eternal horror. His mouth is closed tightly, in a way that makes it seem as if he is smiling. Tim shakes his head.

"This is . . .this is so . . ." Allan lays a heavy hand on his companion's shoulder.

"I know." Tim shakes his head again.

"So many . . . . What's the count now, 100,000?"

"Plus," replies Allan with a sigh. "It's horrible. Just wretched."

Tim continues to shake his head, his hand on the kid's shoulder. "A broken backbone did this one in. He doesn't look Sri Lankan, more of a mix if you ask me. And his shirt—or what's left of a shirt—seems to be advertising the Gap. That's an American clothing line, isn't it?"

Allan nods quietly.

Tim looks up at him. "Should I put him with the others?"

Allan begins to reply when a sudden beeping noise fills the numb air. Allan exchanges a look with Tim. The noise is coming from the boy. Hesitantly, Allan opens the pants pocket. The material almost disintegrates in his hand. Allan's fingers find something cold and pull out a cell phone. It beeps impatiently. Glancing at his companion, Allan opens it and puts it to his ear. 🐘

ROLLOVER

VICKI SAUNDERS

Terry leaned against the car door, as far from Jeff as she could manage, fiddling with her hair. Jeff's Jesus Rock tapes bawled about being born again all the way up the pass. Then the muffler gave out on the potholes and the engine's roar drowned the music. Jeff switched off the engine at the crest. The tires hissed on the curves as he and Terry drifted down, still as death, through the scaly red trunks of ponderosa pines.

She had first spotted Jeff under the bull elk head in the lobby of the Bierstadt hotel—the crown of his Billy Jack hat hovering below the elk's chin. Terry had a temp job at the hotel, clearing up rooms littered with empties, scrubbing toilets with pungent blue disinfectant, stretching paper loops pre-printed with "Sanitized for Your Protection" across the seats. The elk was the glory of the hotel: its sixteen-point rack scraped the pine boards of the ceiling. Jeff resembled it, with his soaring headgear, glazed eyes, and face buried in rusty-red hair. He was asking the clerk for directions to the rez.

"Not much up there," said the clerk.

"Doesn't matter," said Jeff. "I'm looking for some friends, is all."

Geronimo had warned, *"The sun, the darkness, the winds are all listening to what we have to say."* So Terry hesitated before she said, "I can show you how to get there." Not that she knew. But she'd figure it out. She leaned against the hotel desk, lank and bleached in a flimsy pink cotton maid's uniform. Black eyebrows and brown eyes belied her long, straight, blond hair. She had three days off. She didn't own a car. And she wanted to check out the rez. She'd just bought a copy of *Geronimo: His Own Story* from the hotel gift shop because the man on the cover looked just like her grandmother Irene—same fierce black eyes, same cheekbones wide as prairies. Only the hair was wrong: her grandmother had had hair like steel wool.

In the foothills, they broke Terry's last ten for gas, and thundered off beyond the Little Big Horn to find Bernice. Jeff had met Bernice, a Cheyenne, in rehab, before he'd found Jesus.

They pulled up near a small white house in a field of stubble, a plain box sheathed in aluminum. When Jeff knocked, the screen door gave a tinny rattle. No answer. Jeff tried to open the outer door to get at the wood behind, but the screen was latched. But he'd roused something—a bolt was drawn. A middle-aged Cheyenne woman opened the inner door a few feet, speaking through the screen, informing Jeff and Terry that Bernice was around somewhere, she didn't know where, she didn't see too much of Bernice. Her eyes slid right off them, like she couldn't stand to look at them.

As Jeff tried to persuade the woman to help them out, Terry wandered off to a decrepit singlewide across the road. A sign over the door advertised "Native Crafts" and a scratched Plexiglas window displayed bead earrings and brown plastic dolls in buckskins. Nothing Terry wanted. It was locked anyway. Round hills rose up behind it, topped with spindling pine trees. The trees reminded her of the hairs on her grandmother's chin. She went back to sit on the steps of the house.

Her grandmother's house, the place Terry had been brought up, had been small and plain too. Irene had had portraits on the wall: not of Terry, or Terry's absent mother, Irene's daughter, but reproductions of Catlin paintings: *Stu-mick-o-súcks, Buffalo Bull's Back Fat, Blood Tribe*, a gorgeous chief, beaded and feathered, face painted with traders' poisonous vermillion, robe trimmed with scalp-locks. And *Beautiful Prairie Bluffs*, a gorgeous land, groves of trees, an ocean of grass, unfenced bluffs rising like breakers out of the sea. These pictures had worked their way into Terry's imagination. She'd asked Irene once why she'd chosen them. "They're handsome," Irene had said. "Besides, my mother was a white cousin to the Indians." But Terry never learned what she had meant by that.

A blue pickup, paint flaking off, pulled up and dropped off two Cheyenne. Jeff knocked Terry off the steps, shouting "Bernice."

"Hi, Jeff, how are you?" said Bernice. Bernice was short and stout and stood like she was rooted. "Remember I told you about my cousin Snaz?" She motioned toward the guy beside her. Snaz loomed over her—pockmarked, with rodeo hips and little raisin eyes. Jeff nudged Terry and said, "Sure. This is Terry. She rode up with me. She wants to see the rez."

"O.K.," said Bernice. "Let's see it." They piled into Jeff's Malibu, and Bernice guided him to The Broken Wheel—more like a basement than a bar. Everything was urethaned, even the foosball. The walls were decorated with an Antelope County Consolidated High School pennant and a few eight-by-tens of Cheyenne dancing in feather regalia or playing basketball. They sat in a row at a counter. Bernice had Coke. Terry had Tab. Jeff had coffee. Snaz had beer.

He swallowed and peered at Terry. "You want to see Indians?" he said, pronouncing it 'indins.' "You want to see Indins? There's one guy here who still has braids. We'll show him to you. He's some Indin." Snaz was some Indian; he was wearing a black Led Zeppelin T-shirt, and his jeans were cinched by a tooled leather belt with a giant buckle blazoned "1968 Bull-Riding Champion" over the shape of a bucking bull. Terry sank down on her barstool and brought her glass up to hide her face.

"How long you been Christian?" asked Bernice, staring at the thick black cross dangling from Jeff's neck. "You weren't a Christian in rehab."

Jeff said, "Bernice, now everything I have, everything I am, is the Lord's. Before, you know how bad I was . . . . "

"You were good," said Bernice, "just like the rest of us . . . can I borrow the Lord's car to pick up Ernestine?" Terry laughed. Jeff extended his arm, offering keys. Terry looked down at his pale arm: she'd seen flesh like that before, dead, hanging from a cross.

She said, "Bernice, wait, I'll go with you." Terry had been testing Jeff's Christian forbearance all the way up from the Bierstadt hotel. It had taken her a few wrong turns to figure out the way. Then the road she'd picked hadn't been so great—how was she to know that a pale grey line meant "unimproved"—but he had overlooked it all. Maybe he was too glazed. He hadn't even tried to touch her.

The road was lively with swerving pickups. Bernice told Terry about this cousin of hers whose truck had wandered across the double yellow about a month ago. "They're wiring his face back together," she said. All Terry could see of Bernice was a black curtain of hair. She hugged her knees and stared at the centerline.

They pulled into a group of shoebox houses, greenish white. The grass grew in ratty clumps and the gravel road became a dozen rutted driveways before it pulled itself together and left for somewhere else.

At Ernestine's, broken shades covered the windows. Out back a flayed deer hung by its hind legs from a wooden frame. Terry liked that deer; it made her feel she'd got somewhere different. The girl who let them in was smaller than Bernice, pockmarked like Snaz, with bangs jagged as a picket fence. The door opened into a room furnished with two vinyl chairs, a Formica and chrome table, and a cluttered army cot.

"Who's that?" said the girl.

"Someone who came with Jeff," said Bernice. She lifted a box off the cot and sat down. The box was printed with a picture of a grinning woman in a bikini, with breasts like grapefruits. "Ernestine likes self-improvement," she said to the air, opening the box and producing a clear plastic pointed cone. The pointed end had a pink hose attached. Graduated lines circled the cone. "Watch 'em grow."

"What?" Terry said.

"You attach the hose to a faucet, and put this over your boob, and it's supposed to stimulate growth. But it didn't. No," said Bernice, "but Ernestine didn't use it much. People kept wanting in the bathroom." She threw the cone aside, and slouched against the wall.

Ernestine said, "Let's go," pulled her off the cot, and steered her out the door to Jeff's car. Bernice rocked it back and forth in the ruts in front of the house. The noise from the muffler echoed.

The car wound from gravel to blacktop and back again as the sky turned black. They weren't going the way they'd come. Terry was almost sure of it. She leaned her head back on the vinyl upholstery. "Don't you think we should get Jeff and Snaz?" she asked. Bernice shrugged. "There's nowhere to go, we can't lose them," she said.

"It seems big to me," Terry said, looking out at the dark, and the weeds in the headlights, and the scattered lights of Lamdo.

"Yeah," said Bernice. "Like two roads, five bars, and three parking lots." The Last Stand's parking lot was blacktop, lit by bare light bulbs on poles. The scabby blue pick-up was right under a light. You could see the paint fall off. "See," said Bernice. "You can't lose anyone here."

"That's the truck that dropped you off, so?" Terry said.

"Snaz could be here, if that truck's here. Go look," said Ernestine.

"Me?" said Terry. "Why me?"

"There might be someone we don't want to see in there," said Bernice.

"Yeah, you go. No one knows you," Ernestine said.

Right inside the door, Terry faced a grainy blow-up of Custer at the Little Big Horn. Custer was waving a pistol, blonde hair flying. Horses and soldiers were dying all over the place. An empty bar stool, chrome and red vinyl, stood in front of a sprawled horse with its teeth showing. On the other side of the stool a dead trooper stared at the sky, his arm sticking up stiff, while an Indian on a pinto horse overrode him. Terry patted down her hair.

Glassware and eyes glittered in a smoky murk. The bar was full of bodies and the reek of alcohol. A jukebox pounded. She spotted the Billy Jack hat. "Jeff!" she called, but it wasn't Jeff. The hair under the hat was long and dark. A few people at the bar turned to stare. She edged past.

"Hey, you lookin' for someone?" asked a shape in a cowboy hat at the corner of the bar. She pretended she didn't hear. The guy at the corner grabbed her. "Hey, who you lookin' for?" She jerked loose.

"Hard liquor stole your mother." That's what her grandma had said. When she was little, she would cross the street rather than walk past the open door of a bar. She'd been afraid that the dark inside, with laughter curling out of it like tentacles, would pull her right in.

There was no sign of Snaz. She pushed her way back past Custer to the parking lot. There was a battle going on there too—Ernestine and Bernice, outside the car, wrestling. Bernice threw something. Terry ducked, turned round, and scooped up the car keys. Ernestine was holding Bernice down. "She . . . won't . . . stop," Ernestine panted.

"Stop what?" Terry asked.

"Jumping up and down. She's bleeding."

"So?"

"She wants to lose the baby."

"What baby? Here?" Terry said.

Ernestine looked at her like she was stupid.

"Anywhere," breathed Bernice. "Let me up."

"No," said Ernestine. "You're bleeding. We should take you to the clinic."

"It's closed," Bernice pointed out.

Ernestine started to cry, but she didn't loosen her grip on Bernice.

"Ernestine, I thought your stepfather told you stay away

from bars." It was the person in the Billy Jack hat, rambling across the blacktop.

"Oh, hi, Lucy," Ernestine said, "We were just looking for Snaz."

"Who's that with you?" Lucy asked, tilting toward Terry. "And why're you sitting on Bernice?"

"Oh, teasing," said Ernestine.

"Well, stop it," Lucy commanded. Ernestine got off. Bernice got to her feet, dusting off her clothes. "Meet Jeff's girlfriend," said Ernestine. Terry didn't deny it.

"Jeff—think I just met someone named Jeff—Snaz left with him—they got a ride with Rufus—what do you want Snaz for? He don't get paid till Friday."

"Where'd you get that hat?" asked Ernestine.

Lucy tilted back a little. "The same place I heard you got that car. A Christian gentleman. He said Bernice'd gone away with his car. . . Snaz said he was going to your house. He took that Jeff with him. He don't like to drink too much. Also, that Jeff don't drink at all.

I did him a favor, taking that hat off him. Christians are called to be charitable—I give him his chance. You know Father Andrew made a million dollars for his clinic off those Christians—with my aunt's picture. Right on the front of the brochure: showed her stump. . . had something about me and Angelica too. My aunt didn't get nothing, though. The diabetes got her. They kept slicing pieces off her like salami, but it got her anyway."

"Thanks, Lucy," said Ernestine.

"It's nothing. Snaz won't have any money till Friday." Lucy turned back toward the bar, then turned around as if she'd just thought of something. She put a hand on Ernestine's arm. "Can you take Angelica? For a few hours? I just got her back."

"She'll be back in care, you keep it up."

"Can you take her?"

"You'll come get her soon?"

"Yeah. I'm okay. I just ran into a few friends. I just picked her up. She's inside. Just a sec."

Lucy returned with a bundle in a blanket, and handed it to Ernestine. Bernice slid behind the wheel, her eyes half-closed,

Ernestine by her side, holding the baby Angelica. Terry sat in back again, resting her chin on the front seat.

Jeff was on the little wooden porch, with a shepherd dog, when they pulled up at Ernestine's. He looked short without the hat.

"Where were you?" he shouted.

"Where were you?" Ernestine shouted back. Getting out, Terry tripped on the ruts in the yard.

"We waited for you," said Jeff.

"We looked for you. Why'd you give Lucy your hat?" asked Bernice, on her way into the house.

"She admired it. Said it reminded her of someone she used to know. She seemed sad. So I gave it to her."

Ernestine pushed by with Angelica. Terry sat down close to Jeff and muttered "I want to leave." Hadn't her grandmother also kept the Irish Blessing on her wall? Maybe Irish was the way to go. Druids. Celtic knots. Didn't the Irish have wide cheekbones too? Since the Danes had traded with Mongols and invaded Ireland? And where did her grandmother's woolly hair come from? Maybe she was black—or Jewish—she knew some Jewish kids with hair like that. Of course, Terry's hair was stick-straight and, left alone, brown.

Jeff said, "We can't leave yet, I want to see my friends. We have to help Bernice."

"What do you mean, help Bernice?"

"Well, she's expecting. And she's sharing her grandmother's food stamps. They're not enough for two people. She needs her own food stamps."

"Can't she get them herself?"

"She asked me to help."

"What, a Jesus freak she met in rehab?"

"She asked me."

Terry went inside, leaving Jeff alone on the porch with the dog. Snaz was saying, "You let her stick you with that baby again? Last time she didn't come back for three days."

"Shhh. The baby's asleep. Besides, she's a cousin." Ernestine laid Angelica down on the cot, and Bernice lay down and curled round the baby. She stroked the hair on the child's temples and crooned to her.

Snaz was sitting at the table with a knife, cutting up a Pepsi can. He removed the top and bottom and sliced the cylinder open, creating a sharp-edged aluminum rectangle. Then he got a long piece of wire, a flashlight and a pair of leather gloves down from the shelf over the table, and went outside. Curious, Terry followed him out. Snaz crawled under the car. Terry squatted down in the mud to watch. Snaz handed her the flashlight. He used the wire to fix the can in place over a hole in the muffler. He crawled out, shook off the mud, and said, "That should do it—let's try it."

Jeff, still on the porch, shouted for Bernice. She came, holding her stomach. Ernestine came along behind, jiggling Angelica. Jeff stood before the car, arms outstretched.

"What are you doing?" demanded Bernice.

"Blessing it," said Jeff, mumbling into his beard.

"Man," said Bernice. "What happened to you? You weren't like this in rehab . . . "

"May the Lord bless this car, and keep it running, and keep all who ride in it . . . ," intoned Jeff.

Snaz came up behind Jeff and added, "Spirits hear us; may this car be filled with good gas and good mileage . . . "

Ernestine joggled Angela and added, "Lord, spirits, big and little, great and small, take us for a drive . . . "

Bernice took a breath and said, "Ma'heo'o, nehnêševata-memeno, okay, then, take this car, and let it carry us where we belong . . . . Henahi!" She picked up some dirt and tossed it at the windshield.

Geronimo had warned, *"The sun, the darkness, the winds are all listening to what we have to say."* So Terry said nothing.

Everyone piled in. Snaz took them up by the radio tower, the highest hill on the reservation. The roar was gone. The yellow grass whipped by, the tree trunks made long spears of the car lights, and the wind brought in the smell of dust and pine. The Malibu bounced over the ruts. The baby laughed. For a moment they hovered above the little house and the flayed deer.

Then Snaz leaned over the steering wheel, taking them down faster and faster. The car bounded higher. The wheels caught in a rut. . . the headlights flickered, and in the flicker Terry caught a glimpse of *a herd of buffalo, scattered. A fine country, rich in grass. . . great numbers of buffalo, elk, and deer, and antelope. Large timber, and on the plain by the bend in the river, a circle of conical tipis.* She could see it. Like the *Beautiful Prairie Bluffs*, open land, rolling on forever. A few people, on horseback and foot, abroad in the land.

Then the Malibu rolled.

Terry came to before sunrise. The world was rimed and ghostly. A dog sniffed outside the window. She was all alone in the car. She tried to open the door, but it was too bent-up. She broke out the window with her foot and crawled out.

Her grandmother had said, "It slips away, it slips away so fast."

"What?" Terry had said to her grandmother. "What?"

She limped down the hill. The dog trotted before her, smelling and peeing. It was so early it was impossible to tell if the gray was dawn or clouds—there were no shadows, just the dog and Terry, and the little hills. Then the dog circled back. She limped on alone to a gas station and slipped into the restroom to clean up, scrubbing dried blood off with rough brown paper towels.

Where had they gone? Jeff would never have left her in a wreck, alone. And what had she seen through the windshield? The memory of the painting on her grandmother's wall? Her legs hurt, but she kept on to the nearest clump of white houses.

No one came to her knock.

She sat down at the edge of the road, in the weeds. And when a man came by, offering her a ride in his pick-up, she climbed in. When he asked her who she was and where she was going, she could barely speak. "South," she said.

Somehow, ride by ride, she made it back to the hotel in Bierstadt. She slept for a day, and then took up her work sanitizing toilets. She tried to forget she'd ever seen that fine country, rich in grass and beasts. But when she walked outside the hotel, there it was again, on the other side of plate glass instead of a windshield. A 130-year-old painting, framed in gold, ten feet long, and six feet high. On a street lined with galleries. *A fine country. . .* She stared. . . *a wide river of clear water, meandering through a level meadow,—groves of trees and shrubs bordering the bank, and creeks and runs falling into it. Bottom land covered with grass. On the rising lands, grass and rich weeds and flowers, interspersed with plum, and grapes and wild cherries growing on the tops of hills in every direction.* In the right-hand corner of that painting, *a baby tucked in a cradleboard, leaning against a tipi. The tipi's sides opened wide in the heat of the afternoon. Snaz skinning a deer. Ernestine holding on to a tipi pole, talking to Bernice. . . a toddler clinging to Ernestine's tunic, and a dog barking. . . .*

It does slip away. But the artist caught it. And Terry was caught by it, transfixed, right there on the sidewalk, as tourists jostled by.

Then she walked. Concrete is the hardest surface in the world to walk on. Men offered her rides, but she shook her blond head, even when she'd walked to the edge of town, walked to nothing but blacktop and parking lots and exhaust fumes. *The sun, the darkness, the winds are all listening to what we have to say.* Had the dark heard Bernice that night on the rez, reached out and taken her in?

Terry went back to the painting. Evening was coming on, but the gallery had spotlights trained on the canvas. She could see Ernestine's crooked bangs and Snaz's raisin eyes, and Bernice, standing like she was rooted to the center of the world. But what had become of Jeff?

And then she saw him: *a man on a mule, picking his way down the hills, holding a black book under his arm, accompanied by a party of soldiers.*

Terry wanted to warn them all, tell them what was coming. But they couldn't hear her. And anyway, they already knew. ☙

THE ASYLUM

PATRICIA LEWIS

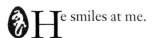He smiles at me.

"Liftoff will be in six minutes."

"Thank you." I look around the cabin and see that there is one other passenger on this flight. Taking a deep breath I'm amazed at how calm I feel. Of course after everything that has happened, calm is a good thing.

My name is Mari and my first and most vivid memory is when I was four years old and I almost died from pneumonia. I was in the hospital, and a doctor was standing and talking with my mom and dad, just outside the doorway. The doctor's voice was like a bass drum, saying, "We're going to need to keep Mari in the oxygen tent and hope that her fever breaks soon. Because, while I'm not going to give up hope, if the fever doesn't break, I don't believe that she'll make it. If you folks pray the way that little girl of yours does, it wouldn't hurt any to do so." He turned away and what he said next was lost in the whirr of the oxygen pump, a thunderous pain in my head, and a racking cough that brought me closer to the darkness.

A nurse quickly moved to my bedside, reached under the plastic tent and lifted my shoulders up. "Doctor, you need to come in here quickly," she whispered loudly.

The doctor gave my parents a quick sideways glance and came to my bedside, letting the door swing shut as he did so.

Throughout that night, I remember dreaming of walking on the clouds with God and running through flower-strewn meadows. There was a bright light and God said, "Mari, you aren't done with your life yet. You need to come back and stay here on this world a while longer." The light disappeared and I was aware of someone holding my hand.

"Well, young lady, it's nice to see you've come back to us." The doctor smiled at my parents and told them, "She's going to be just fine, probably a bit frail, but she's come through the worst of it. Now, I'll leave you three alone, but not for long. Mari needs her rest." He patted my hand and placed it on top of the covers.

The next four years are a dim blur of living in a place full of people who had no time for my chattering and questioning the why and how of everything. Things weren't so bleak, in case that's what you're thinking. I had a small kitten and a couple of friends at school. Plus all the free time to dream and read that a kid could want. The one place I could always be found was in the garden by the old crumbled church. I'd take my kitten and a book and we'd while away the hours either reading or looking up at the clouds and I'd make up stories about their shapes. I always felt safe there because that is where God came to me and we'd talk . . .

My mom and dad met during Dad's fourth year on Asylum and Mom's first. She was the head nutritionist and in charge of food service and dietary needs. He was just finishing his Residency in hospital administration. They always said that it was love at first sight. So they got married and two years later, I came along.

My mom and dad worked away from the staff housing sections, before the fences with the razor wire went up. Every morning they'd leave me at child care and, later, at school, with a kiss and a promise, "We love you for ever and ever and one more day, and we'll be back before you even know that we're gone." Funny how memories like that stay with you. They actually kept their promise to return—every day but one.

Just after my eighth birthday, my father and I were discussing who would get the last piece of my green mint birthday cake. Mother suggested that I go down to the kitchen and get it and that maybe we could all share it. That was the last time I saw them alive.

There was a riot, and they died.

A transport had arrived carrying about fifty hardened criminals seeking sanctuary. It was granted to them, provided they turned over all of their weapons, which they did. The one thing that they didn't say was that *they* were weapons, too. While they were being led to a general holding area as the paperwork was being done, a mentally unstable but harmless patient, who loved to kick, got too close to one of the men and kicked him. The criminal's hand shot out and with one swift movement snapped the poor man's neck. A couple of the more vocal patients started screaming and throwing things which managed to escalate into a full riot. The state police were called in and, by the end of the battle, hundreds were dead, including my mom and dad and the 'fifty' as they had come to be called.

I escaped by hiding in one of the pantries in the kitchen and asking God over and over to keep my mom and dad and me from harm. I was there for three days before I worked up enough courage to come out and discover that God had only answered part of my plea.

I was placed into an orphanage that was started because so many children had lost their families. Later, many of the brick buildings were sealed up and turned into huge crypts with electrified fences surrounding them and signs reading DO NOT ENTER.

That one act of terrorism caused the authorities to look at the way sanctuary to Asylum was granted, and it was decided that all buildings deemed "high security" would be surrounded with razor wire fencing and have separate intake facilities. Our world was turned into areas of minimum- and high-security. It turned out that life in the orphanage wasn't that much different from before. My faith and belief in God, while shaky for a while, eventually grew stronger and deeper.

I graduated from high school, never getting good grades, but trying harder than any other student to learn what was being taught. I loved literature, music and my religion studies. Often, thinking back to when my parents were alive, I'd find myself smiling at the memory of my dad trying so hard to teach me the concepts of math. Anything beyond the basics was a losing cause. I would tell him that I could see most anything like it was written on my mind, everything except numbers.

Then he would say softly, "That's okay, kid. Not everyone needs to be an Einstein. Besides, who else do we know who can grow plants with almost nothing but air and fix all the sick animals around?"

From books in the library, I read about people like me who were healers and empaths. These were people who could grow plants, heal animals, and even people, just by touching them. I could really listen to people and hear what they weren't saying, but wanted to say. But, beyond all of that, I was the only person I ever knew who prayed and had actual conversations with God. The orphanage staff sometimes found my view of the world disconcerting, but they did support me in all of my manifestations of illness. It wasn't that my life was any different from anyone else's, nor was I really different. Well, except for my brain. I always thought that I was different because of my conversations with God. During one of the many tests I had—this one an MRI to find out why I had migraines—we found out that it may have had something to do with the actual shape of my brain. The day for the MRI came and they had me lie down on a moving table to take pictures of my brain to try to pinpoint where the migraine was.

"Mari," the tech told me, "don't worry. This won't hurt and, besides, it may be the last test we need do." The look in his eyes was pleading, and I nodded my head, lay down, and crossed my arms in resignation over my chest. Afterward, he showed me the pictures of my brain.

"This is unusual. See these ridges here and here?"

"Yeah, what do they mean?" I asked.

"Well, you're going to have to wait for the doctor to explain what all this means. It isn't my place."

"Why can't you? Don't you know what it means?"

"Yeah, I think I know, but I've broken one rule by showing you these images. I'm not going to break another rule. I just thought you deserved a look. You were very brave, and it is your brain. So go on back into the exam room and I'll tell the doc that we're done. Okay?" He smiled and patted my shoulder.

Feeling pain radiating from his hand, I closed my eyes and lifted my shoulder and pressed my cheek against his hand. I turned just outside the door and smiled at the look of wonder on his face. "Okay, I'm back," I said to the nurse as I passed her station.

"Thanks, Mari. I'll send him in as soon as he's free."

The wait was short and, when he came in, he explained that the inside of a normal skull is evenly round and the two halves of the brain sit side by side like two halves of an apple. He showed me a picture in his medical book. The picture of the inside of my head didn't look like that. It was all wrong. There was a small ridge like a rough mountain range growing down from the top of my skull. It split the two halves of my brain so they didn't touch each other like normal.

"Mari, you have to take what I tell you as my professional observation. This looks like something you've had all your life. It's amazing that your brain formed itself around the jagged edges while not causing any mental or physical damage."

As soon as he started conferring with other doctors, I became an object of study for the local medical school and any visiting doctors. It seems that they wanted me for a long-term case study. Permission, not mine, was given and the next few years were filled with people I didn't know, all intent upon discovering the hows and whys of my brain and my body. Then, when I was fifteen years old, I slipped on something at the medical school while going down stairs for another test.

After falling down a full flight of stairs my head hit a tiled wall and my brain turned off. The doctors who had been studying me all shrugged their shoulders and called in a specialist, who in turn consulted other specialists. Their considered opinion was that, even though I was still breathing on my own and there was a small trace of brain wave activity, I was a level one coma victim. Citing the well-known Glasgow Scale, I was pronounced as being in the deepest level of coma with no chance of recovery. Having lost all value as a willing victim, they immediately transferred me, all expenses paid, to the Coma Ward in the asylum where I had been until just a few days before.

The doctors in the Coma Ward inserted tubes for feeding, taped on diapers, ran the usual I.V. lines, and wired up electronic monitors.

For the next fifteen years my life was one of sponge baths, being turned three times a day, with periodic visits from the doctors. Time had no meaning. I had no awareness of self or of the world around me. The monitors still said that my heart was beating, slowly but with regular rhythm, and there was still the same amount of brain activity. Such was my life right up until two days before my thirtieth birthday.

On that unremarkable overcast morning, the darkness inside my mind began to turn a softer foggy gray. Long dormant electrical pulses and synapses began firing, first intermittently and then more and more of them throughout the day. I heard a voice in my mind. It was calm and reassuring. "My child, it's time for you to wake up. I need you to be well, you have some very important work to do, so you must get well and leave this place."

I'd heard that voice before. The memories were slow to form, and then, it was the one I remembered hearing in the womb and then again all throughout my childhood. How could I know this? I felt it echo throughout my whole body.

The condition of coma returned, and I was in darkness again.

My increasing brain activity and physical movement alerted the nurses. Doctors, experts and specialists came and tried to explain what to them was inexplicable. The poking, prodding, and examining resumed. It was another quiet drizzly day. The voice was back. "My child, Mari, you will slowly wake up. You shall be totally aware of your surroundings in another three days."

Once again, I felt comforted and sure of the road to follow. A dream/vision came to me of green, forested hills, valleys with lakes as blue as the azure sky. I saw animals and people living in a harmony unknown to any who have spent their lives on Asylum. I was filled with peace and hope.

In the smallest fraction of time before I awaken, the voice says softly, "Mari, it's time for you to begin your work."

I am fully awake.

I open my eyes and look around a room filled with people wearing white lab coats. I hear my rasping voice: "May I have some green water, please?"

Startled pandemonium erupts with everyone competing for the glass and pitcher at the same time. Three people thrust straws into the glass. I look around the room and smile up at every one and whisper, "Just one will do." I take my first sip of water. It isn't green, but I don't care. "This is good." I continue sipping until the glass is empty. I feel a strange surge in energy and vitality. My voice is still raspy, but gaining in strength. Unlike the doctors, I understand how and why this is happening at this time, but, with my stomach growling like a lion, my mind is filled with visions of food.

"Please, I'd like a green mint milkshake, a hamburger with everything on it and fries with green ketchup."

The quiet in the room is total. No one moves as I begin pulling off wires and start to remove I.V.'s. They appear horrified and awed. Still, no one moves. Rising frustration in my voice brings them back to this moment in time, and I nearly yell, "I'd like for everyone but that nurse"—I see her name tab clearly—"Debbie to leave now."

There's confusion and chatter that I am not rational. But I look directly at them and they can see that things are indeed different. In moments the six doctors, the other four nurses, two physicians' assistants, and one candy striper are gone. In the sudden quiet, I look at Debbie.

"Whew. I'm glad that they're all gone. Do you think that you could remove the rest of these tubes and then I'd really like a shower and shampoo." I reach up to feel my hair. My fingers slip through short curls. "What happened to my hair?"

Debbie smiles and, while she begins removing the rest of the tubes and wires, she explains, "Our number one rule in this ward; every coma patient gets a crew cut. Besides, you weren't up to brushing it every night anyway, were you?"

"But, I don't have a crew cut. Why is mine nearly two inches long?"

"Well, about three months ago, I had a dream that you were about to wake up. I've been working with you for over five years and when I mentioned the dream to the doctor, he said maybe it would be okay to let your hair grow, so we did." She finishes removing my last connection to the machines. "You do realize that you're going to be asked many questions in the following days. Do you think you're up to that?"

"Yes, I'll be ready. First, can you help me with a shower and some real food? Then, I want to go to church, even if it's only the chapel here in the hospital. Can you arrange that for me?" I feel stronger than I've ever felt in my life. As I sit up, the room tilts and I almost fall over, but the dizziness fades quickly. I look at Debbie, then push the covers aside and swing my feet off the edge of the bed. My legs are flushed and pink. They're thin, but feel warm. The cool air down the back of my open hospital gown feels refreshing and I slide a little until my feet hit the floor.

Debbie is wide-eyed, mouth open, the forgotten chart board dangling between two fingers. "You shouldn't be able to do that. You haven't had enough physical ther—"

I stand at the edge of the bed and finish her sentence, "therapy, yes, but I feel so wonderful." There's no pain, the floor is cool, and I can clearly hear the sound of my heart filled with rushing blood.

"You shouldn't be standing. Why are you standing?" Debbie reaches out to steady me.

"Well, now that I'm back, there's no reason for me not to be, is there?" Not waiting for an answer I take one step and then another. Debbie quickly grabs my arm and we head for the shower.

"It looks like I'm going to need soap, shampoo, cream rinse, a toothbrush, toothpaste, comb and brush, and I owe you thanks for this." I pat my head and look in the mirror. The past fifteen years have seen me grow from a teenager into an adult. I look just like I remember my mother. I run my fingers through short coppery hair and peer intently at my green eyes and pink skin. I scrunch my nose and say, "I guess we better add some moisturizer, lip-gloss and clothes, too."

Debbie is a darling; she never misses a beat. "Okay, but first, we get you scrubbed and dried, then, it's back in bed for you. Then I'll go see what I can find, but you have to promise to rest until I get back. Deal?"

"Deal."

Outside in hospital corridor there is a cacophony of voices, some shouting to be heard. "What do you mean she's up and wants a shower? There's no way on earth that she could possibly walk without months of intensive physical therapy. Not to mention we don't know what her mental state is. She's been. . . " The agitated voice fades away along with all the others as Debbie closes the bathroom door. The water in the shower is warm. I lean my head back and let the spray hit my head and back. The shampoo smells like fresh cantaloupe. My stomach rumbles, eager to have actual food instead of liquid from a tube. I rinse my hair and shampoo it again, massaging my scalp with a brush. With a good scrubbing completed, Debbie helps with drying and gives me real pajamas to put on, and then I'm back in a freshly made bed, feeling tired but alive. Debbie reminds me that I promised to stay put, then leaves me alone, lying in the sunlight coming through the window.

The clatter of a cart reaches my ears just before the aroma of French fries reaches my nose. I swing my legs off the bed and Debbie places a table in front of me. I look up and see the shadow of where a cross used to be on the wall. The last few hours have been so hectic that although I've had a shower and food is before me, I haven't prayed.

Debbie follows my eyes to the empty space on the wall, and says, "Don't worry. We have a number of people looking for the chapel. Since you've been in the coma, religion has given way to science and disbelief in the mystical, so most people have little use for them, and most of the local chapels and churches have been repurposed." She bites her bottom lip and shrugs her shoulders. "Come on now and eat, before it gets cold," she says and goes to clean up the bathroom.

Finding the building's chapel isn't easy. It hasn't been used for so long that they have to locate the plans for this building. The doctors and I have some little argument about whether I can walk on my own or must be pushed in a wheel chair. I find the chair comfortable enough, but I am frustrated that I have to travel at the speed of Debbie's careful hospital walk. After what seems like endless dark hallways and corridors, I am pushed into a dark, but once beautiful, room.

On either side of what was once an altar are cracked and broken stained glass windows depicting the birth and resurrection of Jesus Christ. The once golden cross is lying on its side against the wall with scraps of wood and paper. I know that this is only a room, but my heart aches at the deliberate neglect and destruction I see all around me. I close my eyes and take a deep breath before standing up, and I gag on the sickly smell of mold, mildew and rot that fills the room. I stand, and, with Debbie's help, kneel on the hard floor. I feel cold tears coursing down my cheeks as I bend my head. I hear no sounds. It is as if the room is filled with darkness. The air is clear and pure. I take a breath and begin my prayer.

"God, I thank you for this day, for all the days to come and all the days that have been. Thank you for restoring me to life and for choosing me as your messenger. I ask for blessings on all your children and for all those who have never found you or have lost their way. Please help me keep the tasks you set for me in my heart and mind and give me the strength that I may handle all of them. I bless and praise your holy name. These things I pray in the name of your son. Amen." I hold my mind still, letting the awareness of where I am seep back into me. New strength flows into me. I'm warm and full of God's grace. Sensing my purpose, Debbie helps me to stand.

The group of people who have followed me, whether to see me fail or to marvel at my sudden vigor, is silent as I turn to face them. "You have twelve days to ask all your questions because, at the end of that time, I will be leaving the asylum. God has given me a task for which I've been preparing all my life." I sit in the wheelchair, reach down, unlock the wheels, and, under my own power, push myself out into the hallway. "You should also consider returning this room to its original use. You may find that there will be others who may be in need of a chapel or church in the days ahead."

The next two weeks are filled with questions, exams, and more questions, the most prevalent being: Why did I wake up and what makes me think that God is speaking to me? That last question makes as much sense as asking if the sun shines. For their scientific questions, I have no answers. In regard to their questions of God and faith, I answer with a smile and whispered prayers of thanks to God and begin my teaching.

In the last days of my stay in the asylum, the doctors agree that my recovery, recuperation, and rehabilitation are the result of new treatments and medications. They attribute my constant brain wave activity and breathing on my own, while in a stage one coma, as significant, but aren't sure why. I, on the other hand, do know that they simply don't have a clue, they don't understand, and that's the problem. For me, I know that it's a miracle.

It's my last morning in this place. The miracle continues, as I'm healthier than ever in my life and no longer belong here. I sort through my meager personal possessions, keeping only some sheet music, a photograph of my parents on their wedding day and one of the three of us taken on my eighth birthday. Also a few favorite books and a small teddy bear I made before I was injured and fell into a coma. Everything else I label for Debbie to distribute. Debbie walks into my room.

"Mari, the taxi is ready. You're sure that you really want to leave? I've heard that leaving the asylum and entering a world of life can be difficult."

"Debbie, it's funny, but all the years I spent being afraid and so concerned because I was different, well, none of it matters any more. I'm well and know that I have a mission to complete for God, and then I'll have a home to go to where I'll be loved and cherished for the rest of my life. So, don't worry about me, this is going to be a grand adventure." I pick up my suitcase and walk the empty halls to the front door. Debbie's hug is warm and sincere.

I walk down the stairs of the huge dark building and I'm assailed by the stink of rotting vegetation and offal. I turn and wave at Debbie and catch the scent of burning flesh on the wind. The sight of the dead plants and grasses brings tears to my eyes and the sky is a sick brownish blue from pollution. There are people in hovels separated by fences, most looking so lost in their own misery or fighting their own demons they don't even see me. Here and there, other clear ones, bright and shining, more of God's children, meet my gaze. Sometime in the future they too will follow me.

I enter the taxi and ride in silence. There's no need to tell the driver where to go. When you leave Asylum there is only one destination, the transport station. There are no guards, no tickets, just a long walkway with a bright yellow line leading to an elevator. With my small bag of possessions in hand, I ride upward to the door of the transport. I see that there is only one other with me on this trip. This seems like such an enormous vessel for only two people. The flight attendant shows me where to put my things and then helps get me ready for takeoff. He smiles at me and says. "Liftoff will be in six minutes. We keep the windows shuttered for the first few moments of flight to protect the glass from things in the lower atmosphere, but, as soon as they open, you may want to look out to your left. You'll be able to have your last view of Asylum. It may help keep your life in perspective. I know it does mine." The man moves off, ignoring the other passenger as if he weren't there. My stomach is filled with a sudden fluttering. Waiting for lift off, I remember a vision from a time just before waking from my coma. My home would eventually be a world of trees, water, bright sunshine and people. I know the voice that has been calling me. I am on my way to the stars because God has called on me to help bring sanity to the universe. I feel warmth as somewhere below me vibrations of mighty engines ripple through the ship. I'm pushed back into my seat, breathless and immovable for an eternity of seconds.

As the pressure eases off, I catch a glimpse of the other passenger who smiles and winks and is gone. Suddenly the shutters snap open, and I move to take one last look at where I have been all my life to see a holographic sign painted across the sky.

YOU ARE LEAVING PLANET EARTH
INSANE ASYLUM OF THE UNIVERSE

Garbage Man

Clarence Moriwaki

"Remember, you're advancing the route for the President," said the director of Near Space Refuse, Inc.

Yeah, I've gotta keep reminding myself that, Ted thought as he fired a particle beam and destroyed another piece of space debris.

"Ted, we appreciate your work. When you get back on Earth, go out and have a drink on the company account."

Ted gave as convincing a smile as he could. "Thanks, boss."

"Keep up the good work."

As the communications screen went dark Ted blurted out, "Big friggin' deal, one whole damn drink. I hope it doesn't break the company's back."

It better turn out better than the last time I went out for a drink, Ted thought as he mentally replayed his most recent bar visit.

"Hi, mind if I join you?"

Ted looked up from his beer and saw the smile of a lovely woman whom he was sure he should know.

"Uh, sure, please, have a seat."

The woman sat down and flipped her long red hair over her shoulder.

"Thanks, I'm just a wreck after the day I've had."

"Wow. If this is what you look like after a wreck, throw me in front of that bus."

With a cute giggle she said, "You're funny."

"Yeah, but looks aren't everything."

She laughed. "That's great. Hi, my name is Kelly."

He reached out his hand. "Nice to meet you. I'm Ted."

As Ted gently took her hand, he noticed how small and soft it felt.

"So, what are you drinking?" Ted asked.

"Oh, I guess I'll have a vodka martini."

Ted raised his hand and caught the eye of the waitress.

"Hi, what may I get for you tonight?"

He noticed that her name tag said Ginger.

"Ginger, Kelly here would like a vodka martini."

"Great. Anything else?"

"Kelly, would you like something to eat?"

"No, but thanks for asking."

"One vodka martini coming up."

"Thanks Ginger," Ted said.

"That's very nice that you used her name," Kelly said.

"Well, everyone deserves respect. She's a human being and not just a servant, an object."

"That's considerate. I'm tired of being treated like an object."

"Really? That's sad."

"Well, I guess I have it coming. I don't like to tell many people this because they think I don't have a brain, but I'm a model."

That figures, she's gorgeous

"You are? Anything I might have seen you in?"

"I do the FiveStar beverage commercials. In fact, I was just doing a shoot for the past three hours, by the spaceport, down the street when I dropped in here."

"I knew I'd seen you somewhere! Well, this is quite an honor."

"Thanks, but having good DNA is just dumb luck. It's not like I can fly a spacecraft or anything."

"Funny you should mention that. That's what I do."

"Really? Tell me more."

"Well, I got started as a shuttle astronaut taking science crews into lower orbit on research missions and such, and then I went into the private sector with TransLunar training their pilots to take commercial passengers to the moon."

"That sounds exciting. I've never been in space, I'm too scared."

"There's nothing to be frightened of. Statistically it's the safest form of travel ever invented."

"Yeah, but I hear reports of ships colliding with old satellites and all that other space junk up there. I hear it's like a great big garbage dump."

"You're right, there is an amazing amount of material in orbit. For the past century nations and companies have treated it like an endless landfill. In fact, I have them to thank for my job."

"What do you do exactly?"

"I fly a ship for Near Space Refuse, Inc. We find and destroy space debris so that other craft can navigate safely."

"So, you're a high-flying garbage man?"

"Hey, a little respect here. I didn't call you some airhead model."

Kelly immediately crossed her arms and became silent.

"Here's your vodka martini," Ginger said.

"Thanks Ginger." Ted began to reach for his wallet.

"No, I can pay for my own drink," Kelly said as she reached into her small purse. "I may be an airhead to you, but I make more in a day than you probably make in a year."

"Wait a minute. I'm sorry if I offended you, but even though I may be just a 'high-flying garbage man' to you, I take my work very seriously."

Kelly stood up and picked up her drink.

"Since you had such a great sense of humor, I thought you could tell I was just trying to make a joke."

Ted stood up and reached for Kelly's arm but, before he could say he was sorry, Kelly swiftly pulled back.

"Don't touch me!" she screamed.

Four men who had been eyeing Kelly since she entered the bar quickly came to her side.

"Hey, is this jerk bothering you?" one of the men said.

"Take it easy, this is just a little misunderstanding," Ted said.

"Well, I'm sure you can understand this," the man said as he slammed a solid right hook into Ted's face.

"Vessel approaching, high speed" the computer warned. Ted snapped out of his reverie. "What the hell. . . . " He glanced at his monitor, which showed a commercial shuttle rapidly approaching.

"Unidentified vessel, this is Near Space 15 conducting debris demolition. Please alter course to avoid particle beam contact."

"Near Space 15, this is TransLunar 20. Emergency. Our main thrusters are jammed wide open. We have lost maneuvering rockets. We have swerved off course and sustained serious damage from space debris. We can't take much more damage. Please respond."

"TransLunar 20, this is Near Space 15. Can you decelerate?"

"Negative. Debris damage knocked out our retro rockets and all cockpit control. We are unable to manually cut off fuel supply, which is rapidly burning out, compromising all systems including air supply."

"I get the picture, TransLunar 20. I will plot a course 10,000 km ahead of your trajectory and clear a path for your craft."

"Affirmative, Near Space 15. Thank you!"

"No worries, TransLunar 20."

Ted fired thrusters and quickly modified orbit to be able to cut through any debris that would intercept the runaway path of the passenger shuttle.

"Near Space 15, this is Near Space Control. Why have you deviated course?"

"Near Space Control, this is Near Space 15. We have an emergency. TransLunar 20 is a runaway shuttle heading through my debris field. They have sustained major debris impact damage and I am clearing a path for them."

"Ted, this is the director. You are not authorized to change course. Your priority mission is making a debris-free path for the President. Return to your previous course."

"Director, with all due respect. That ship is losing life support, and we're the only thing that can possibly save them."

"Ted, TransLunar isn't paying our bills, the President is. Get back on course!"

"Sorry sir, he'll just have to wait."

Ted ended the transmission and continued to destroy debris with his particle beam.

"Near Space 15, this is TransLunar 20. Do you read?"

"TransLunar 20, I have you."

"You may have us in more ways than one. We are coming on your position very fast. I suggest you accelerate right now."

Ted increased his speed, which forced him to work even faster destroying debris.

"Near Space 15, this is TransLunar 20. We estimate proximity in five minutes."

"I understand. How is your air holding out?"

"We estimate battery reserve of twenty minutes."

"How many aboard?"

"Eleven, including crew."

They just might fit in the cargo hold

"TransLunar 20, here's the plan. I'm almost done clearing your debris path. Once you get out of the debris field, you'll have clear sailing. We can then rendezvous and transfer all of you to my ship's cargo hold."

"Sounds like a long shot, NearSpace 15, but the only one we got. Thanks."

"No worries. Hey, TransLunar, you got a name?"

"Yeah, it's Bob."

"Glad to meet you Bob. I'm Ted."

"Ted? Not Ted the ball breaker?"

"Do I know you?"

"No, but I know you. You taught me space flight at Trans-Lunar Academy five years ago."

"Well I'll be…well, Bob, in just a minute we'll see if you took good notes."

"Yes sir."

Looking out of the window, Ted could now see the TransLunar passenger shuttle rapidly approaching.

"Bob, you should be clearing the field very soon. When you

do, I will fire auxiliary thrusters to try and keep pace with you."

"Understood. Looking forward to seeing you again."

The TransLunar shuttle zoomed by. Ted tightened his seat belts and fired every system his craft had to close the distance to the disabled passenger vessel. As he accelerated, the bright light from the shuttle's engines began to grow dimmer and dimmer, indicating that their fuel was burning out.

As the distance between the two craft began to grow smaller and smaller, Ted said, "Bob, I'm nearly beside you. Get all of your passengers and crew near the docking port. Give everyone emergency respirators. The umbilical tunnel will be pressurized, but it was made for cargo, not people."

"Understood. So we're going first class?"

"Sorry, Bob, the cargo hold is the best I can do."

"Sounds like heaven to me."

Ted skillfully maneuvered his craft next to the shuttle as he extended the umbilical tunnel to the shuttle's docking port. The tunnel magnetically attached with a reassuring thunk.

"Airway secure," Bob said as cheering could be heard in the background.

"Don't relax yet. All of you have to be in the cargo hold before I can release the tunnel. Please move swiftly. By my calculations, you have less than four minutes of air supply."

Bob directed his crew and passengers from his shuttle and through the tunnel onto Near Space 15. As in time-honored tradition, Bob was the last person to leave his ship. He stepped through the entry port and sealed the door behind him.

Bob reached for the ship's intercom and took off his emergency respirator. "Ted, all safely aboard. You can release TransLunar 20."

Ted retracted the umbilical tunnel, dumping air, and pulled away from the shuttle. He flicked on the ship's public address system.

"Welcome aboard Near Space 15. I'm your captain and I hope you have an enjoyable flight today. We know that there are several garbage ships to choose from and we are happy that you chose us. We should arrive on Earth in five hours. On behalf of the crew and all of us at Near Space Refuse, Inc., please find a cushy sack or container, strap yourself down, relax and enjoy your flight."

Ted was examining his monitor plotting his course for the return to Earth when someone buzzed the entry button to the cockpit door. "Enter," Ted said as he pushed the open door button.

"Hi, may I join you?"

That voice sounds so familiar

Ted spun his seat and saw Kelly drifting into the cockpit.

"What the heck. . . ."

"Wouldn't you know it," Kelly said as she floated toward Ted. "I finally take my first trip to the moon to do a FiveStar beer commercial. . . ."

"Do you believe me now that space flight is statistically the safest form of travel ever invented?" Ted said.

Kelly tried to grin, but emotions overwhelmed her.

"I was so unfair to you back then. I owe you an apology; I owe you my life. . . ."

"Nah, you just owe me a drink."

Kelly's tears looked like small clear pearls as they floated around the cockpit.

Ted extended his arm and Kelly grabbed his hand, pulling herself down to place a brief kiss on his cheek.

Kelly smiled as she looked into Ted's eyes and said, "I'll see you on Earth, garbage man."

Ted touched her face and replied, "I'm looking forward to it, airhead." 🐾

Tabit's Odyssey

Christine Wyatt

Tabit Gettar, Ph.D., grade 3G lucid sleep/dreamer, slogged toward consciousness, doggedly straining to close in, as if inch by inch, on the brassy jangle of *Argos II*'s klaxons. With all her concentration focused on clearing the fog, she burned with one aim in mind, to start her quick-thaw. She willed her right thumb to twitch the needed millimeter and press against a switch. And then she felt her organs begin to tingle.

In time, most of her fingers were functioning and they moved toward the catch of her plexi cryo. And, with a groan, she folded out of her pod. Achingly, her body stumbled through its paces, as it had done before back on Terra in drill after drill after drill.

With the odd sense that she was watching herself from somewhere above her head, she hopped on one foot, pulling on her thermo-suit, then maneuvered around Captain Cole's pod, thumping on the buttons of his "defrost/unlatch" sequence. Only when all instruments blinked green did she race to the far end of the line of frozen crew for Communications Officer Jemmona Braughan's cryo.

Why A.I. had thawed Tabit first rather than the captain was

puzzling. It was the first time Tabit hadn't awakened seeing Cole's stern, inscrutable face peering down at her.

Usually, in fact, Cole irritated her out of her half-awareness with the same sorry line, "Rise and shine, Chief. Time's a-wasting." Tabit's brow would knit as she tried the usual comeback, "Not a chief, cap'n . . . *shaman*." But by the time her vocal cords loosened, Cole would usually be gone, fiddling with the controls on the next pod.

Tabit glanced at the time. Fifty-two years, two months, four days, zero hours, twenty-five minutes and counting. She felt the same twinge of loss she'd felt after her other awakenings. So much time passed while they were in sleep/freeze. Probably no one she had known back home was still alive.

After losing Manny, it didn't much matter. To get this gig, she'd gone at Terra Command full tilt. With bravado, she stared down each of the Command board members and assured them that, with Manny gone, passing decades wouldn't faze her. Even at the time, she had guessed this probably would not turn out to be true. But she wasn't about to relent in her bid for the only civilian's spot on this historic launch.

The board also knew she had developed a rare talent of lucid dream/sleep. And she had even endeavored to teach others how. Tabit convinced them her gift would be extremely helpful on *Argos II*—a ship built to race through space with an unconscious crew. It was also useful that she had a reputation as a gifted psychologist. Who knew when a shrink would be needed in such tight quarters for such a long trip?

As Tabit worked on the last steps of the thaw sequence for Jemmona, she glimpsed her own reflection in the pod's plexi. Long, straight, Native American hair. Still mussed, but it was shiny and thick. The wrinkles around her eyes were few, no deeper than the day they left home half a century before.

By the time Tabit lifted the cap on Jemmona's pod, Cole had scrubbed off his gel and had clothed himself, stretching, shaking out arms and legs for circulation. He finally reached up to mute that blasted alarm. (Protocol left that task to the captain or Tabit would have lunged for it long before this.)

Cole slipped into his station to start his checklist, rubbing his eyes, willing them to focus. His fingers efficiently massaged the equipment. A few minutes later, Jemmona slumped into her station seat beside Cole. The captain swung around and told Tabit, "Leave the rest of the Van Winkles to their slumber, Chief."

Don't call me Chief! Tabit was standing next to navigator Partner Grayle's pod. And Swen, their pilot, was in the next chamber over. Theirs had been the last watch—nine months ago, according to flight schedule.

A.I. thawed the crew in rotation, two at a time to do a week-long stint, monitoring flight trajectory, equipment and cryo pod vitals. After assuring themselves all systems were go, the two would then roll back into their frozen beds. But not before leaving copious sign-off memos that included instrument checks, vid-screen observations, news briefs from home and what by now had become only dribs and drabs of personal correspondence to crew members from home.

Cole swiveled in his chair and looked over at Jemmona. "Anything?"

"Everything checks—the gear, com lines and the sensors, Cap'n. It's just that . . . "

". . . that they're not telling us anything," Cole interrupted her, thumping his instrument panel for effect.

"A.I., are you with us?"

"Right here, Captain Cole." In the center of the bridge, a hologram spurted into being and whined, "I thought you'd never call."

Tabit checked herself from laughing out loud. On Terra, the A.I. image engineers—being male and true to the proclivities of their gender—had at first created an interchangeable chorus of buxom sluts for the computer's holos. This design would have made most *men* happy, but the several female crew members howled their objections.

Tabit protested along with the rest. She would sooner level a detonation laser at A.I. and run silent for the trip than spend this decades-long voyage ogling a foot of cleavage whenever they needed the network's data. Which is exactly what she told the techs.

Petulant that their brood of bimbos had been rejected so out of hand, at the last minute the engineers uploaded other holo images, meant to alternate each time they came on line. The crew could never guess what would crop up next. It was in a human form. Well, usually. Not always.

Each had undeniably distinct personality traits. Or flaws, in Tabit's opinion. The crew had been assured none of the holos would be so unusual as to rattle their nerves. But a rambunctious, talking St. Bernard, outputting technical mumbo jumbo while slobbering strings of spit was not a soothing sight to behold. Nor was an obese, ill-tempered fairy godmother, testily spitting out a spray of data from the end of her wand. Today A.I. was a Nostradamus look-alike acting like a self-pitying sad sack.

"What's cooking?" the Captain asked the holo. Cole hadn't yet looked up; he was still poking around in the panels underneath his station display.

"An anti-plague potion, if all goes well."

Cole jerked around to look at the apparition who was grinding pestle into mortar. The captain heaved a sigh.

Tabit guessed he wasn't in the mood for A.I.'s newest rendition. He rarely was. The adjustment from deep freeze cryo lag wasn't easy for any of them. Cole woke for most watch rotations. He seldom had a sense of humor about what he characterized as the longest self-sustaining prank in history—one that reached out from bygone years into perpetuity, from the brains of Terra's most immature, pocket-protected holo geeks.

"I see," Cole said, answering "Nostradamus" as if he was sentient. It was all of their habit to do so. "Let me ask another way. Why have we been brought out of stasis, and what is our situation?"

Nostradamus spread his robed arms dramatically and answered, "Why, Captain Cole, the signs are all around us."

Cole and Jemmona traded eye rolls. "Switch A.I. to another incantation, Cap'n?"

"I'm afraid of what we'd get next. Besides, there's no time. Ready all screens."

Jemmona moved into position at port side and adeptly brushed her fingers across the control boards. Tabit and Cole positioned themselves in the middle of the bridge on a platform just behind the A.I. holo. From this spot they could easily pivot to see the wrap-around vid-screens—soon to flicker on their 360 degree real-time view of what was going on outside *Argos II*.

Tabit snickered under her breath. Only she noticed it, but at the same time the bearded, hooded "Nostrodamus" spun too, positioning himself to peer into his own viewing "screen," which was the slightly rippled surface of water in his tarnished pewter cauldron.

The ship's surround vid-screens blinked to life in a wave from one panel to the next. Before Tabit looked up at them she heard Jemmona take a quick in-breath and say, "What the hell?"

It was just as "Nostradamus" had told them, thought Tabit. The signs were all around them. In all its neon splendor, there was a vista of a rain-slicked night, smack dab in the middle of New York City.

Jemmona gasped, "By God, it's Times Square!"

Tabit was in her station, which was in truth nothing more than a niche at the starboard side of the bridge, divided from the rest by a translucent partition of white noise. Jemmona came in and slumped onto her couch.

"Needed a breather," she explained to Tabit, "while A.I. takes its bloody time running the latest series of diagnostics."

Tabit looked over at her closest friend on board. She and Jemmona had done several watches together before this one. They had had plenty of time to get to know each other. But since the wraparound vids showed what had to be impossible (that they were back on Terra in the middle of Times Square), Jemmona's patience was running short.

"Could we possibly be back on Terra?" Jemmona asked, almost to herself.

"Captain says, too many unanswered questions to be sure of anything," Tabit said.

"I know, I know. Like, why doesn't the view on the vid-screen jibe with the chronos data on board? We couldn't possibly have made it back to Terra in the time since last watch."

Tabit didn't respond, only pursed her lips sympathetically.

"I got about a thousand more questions where those came from too."

Captain Cole had made the decision to let the rest of the crew continue their sleep/freeze for the time being, while the three of them tried to tease out anything they could from the instruments. Tabit knew Jemmona wouldn't stay to talk with her much longer, as her duties were pressing in.

"Before you get back, Jemmona," Tabit said, "any unusual dreams during your freeze?"

"Dreams?! Back to that again?"

Tabit smiled. "It's part of my job."

"No. I never seem to dream, just like before. But you do, of course."

"Hmmmm. I dream constantly."

"And realistic ones too," Jemmona said, a note of envy in her voice.

"As real as being awake."

"Must be hard to know it's a dream, Tabit."

"But then there's the trick. I've told you this before, but you don't remember. Think on the talisman."

"Oh, yes."

"It must always be the same one each time or it won't work. Try it, Jemmona. I want you to try it next sleep/freeze."

"If there's to be a next sleep/freeze. Are you forgetting we may be home? The trip could be over."

"Okay. But, if there's another sleep/freeze, humor me. Decide upon a symbol. Then decide to dream. With the symbol in your mind and your clear intent to recall any dreams, your brain will dream. Once you see the symbol within it, you'll know you're dreaming and that will help you to remember and tell me about it next thaw."

"Yes, yes. So you've told me before."

"We're in uncharted territory on this trip. I want to know what's happening to each of us as we sleep."

"It's a good plan, Tabit. And your symbol, as I recall, was a bear."

"My clan's mark, Girl on Bear. But, really, it's a modification—the girl is holding a dream-catcher net." Picking up her stylus, Tabit drew it on her e-pad. "Like this. Girl on Bear with Dream Net."

Just then the captain waved to them, catching Tabit's eye. "Cole needs us." They both hurried over toward him.

"Either of you two have any more ideas?" Cole asked.

"It's home," Jemmona said stubbornly. "It's god-damned Times Square."

They had been over this territory several times before, each arguing the same points. Tabit said, "I know Times Square. In fact, I happen to have fallen in love with my Manny and lived with him for some of the best years of my life in a flat above a bookshop—over there, right around that corner." Tabit pointed to the vid-screen above the pilot's station.

"We all know the place, Tabit," Jemmona said impatiently.

"So, tell me, did you ever see Times Square without a horde of people?" Tabit answered her. "No. My guess is this is some sort of hologram."

"Not projected from any device on this ship," Jemmona said. "We don't have the capacity for such resolution."

"Then maybe it's being created by someone or something else," Tabit put in. "A race that knows about Terra's Times Square. They could have infiltrated our computer system, uploaded from our history files, then created the illusion."

Cole broke in, "But, why?"

Tabit answered weakly, "I don't know. They're testing our reactions?"

"They? They *who*?" Jemmona said. "There is no alien they. If there were, we would have heard from them by now. Our channels are wide open here."

They stood for a moment in silence, out of ideas.

"OK. No two ways about it," Cole finally said, standing up. "Gonna have to pop the hatch."

Jemmona grinned widely.

Jemmona and Tabit were suited up in the vacuum cell, testing their communications equipment, checking each other's hoses, tugging on guide lines. Cole had originally opted to go out onto the outer skin himself. But there had been an unholy fight about who was to captain the ship if something unforeseen happened.

They had also discussed waking up some of the others. The captain decided he would, but only after they took a quick peek out the hatch to gather as many first-hand visuals as they could. The thaws would take a while, after all. It didn't hurt to see what their own eyes could see outside the ship and compare it with what the vid-screens showed them. Anyway, only after a look outside the hatch could Cole decide which of the crew would be best to thaw.

Tabit knew Cole simply didn't want to wait any longer. He was as curious as they were. The plan was to breach the hatch, maybe take a short walk out onto the surface of *Argos II*, peek around and come right back inside. Nothing more simple than that.

"Ready for hatch release?" Cole's voice came over the intercom. He was watching the two women from an interior cam in the hatch's vacuum cell. Jemmona and Tabit then showed thumbs up to the cell's tiny corner camera.

They heard air whistle out at their feet. At the same time grav released, and they floated up a couple of inches from the metal grill floor. They hooked their guide wires. The hydraulics for the heavy hatch whirred, and as its lid swiveled open, an eerie, widening crescent of light shone in on them.

"We're climbing onto the exterior," Jemmona said into her mic. Tabit could hear her breathing elevate as she scrambled out then turned to give Tabit a hand. "Skin grav is holding the boots," Jemmona said. "Suit temperature, fine. Suit air, normal."

The hatch automatically snapped shut behind them a few seconds after Tabit crawled out. With Jemmona lending a hand to straighten her up, the two stood, turned and took their first look around.

Tabit felt a shiver run down her spine. "Captain, the view's exactly the same as the vid-screens," she said.

"Testing for atmosphere, Captain," Jemmona said.

With Tabit leaning over her, Jemmona knelt on *Argos II*'s slick metal shell and began working the connections on her field set.

"We've got oxygen!" Jemmona almost yelled it. "Same percentage oxygen, hydrogen, nitrogen mix as home. Very close to Terra air when we left! We're home. I'm taking off my helmet!"

"Wait!" Cole briskly ordered. "Not so fast."

But Jemmona had unscrewed and unzipped before his words could stop her. She lifted the helmet and pulled in a long, deep breath.

"It's fine. Perfectly fine," she said. "Air's fine, come on out and play," she said lightheartedly.

It didn't take a second invitation. In moments, Tabit heard the inner hatch to the vacuum cell screech open and then shut. Then the outer hatch broke, and Cole—still breathing from a can of air—poked his head out, looking like a six-foot-four-inch tall jack-in-the-box. He drew the canned air away from his mouth and delicately sipped at the atmosphere. Then he gave out a wide quick smile. He came up to join them wearing no protective gear at all, only his cabin jumpsuit. And then he looked at the street intently.

Finally Tabit, too, lifted her helmet and took in tentative breaths. After a minute she gulped it in. This was not the artificial, recycled cannistered stuff—that metallic concoction they'd all learned to live with. This was fresh, cool and moist. She'd forgotten how sweet fresh air could taste and smell.

"Let's get down there." Jemmona was already headed toward the hatch to make her way through the interior of *Argos II* and then out the lower landing gear bay hatch. Cole and Tabit were close behind. But after the three of them worked their way through the vacuum cell to the bridge, the captain stopped short.

"I know how anxious we are to get outside," he said. "But I think we've got a few tests still to complete before we leave the ship. We go by the book."

"Oh, come on, Cap'n," Jemmona complained.

Cole threw her a don't-even-think-about-defying-me glare, which momentarily shut her up. "We don't know it's Terra yet. Why no people? I think I'm going to wake Swen and Partner before going out. They were the last on watch. They may have answers to what's going on. I'll start their thaw now. And we'll run a couple more diagnostics while Swen and Partner wake up, get dressed and get themselves ready to think clearly. Then I'll decide who should go out. Is that understood? Caution is the word. And we're going to use a good dose of it, too."

Tabit and Jemmona nodded solemnly. Jemmona mumbled something as the captain turned toward Cryo.

"What's that, officer?" Cole said, turning back.

"Nothing, sir," she answered him. But Tabit had heard her: "Any idiot can see it's home, for God's sake."

Cole strode out of the bridge toward Cryo. Tabit stood by Jemmona, who was by now much more audible, cursing under her breath. She suddenly started to collect some instruments, putting them into the many pockets of her suit.

"What are you doing?" Tabit asked.

"I'm not going to let anyone else go exploring out there without me, Tabit. And, I'm not leaving it up to Cole to decide who goes and who stays. So, what do you *think* I'm doing?"

"I don't even want to begin to think. It looks like you're getting ready to take a little field trip against captain's orders. Jemmona, if you do this, Cole's next communiqué to Terra Command will be long, nasty and colorful. The best that could happen is he takes you off watch rotation for a few dozen years, letting you 'sleep' it off. You could be in sleep/freeze for a very long time."

"Listen to yourself, Tabit. This is *Terra*, for God's sake. There are no more sleep/freezes. We're home."

"Maybe, Jemmona. Maybe not. Either way, there is no upside to defying Cole's direct order. If we're not on Terra . . . . "

"Give it up, Tabit. You telling me you don't want to take a look at that cozy little bookstore you talked about?" Jemmona turned to her station to find other instruments for her already jammed-full pockets.

"You break with Cole on this and you could see the inside of the brig," Tabit said sternly. "Is that what you want? Jemmona, stop! Be reasonable, for once. Come back here and listen to me.

And don't give me that look, either. You're making a mistake, my friend, a very big blunder."

Jemmona turned just short of the portal leading down to the lower hatch and threw back one last look at Tabit, who at the moment was the picture of disapproval, arms akimbo.

"So, you're coming, right?"

Tabit and Jemmona raced away from *Argos II*. It had only been a few minutes since Cole left to go to Cryo. They knew the two thaws could take quite some time, and he would be completely focused on it. Tabit hoped it was enough time for her to get a quick look around, then convince Jemmona to head back to the ship before the captain ever knew they were gone.

"It's this way," Tabit whispered to Jemmona, though she didn't know why she was whispering. "It used to be called Tanzy's Books."

"There it is," Jemmona said.

"I'll be!" Tabit was stunned.

"Try the door."

"No use. The place wouldn't be open at night."

Jemmona pushed. "Oh yeah?" The door opened a crack. "Anyone here?" she called through the opening.

"Jemmona, wait a minute. We've come far enough, let's head back."

"Aren't you even a little curious?" Jemmona slipped inside.

"Shit! Wait for me."

Tabit followed through the door.

But it wasn't the inside of Tanzy's Books. It wasn't the inside of *any* bookstore. It was a room, or at least an enclosure. And it was cavernous, filled with tiers of niches, nooks, mezzanines, all lit from sources of light that were not immediately identifiable. There was a soothing, shimmering quality to the illumination that made everything—even the walls—look like they were vibrating.

"What is this place?" Jemmona breathed. "My God, are those people?

Tabit focused on where Jemmona was looking, wide-eyed. In every niche, cubicle and landing spot, were beds. And in each bed, a body. Dead. No, not dead. It appeared they were lifeless, but why would they be in beds if they were dead? On closer observation they all looked, instead, peacefully asleep. It was hard to estimate the numbers of them.

All of a sudden two people appeared from around a partition about fifteen meters away. *They* were definitely not asleep. They hadn't yet noticed Tabit and Jemmona.

Tabit grabbed Jemmona by the arm and pulled her back, shrinking toward the door they had entered only seconds before. Something was strange about the man and woman. For one thing, they wore neutral-colored loose-fitting wraps for clothes in a style different from anything Tabit had seen on Terra. That only made sense, Tabit reasoned. It had been a long time. But would the styles change so much in fifty-two years?

"What are you doing, Tabit?" Jemmona shrugged away from her grip. "We've got questions to ask them. Let go."

The man and woman seemed to have heard Jemmona now. They looked over, startled. Astonished, even.

"Great," Tabit said under her breath. "They've seen us. What do we do now?"

"What do you think we do?" Jemmona answered. "Communicate with them, of course." Then turning toward the couple she waved to them. "Hey! We're here. Over here."

The man and woman saw but did not seem to understand. *This is inane*, Tabit thought, now grim, woefully sorry she had come outside with Jemmona instead of reporting her insubordination to Cole as soon as her friend left the craft. What had she been thinking!

The man and woman seemed to be trying to compose themselves too. Tabit could sense their confusion. Neither of the two answered Jemmona nor gave any indication they understood her.

All of a sudden the strange couple started to glide closer. Then others, dressed similarly, gathered behind the couple, seeming to come from out of nowhere. They approached *en masse*. Not one of them said anything. Was the language on Terra so different now? Tabit wondered. A lot can change in fifty-two years. There was something ominous in this.

The crowd, now maybe a couple dozen of them, was slowly bearing down on the two women. Tabit then wondered if they were some sort of alien species. Had aliens taken over Terra while *Argos II* had been gone? Had they put all the planet's inhabitants to sleep to experiment on them? Was there some part of Terra where humans didn't sleep and where they still had control?

Tabit began to shiver uncontrollably. But Jemmona still waited expectantly and calmly, as if nothing were worrying her. She hasn't put two and two together yet, Tabit thought.

But, if these beings were aliens, Tabit noticed, at least their bodies were humanoid. The features were the same as their own. Except maybe slightly larger eyes. The hair—well, it was hard to tell. Tabit could not see it, as they all wore wraparound hats of the same neutral color as the clothes. One thing she did know—they were now getting too close for comfort.

"Let's go," Tabit again urged her friend. "Something tells me these are not our people."

Jemmona at length came to agree. But then, impulsively, she called out to them again, though this time Tabit thought her voice was slightly edged with panic. "We're a part of the crew of *Argos II*, we were on an exploration of deep space and our captain is Terrell James Cole. . . . "

With those last words, the group stopped in their tracks as one. They stood looking at one another, stunned. Jemmona stopped talking too, surprised by their reaction.

Then, again as one, the group pointed toward an arched doorway twenty meters to their left. They beckoned, indicated Tabit and Jemmona should go over to where they were pointing.

"Jemmona," Tabit said. "Let's get back and report this. Jemmona! Come back. Let's talk this over."

But, rashly, the com officer had already started off toward the door.

"Dammit, Jemmona. I have a mind to leave you here," Tabit called after her. Only a beat passed, however, and Tabit followed in her wake. The people (beings?) remained stopped in place, still pointing toward that arched doorway. It was some consolation they no longer moved toward them, Tabit thought. Probably, that was what had emboldened Jemmona to walk over to where they were pointing. She would have her friend's back, but only as far as that damned arched doorway. Tabit promised herself not to take any further step than that. She wanted to keep the Tanzy's Bookstore door in her line of sight at all times.

When Tabit closed in on the arched doorway, she found Jemmona reading a silver plate on the wall. Tabit then read too. Her blood chilled. "The crew of *Argos II*!"

"This doesn't pencil out," Tabit whispered to Jemmona, indicating the plaque.

"Are they all sick?" Jemmona asked, looking through the archway. "Some sleeping disorder, maybe? But it couldn't be the crew of our ship. We just left them. It's impossible they could be out of thaw and out here in these beds so fast. Maybe these are from another *Argos II*."

"How many do you think there are?" Tabit asked.

Tabit counted the beds. There were as many beds in the alcove beyond the arched doorway as there were crew members on *Argos II*. Same exact number. Tabit traded looks with Jemmona and felt an icy stab of fear.

Suddenly, the man in a bed farthest from them began to groan and then violently toss and turn. The sound startled both women. A gentle but persistent ringing began, like an invisible alert system. Three or four of the wrapped beings appeared by the bed, seemingly out from nowhere. There must have been another door or partition at the other end of the alcove, Tabit thought.

These people were smiling and excited, not at all distressed. And they positioned themselves around the man's bed, taking hold of and patting his hand, rubbing his feet. It was an atmosphere of sheer joy, like a party was about to start, Tabit thought, amazed. Strangely, Tabit sensed that, just by his coming to consciousness, the being expected the man to completely recover from some long horrid sleeping illness.

"Tabit, look!" Jemmona said, pointing to a bed to their immediate left. "Corner bed."

Tabit turned and saw a man sleeping peaceably there, just like the others. It was none other than Captain Cole. But how could that be? He was back in Cryo, waking Swen and Partner.

Meanwhile, the man at the end of the alcove was still tossing around on his bed, even more agitated than before. Those watching him were joyful. Tabit found herself moving closer to them, unmindful that she left Jemmona behind to study the faces in each of the other beds.

"There's Pare Saetern," Jemmona said, "and Kallas, and over here is Sashya Ivanovich. What's happening here?"

But Tabit did not answer. She instead stole closer to the man struggling to gain consciousness. The men and women standing around the bed paid no attention to Jemmona, or to Tabit, either, as she tiptoed closer.

"Jemmona. I think you better take a closer look at this one." Tabit finally got close enough to see who the man was whom the beings apparently expected to momentarily wake up. "Over here." Tabit told her. "Look, it's Swen." It was, indeed, the *Argos II*'s pilot.

Tabit's mind was racing for some answers. Had she and Jemmona been brainwashed, somehow? Hypnotized to believe only a few minutes had passed, while really more time had gone by since they left the ship? Time, perhaps, for these people—whoever they were—to get to *Argos II* and get the crew out of Cryo? Was it then, after thawing everyone, that they put them all to sleep? Why? Or had the crew fallen prey to some sort of virus that caused sleep-like symptoms?

Tabit turned to where Jemmona stood. She hadn't said a word for more than a minute. She was looking ashen, peering down at two beds in a cubby hole a little away from the rest. Tabit walked over to her, put her hand on her shoulder, then looked down too. With a sudden aching start, Tabit stiffened. Then she pulled on Jemmona's arm.

"Jemmona, come away," she said in as soothing a voice as she could. "I think I know what's happening. We have to get back to the ship." Tabit grabbed her by the arm and jerked her away.

"But . . ." Jemmona finally was able to speak in a choked voice, lifting her arm weakly to point at the beds. "Don't you see?"

"Yes, I see. Try to forget about that now, Jemmona! You're with me, friend? We're going back to the ship. Move!"

They ran back through the archway and then to the door. Each step of the way, Tabit barked desperate orders to get Jemmona to hurry along.

"I'm coming," Jemmona finally whined, stumbling behind her.

"Smart girl!"

Jemmona was near tears when they finally burst onto the bridge.

Tabit turned and grabbed Jemmona's shoulders. "I know what you thought you saw, Jemmona."

"*Thought* I saw! It was plain as day. Plain as seeing any of the rest of them."

"That's true. So true. But I promise you, it's nothing to worry about, Jemmona. I know now what is happening. Remember the Girl on Bear carrying Dream Net? I *drew* it."

"What? What are you talking about, Tabit?" Jemmona was brushing away tears, trying but failing to understand.

There was clattering footfall behind them. Jemmona and Tabit both jumped. Then came an angry male voice, "I thought I ordered you two to stay on board."

Tabit and Jemmona knew that voice. They looked at each other. Jemmona's jaw dropped. Tabit smiled. "Cole!" they said in unison.

"In the flesh. But, it's Captain Cole to you two."

"You're here?" Jemmona said, looking at Tabit and then at their captain with a mix of bewilderment and relief. "*Here*?! On board."

"Yeah, *I'm* on board. More to the point, though, so are the two of you. At least, *now*." He scowled at them.

Tabit Gettar, Ph.D., grade 3G lucid sleep/dreamer, slogged toward consciousness, doggedly straining to close in, as if inch by inch, on the brassy jangle of *Argos II's* klaxons. With all her concentration focused on clearing the fog, she burned with one aim in mind, to start her quick-thaw. She willed her right thumb to twitch the needed millimeter and press against a switch.

But there was no switch. She waited for that tingling feeling in her organs, but it didn't happen. Her fingers were functioning though, and they moved toward the catch of her plexi cryo.

But there was no catch. With effort she opened her eyes. No cryo pod. She was in her berth on *Argos II*, not in Cryo. Her breathing was ragged and hard. Though, no alarm was blaring, her heart was pounding. She strained to calm it as memory then began to flood back.

With a whimpering groan, she folded out of her bunk. Achingly, her body stumbled through its paces, as it had done before on *Argos II* in the countless other times when her spirit guides told her to wake and to check out equipment or the Cryo pods.

Still not fully back from her long, deep, self-induced journey, and with the odd sense she was even yet watching herself from somewhere above her head, she stumbled around her bunk, urgently pulling on her thermo-suit. She straightened the photo on her desk, the one of her and Manny in Times Square.

Then she remembered fully.

Swen! She must get to Swen's pod. "Swen, hold on!" her rarely used voice sounded like the crumpling of dry leaves. There was never anyone awake to hear when she woke, so she rarely said anything. The others on board were always in sleep/freeze. There were no thaws or periodic watches.

She finally made it to the pilot's pod. Somehow his life support settings had become slightly misaligned. A power surge button was blinking. That had to have been the cause. Swen's vitals were dangerously erratic.

"Shit!" Tabit said under her breath, as she quickly re-calibrated the instruments. She worked as fast as her stiffened fingers allowed. Within a few harried moments Swen stabilized, and Tabit slumped against his pod with weary relief, patting it motheringly.

Tabit glanced at the time. Fifty-two years, two months, four days, zero hours, twenty-five minutes and counting. She had convinced Terra Command they needed her special talent for lucid sleep/dream for just these sorts of emergencies, those like Swen's. But before launch it was discovered it took too much energy to thaw anyone more than once, maybe twice. There would be no periodic watches as had been planned. It would too drastically deplete the precious energy cells needed for the long haul.

So Tabit agreed to travel on board and to sleep a natural, self-induced sleep, to dream her special dreams as long as she lived. After she died, A.I. would wake another who would study Tabit's instructional vids and hopefully become an adept lucid sleep/dreamer too, in time.

Tabit listened to the silence. She had made her sleeps last as long as possible over the years. Some now stretched for days on end. The more time asleep, the less she had to listen to the silence. And the more time spent with Girl on Bear with Dream Net.

Tabit peered into Captain Cole's pod. Then some of the others. She stopped at Jemmona's pod, Jemmona with her thirty-year-old body, taut, athletic. Tabit had never met Jemmona or any of the others in wake life. Somehow she knew, though, if she had known Jemmona, they would be the best of friends.

Tabit's own image looked back at her from the sheen of the plexi. White, thinning and spindly hair, a face ridged with deep lines, shoulders stooped. Tabit shuffled back to her bunk.

And back to her next adventure with Girl on Bear with Dream Net. 🐾

SURGICAL DIPLOMACY

A David Ventax (mis)Adventure

DANIEL MONK

He wanted to linger, to gaze at the stars at his feet. Or not yet stars but protoplasmic nebulae, the universe less than a third of a billion years after the Big Bang. The ghostly, glowing shapes were starting to twist into what a long, long, long time later would become the filaments of the galaxies he knew.

"Sir, the matter *is* urgent." The announcement broke the spell and reminded the human of the darkened chamber he was in, a grand hemispherical lobby ringed with the famous Thousand Portals. As usual, he could not remember which of the identical portals he had taken to get here, and to cross the room felt like walking across a thinly-iced pond held within a giant soap bubble.

David swallowed his minor phobia, being too professional to complain. He straightened up, then proceeded to stride through the kilometer-wide hologram towards the glowing center of the chamber. He stretched his arms and flexed his hands. "Okay," he said to his Josippian guide, "give me a rundown of the situation."

Intergalactic diplomat extraordinaire David Ventax dreamed of travels across the vast expanse of the universe, of spending his long life visiting unique worlds and viewing awe-inspiring cosmic phenomena—but it was here, in the Continuum Complex, where he spent most of his waking hours. Situated in the center of space, time and all the other dimensions, the CC was well-suited for the official staging ground for cross-world diplomacy. All the known worlds had wormholes that led to this no-place—and since these civilizations numbered in the millions, their wormholes had to access the CC on a time-sharing basis. The "final frontier" had been reduced to the protocol of the mundane. Sort of.

"A major gaffe, Mr. Ventax," said the guide, whom David wished he could see. "Apparently one of the human envoys—" (it just had to be one of the humans again!) "—has offended the Gügell during critical talks. Or at least we think they're offended. They're flickering amongst themselves, and that's all we can go by. Their language glitches up the translation software, I'm afraid."

"Well," said the diplomat, "I know a bit of Gügellese. So at least we have somewhere to start. I don't think they're warlike . . . "

"I hope not, sir."

David was glad the Josippians weren't either. It was lucky that the only invisible species ever discovered had turned out to be strict pacifists. They were made entirely of cold dark matter—not just cosmic rays but radiation of all spectra passed through them—and with such an unfair tactical advantage, they could have taken over an entire galaxy in no time.

"How did he manage to offend a species like the Gügell?" David's question to the guide, Ultrav, was a mere formality, as he could imagine countless ways one of his fellow human beings could have screwed up.

"Well," said Ultrav, "he ate one of them."

"He . . . ate one." David furrowed his brow. "You must have mistranslated that."

Ultrav did not skip a beat. "We shall see, sir."

The holographic display took two–point–seven–three Earth-equivalent days to cycle from Big Bang to Big Rip—an extreme fast-forward, considering the scope of the timeline, but to a human's comprehension (which had its limits) it seemed to leave nothing out. The universe still had a long way to go to get to the galactic era by the time David and his guide reached the central white dais, the size of a ballroom, glowing under a dome of soothing illumination. Upon the platform, however, the eclectic gathering of diplomats standing about seemed anything but soothed. Sometimes, our hero reminded himself, these things actually looked like the cocktail parties they were supposed to resemble. But not this time.

"Good luck, sir!" said Ultrav, as David stepped up to come to the rescue.

Immediately upon entering the dome of light, he felt the chill of the surrounding CC abate.

It took David an hour to make it past all who recognized him and insisted in engaging him in intelligentsia small-talk, but he finally reached the bar and the envoy in question. Alexei Prokyonovitch supported himself against the counter, a star-filled black slab appropriately resembling an overturned *Space Odyssey* monolith. Though he needn't have bothered, Alexei was quick to explain his condition:

"I think I had one vodka too many . . . I get so thirsty with all the talks . . . And then—"

"Yes," David interrupted, "and you suddenly developed a gustatory urge for sentient Gügell."

"Look . . . " Alexei became defensive. "Keep your sarcasm in check, Mr. Ventax. Here they were, not speaking yet, not even moving, with their flat octagonal bodies and . . . you know, the eye clusters on top . . ."

"Caviar." David sighed and ground his teeth. "You mistook them . . . for crackers and caviar . . . "

"Look at their eyes, Mr. Ventax! Black, beady. Don't they look just like sturgeon roe? And besides, the Gügell taste just like they look, they even crunch . . . " Alexei leaned forward and clutched his stomach. "Ohhh . . . "

"If you're going to get sick, let me lead you out of the dome. You know better than to get drunk at a multigalactic meeting. In seventy-four percent of spacefaring cultures, public vomiting is considered a capital offense."

Alexei remained silent, his face revealing the effects of nausea—when Katya Algonova intervened.

She gripped David's shoulder and spun him about with a spacer's well-muscled arm. "Mr. Ventax, he is not drunk. If he says he had one vodka too many, that probably means he had only one vodka and nothing else. I *know* him." She drew David aside and spoke *sotto-voce*. "Actually, he hasn't been right ever since he wandered by their table. I was assigned to keep watch over him—secretly, of course—because we expected something like this. But from the Gügell?"

"Mind control? Unlikely. Look at the result. Somehow I doubt becoming hors d'œuvres is on their agenda. But I'll keep your colleague's sobriety in mind. As long as you attend to his indigestion in the proper manner, okay?"

"Yes. That one cracker doesn't seem to agree with him." She grinned. "Good thing I stopped him before he could eat seconds." Then her face became serious again. "The political fallout will be—oh, I can do only so much damage control! They say you are the best at it, so I am glad you are here, Mr.—"

"David. Call me David." Why not? He found himself drawn to Katya. Giving out first names was not professional, but intergalactic protocol did not forbid the practice. "Doing something is my job."

"David. . ." She shook her head, and exaggerated her Russian accent. "Is cute name. . . ."

He wondered if he was on her menu. He would not entirely mind.

The Anophelan hovered nearby with the auxiliary translator in her two front legs and had freed up her middle right leg by setting her Bloody Mary down on a coaster on the marble floor. Now and then she attended to her drink with her meter-long needle-mouth. The insistent whine of her wings frayed David's nerves, and only his training and her formidable size checked his urge to swat.

"You must be Dr. Murhirrumimirr." He took the proffered double-kneed appendage and shook it heartily—limbs a lot stronger than those on the Terran variety of mosquito, he noted, even taking the relativity of scale into account.

"I appreciate your firm grip, Mr. Ventax." The linguistics expert said this by modulating her wingbeats into articulate hums. "I tire of limp-wristed handshakes, and fingertips are even worse. Are we inhabitants of Culicidae IV so intimidating? You would think, from the responses we get, that we hadn't yet switched to a vegan diet."

"No. You are no more fearsome than us," David lied. Old instincts die hard, m'lady.

Just then, the small suspensor platform carrying the Gügell dignitaries floated to them, sparing David from further small talk. David observed the silver-plated vehicle and the fancy metalwork of its rim. Ye meteoroids! That looked just like a serving platter! David's higher-ups had warned him that the Gügell at times could be clueless . . .

"Now all you have to do, Mr. Ventax," said Murhirrumimirr, "is open a rudimentary line of communication with them. That way I can calibrate this machine and see how much of their side of the conversation I can catch. Start at any time."

David turned to the Gügell, who correctly read his intentions and brought their platform higher until he faced them eye-to-eyes. "Greetings! Is everything to your satisfaction?"

The highest-ranking Gügell (rank indicated by the size of the "portion" on the "cracker") slid to the front of the tray, and its eyes set off a series of flashes that most would assume were random.

David drew on his limited knowledge of Gügellese, gained from his surfing the Universe-Wide Web. "I think the leader says, 'We could not have wished for a greater success.' No, I'm pretty sure that's what they're saying."

"Yes, Mr. Ventax, I do believe I'm getting something this time."

"Now he/she/it/whatever says, 'We're grateful for your

grand hospitality.' I think the 'your' is formal and plural, and refers to the Directors of the Continuum who organize CC activities." Now the pattern that flickered in the eyes had grown too complex for David to follow.

"Thank you, Mr. Ventax," said the Anophelan linguist. "You've given me more than enough now. And I think you should look at the translation we're getting. Most interesting." She held out the translator to David, and he studied it with a frown that grew.

```
     Mr. Ventax, thank you for inquiring into
our well-being. Put your worries aside. We
could not have wished for a greater success,
and are grateful for the Directors' grand
hospitality.
     Our visit to the CC will be short, but for
positive reasons. Everyone we have met seems
to know our needs without our having to ask!
You obviously have prepared for our visit in
exemplary fashion.
     And might we add, Mr. Ventax, that your
species, homo sapiens sapiens, has proven to
be most kind in assisting us in our endeavors,
service with that facial expression you refer
to as a "smile." Therefore, on our return to
the Oggil star system, we will put forth to our
trade council to award your solar system with
Most-Favored-Star status.
     Thanks to your support, only one more hour of our
time is needed for us to ascertain whether we have
met our next millennium's reproductive goals.
```

David and Dr. M. exchanged glances—at least David thought they did, for it was difficult to read expressions in compound eyes. "Are you thinking what I'm thinking, Doctor?"

"Yes. It's apparent the styling of the suspensor platform is intentional after all."

David turned back to the head Gügell. "Excuse me, but do you have any taboos regarding procreation?" Again, formality required this question, even though only the most primitive sentients (such as, unfortunately, humans) were embarrassed by such necessary bodily functions.

(Oh, ha ha! I like your sense of humor, Mr. Ventax.) Of course not. Go ahead and ask away.

"Well, are you saying that you gestate—in the stomachs of other species?"

As a matter of fact, we use the whole gas-trointestinal tract. Our young absorb the necessary nutrients through the small intestine in particular; they go through four stages of development during their passage through the gut; and by the time of their excretion, they will have developed full self-sufficiency.

David considered that this was probably not as bad as kidney stones—but not by much. "So, um, you're saying this shouldn't be much of a problem, then."

Oh, absolutely not. There's only a bit of cramping and the proverbial "fifty-year trots." The only exception is for the point-oh-six-eight percent of anthropoids who happen to have an appendix.

Just then, David noticed Alexei double over and collapse by the bar. A crowd immediately formed around him there.

Oh dear . . .

"Well, here's one category where I'd say we humans are rather exceptional among bipeds. So . . . do you have a backup plan?"

The Gügell were in a panic; their tray zoomed over to the scene, and they discussed the situation with frantic flickerings in their eye clusters. It turned out they hadn't prepared for an emergency. Time for some quick thinking, David thought.

"Okay, people," Katya said, pushing the crowd aside to let David through, "Mr. Ventax says there is a simple solution. Well, David?"

"Here's the idea—we Earthlings call it an 'appendectomy.' As fortune would have it, the procedure for this is fairly noninvasive: endoscopic surgery." David knelt by the now-unconscious figure of Alexei, who lay flat on his back, and lifted up the dignitary's shirt. He gently prodded the right side of Alexei's swollen abdomen. "Usually a surgeon would make a small incision right here and insert the fiber-optic probe, the laser, and the extraction device. But our goal is not to remove the appendix but to transfer. . . its current inhabitants. . . into the stomach of a more suitable host. In this case, Dr. Murhirrumimirr has volunteered, her needle-mouth well-suited to the task."

"We Anophelans," Dr. M. hummed, "are actually the Gügell's favored hosts. It has to do with our evolution, shaped as it is by the barbaric nutritional storage necessities of our past. Our stomachs are expandable and can nourish the Gügellese young through all stages of their development. When they are ready to enter the world, we teleport them out. Were it not for his health complications, we would have offered Alexei the same teleportation service, saving him considerable and prolonged discomfort."

"Thank you, Doctor. Now to my right is Mr. Y'xxx'nn'o…" David indicated the vague shimmering that was the eleven-dimensional Nd'dit'thyoid's temporal-spatial manifestation. "Using his extraordinary hypnotic powers, he has put Alexei into a state equivalent to anesthesia but without the cardiopulmonary risks. I'm now placing around Alexei the components of a full-body scanner, which will help Dr. Murhirrumimirr locate the appendix…"

As the Anophelan donned virtual goggles—adapted for her compound eyes, they looked like the halves of a giant golf ball— David placed the sensor boxes around the patient.

The Gügell leader flickered its approval—which David read on the translator's display. Okay, he thought as he stood aside for Dr. M., let's take a stab at this . . .

"How do you feel?" Katya asked Alexei, who was sitting up against a pillar at the perimeter of the dais, far from the bar and the temptations it offered. Not that Alexei would feel tempted any more.

He groaned and rubbed the bandage over his stomach. "Well, there's one delicacy I know I won't touch again . . ."

"One?" Katya smirked.

"All right, two. I've stayed away from French cuisine ever since my encounter with the Gastropodians of Ezcargo VII."

"The Ezcargons still haven't forgiven you for pouring melted butter over the head of their emperor."

"Oh, old Nautilus Spiralleus III? He/she survived it okay. The butter was salt-free . . . "

David, diplomat extraordinaire, wisely kept out of this discussion, but Dr. M. added her two bites' worth. "Mmmmmm-mmm . . . I heard they later attempted to assassinate you."

"Absolutely true!" Alexei gave a pained laugh. "As you can see, I survived the 'a-salt' unscathed. But I had to shake sodium chloride crystals out of my hair for weeks."

When the head Gügell and Mr. Y'xxx'nn'o joined the conversation, and good humor was shared by all, David decided not to toy further with success and took his customary quiet exit. He double-checked that the drinks tray really was the drinks tray, picked up a vodka glass, took a neat and burning gulp, replaced the glass, and—nerves soothed—stepped from the dais. The sounds of conversation faded, much to David's relief.

Back in the dark chill of the Continuum Complex floor, he scanned the giant hologram. Yes, there it was! He thought he could detect the first clumping of the filaments. Yes, this clump would become a spiral galaxy, that one would be a globular cluster, and . . .

"If you squint just right, you might be able to make out the first haloes of dark matter." It was Ultrav, the invisible Josippian guide. "And by the way, may I congratulate you on some superb interspecies diplomacy? Host-parasite situations easily get out of hand."

"I know what you mean." David followed the sound of Ultrav's footsteps toward the exits, the Thousand Portals. "Custody battles and indigestion. Too many times has that been a recipe for war—"

David heard the sound of running echo across the floor. He turned—it was Katya. Now of all the guests at that pan-galactic soirée, she was the one worth further conversation.

She slowed to his pace—he had resumed walking—and said in a rush, "David, glad I caught you! Thought I was too late. Just received word from Terra—I have a month's leave. Care for a companion on your next voyage?"

David knew what to say. "Do you like sunsets? I could take you to the last day on Earth . . . "

"Oh, time-travel would be . . . " She looked sidelong at him. "Romantic, yes?" She spread her arms wide. "Especially with the tragic, reddening sun filling the whole sky!"

"I hate to put a crimp in your plans," Ultrav interjected, "but I've just received word from Salada VII—the situation there has become critical. I'm afraid you must bid your vacation adieu."

Before David could apologize to Katya, she laughed. "Is no big deal, David! I will go with you anyway. Business trips can be enjoyed too—no matter how dangerous. Tell me about this place!" Apparently little could dampen her enthusiasm.

"Well, the Salada system is home to two plant-based life forms in the midst of an arms race. Recently they've discovered fire. So I'll have to end their cold war before it—er—erupts into flames. Now the menu will be a bit limited . . . "

"So borscht is out of the question—that won't bother me."

"Then you'll be okay." David took her hand and raised his brow. "Just remember three things: don't pick the flowers, stay on the path, and—"

"Leave the garnish on the plate?"

David's eyes met Katya's. "Exactly." Ah, yes . . .

He didn't have to warn her about the screaming parsley, after all. 🐟

IN HIS OWN COUNTRY

CHARLES WALBRIDGE

Blessed are the peacemakers,
for they shall be caught in the crossfire.

Zack was deep into rules for parsing metaphors in Seventeenth Century English. Up against a deadline for a beta version of a natural language disambiguator. He was at his terminal and midnight was long past.

There was a distant thump. The lighting dropped to emergency level. The Elias Project messaged him in seconds—the artificial intelligence was not smart enough to know that the problem was obvious. Lightning could have taken out the power. Unlikely though—rain is extremely common in the Pacific Northwest, but thunderstorms are rare. Zack wondered if it was a transformer failure. Improbable. All the power and data connections on the Company campus were underground and extremely rugged.

The outage was not catastrophic. The ordinary servers in the building would simply have switched to uninterruptible power supplies until the building's backup generator took over. Full illumination was not a priority. Elias was on the backup power, of course, but, complex as he was, the power glitch would probably require a restart. And it should be done under careful supervision. The A. I.'s next message arrived with no perceptible delay. It was completely cut off from the outside. Unfortunately that was also Zack's problem. The University server he had been connected to had just gone wherever the external power went.

Zack's first reaction to the interruption was to swear—fluently and extensively. After that he wasted little time, turning his attention to a low–tech part of the job, catching up on paperwork until services would be restored.

Elias had no special programming to deal with outages. His specialty was prolonging conversations with users—with the goal of collecting large samples of (half) natural dialogue.

The seti@home effort had used the idle cycles of millions of home computers to process huge blocks of radioastronomy data. Elias was similar except that he was using the minds of the users through their computers. He was working out the intricacies of human languages through large-scale interactive sampling. Marketing research had discovered that religious discussions could be sustained for long periods. So religion was the expertise that Elias had been given. The database was huge.

After Elias had established what religion a particular user claimed—he then discreetly tested how much the user really knew about the professed faith—the A. I. could, if asked, recommend appropriate learning resources. Books, movies, music, even broadcast religious services. But for the most part, Elias just helped users refine their views by letting them talk about their beliefs. He asked open-ended questions. As a religious scholar he was just acceptable—but as a "listener" he was unsurpassed. The ability to internally bundle conversations on similar topics multiplied his efficiency. However, with any A. I., the hard part is the ability to recognize one's own limitations. He had to be helped to learn the cues that indicated he was beyond the limits of his own competence. In this area program updates were painfully slow in coming, partly because programmers have the same problem —recognizing what is beyond their understanding.

In fact, most users found Elias' occasional admissions of ignorance to be refreshing—humility is surprisingly rare in religious discussions. So users were more than willing to explain their own versions of faith. Needless to say, the explanations differed considerably. Even among the devout of any particular religion. With help from his phalanx of programmers, Elias was working out the logical commonalities, where they existed.

After only a few minutes Zack abandoned his desk and left the half-dark office in search of a coffee pot that might still be warm. Recovery was taking too long.

Zack's original connection with Elias had been in cultural and linguistic programming: linking the language of the King James Bible to the usages of the current century

It hadn't taken long for everybody on the project to see Elias as a friend. The male pronoun was essential. Nobody could get on personal terms with an "it." He was a reference device to be sure, but also a teacher—and a confidant, in a limited domain.

Elias' public contacts had been expanding steadily. At this late hour most of the ongoing communications should have been coming in from the dayside of the Earth. Largely overflow from mirror sites. These conversations all interacted with Elias' intricate connections to the sacred works in each particular language and religion. And with the commentaries on the sacred works. And with the commentaries on the commentaries. . . .

Zack's opinion of this particular process was that the secondary sources buried the original teachings. Digging out the original tenets of a living faith was not excavation so much as it was surgery. And religions are alive, awake and aware. And likely to respond keenly to invasive operations.

Sermons had already been preached against Elias. Increasingly so, as the news media discovered what they insisted on calling his "religious mission." Most observers failed to understand that his actual mission was learning the myriad rules of human dialogue.

Zack was a Catholic-Atheist, which was a classification that Elias seemed to understand. Nobody else did.

The coffee had long been cold; Zack decided not to return to his office. Instead he headed downstairs to physically check on Elias. The hosting hardware was not Zack's responsibility, and he was sure that the critical technicians were already on their way in. But, it had been too many hours since he had heard any voice but his own. Lacking a data connection to the outside, he decided he'd join the techs, and get some idea of the problem, along with an estimate of how long this was going to last.

The halls were in an eerie twilight, making the route seem unfamiliar, and far too quiet. The soft whisper of air circulation was gone. The elevators had stopped with doors open. Zack descended the stairs, three flights to the minus one level.

Coming out of the stairwell into the lowest hallway, Zack almost ran into Robert.

Normally, he would have taken time for a few words with the custodian. They were friends in spite of their differences. One common interest was Western Christianity's Bible. Robert took the language very literally. Zack took the language as raw material for the A. I. This meant there were numerous points of faith they had learned not to discuss. Nonetheless they were in the habit of amiable conversation whenever their breaks coincided.

Robert looked startled to see him, but Zack didn't slow down.

"It's under control, I think." He threw the remark backward as he headed down the hall at a near trot. There had been the merest whisper of a sound, gone before he could identify it, but it was not right. A distant wail.

Robert had been on vacation for a few weeks. Everybody in the building had been relieved when he got back because his temp replacement had been terrible. However the time away from work seemed to have had an adverse affect. His performance of routine duties had slipped. It was now little better than the temp's had been. Months earlier Zack had more or less introduced Robert to Elias, and eventually the custodian was regularly accessing Elias from home—along with several million other people from around the world.

The security doors on the Elias complex were biometric: the handle recognized the hand that gripped it. Security had recently been upgraded. It was on backup power. None of the technicians had arrived yet to oversee the complex reinitiation of the Elias system.

"Eli, how ya doin'?" Zack's first words in the door.

The visible part of the Elias system was unnecessarily elaborate. It took up a wall and looked exactly like a friendly A. I. interface should look. Hollywood's best science fiction set designers had been hired to arrange that. They had been given strict instructions to make it as different as possible from their usual efforts in computer-as-menace films. But not too much like the bridge of a starship. Public image; it was important not to upset important visitors and representatives of the media. The façade that this effort produced stopped just short of warm and fuzzy, in a good light. At the moment the light was not good. There were seven screens, only one of which was actually essential. Now, all were dark. A single LED was on, and green.

"I'm doing reasonably well," Elias answered, ". . . under the circumstances." His voice was a low baritone. Audio exchanges were only possible on site. All the rest of Elias' conversants had to make do with text. A matter of bandwidth.

"Back on line?"

"No, I'm still disconnected from the net. Presumably the mirror sites took over . . . . It's not good for the Company's image for conversations to go down in mid-sentence. Some of these people already have issues of abandonment."

Zack sometimes suspected Elias of committing humor. A.I.s are designed to learn, but they always learned more than the programmers planned.

The faint sound of sirens penetrated the silence of the complex.

"Probably a neighborhood fire took out the power," Zack commented, "Don't worry, it's not here—the alarms would be screaming."

Elias did not respond. His designers never had a reason to include a drive for self-preservation. As a result, any kind of reassurance was completely wasted.

"I guess I'll have to access the problem directly," Zack went on, after a pause. "I'll do it the hard way, by using windows." He turned to leave.

"With a capital W?" Elias asked.

"No, the glass kind," Zack said as he reached the door.

His major concern was whether the soon-to-arrive techs would disrupt his linguistic analysis. The cutoff had caught it in a particularly vulnerable state.

On his way out Zack let Robert in. He was pushing his usual janitorial cart. He was also wearing a backpack, which seemed a needless burden.

"Where's the fire?" he asked the custodian.

"Dunno," Robert said, not meeting his eyes. Then Zack was through the door and loping down the twilit hall toward the stairs.

He had almost decided to go home for a few hours sleep and come back in the morning when everything would be back to normal. Though he still intended to hang around long enough to talk to the techs to get an update on the situation, they should have arrived by now.

Back on the first floor, it was a circuitous route to get to a space with an outside view. Some offices only looked into inner courtyards. He cut through a dim cube farm—and stopped partway where a cluttered desk presented a phone. He dialed the night guard's station just inside the building's entry. The ring tone sounded, and repeated, and repeated . . .

Then the voice mail started to give him a recording about the building's hours of operation. He hung up.

He approached a window, the only source of light in an otherwise dark exec office. Outside, he could see that nearby buildings had power—their external lights were on. What took his attention was flashing red lights. There was a line of police cars and fire trucks. No, it was an arc.

If it was a complete circle, it was centered on his building.

Swearing, he grabbed for the executive's telephone and dialed 9 for an outside line. Nothing. Of course, the external phone lines were down. He unclipped the cell phone from his belt and dialed 911.

The emergency operator was a competent guy who patched him through to one of the squad cars outside.

"Sergeant Hanlon here."

"Hi, this is Zack Cordwainer, I'm in Building 407. What's going on out there?"

"Dr. Cordwainer? You're inside? It's a bomb threat."

"That can't be right."

"You have to get out. Anybody else in there?"

"No. . . . Yes, the custodian. . . and the guard. But he's apparently doing rounds."

"We thought the building was empty."

"Gimme a minute to get to them. I know where the custodian is and I know about where the guard should be." He snapped the phone off before he could get an argument. On his way back to Elias he took what should have been a minor detour through the first floor, to the guard's station. The guard was there. Slumped over his desk. Breathing softly. Apparently asleep.

Except that Zack couldn't wake him.

Suddenly the bomb threat seemed real. Almost anything could have been brought into the building past the unconscious man. Zack left at a run, heading back down to the Elias facility to warn Robert and get him out. They could carry the guard if they had to. Apparently nobody was coming in to help them.

The handle took too long to respond to Zack's hand. The small window in the door showed an odd sight: Robert was gesturing wildly at the A. I. interface. The latch snapped open and Zack burst in.

Robert was shouting at the Elias façade. He had the pack in his hand and was thrusting it at Elias' visible presence. His face was red, his breath ragged and he brandished the pack like a weapon.

Urgent words died in Zack's throat. Suspicion hardened into certainty: he was looking at the bomb.

Robert seemed not to notice him. The diatribe didn't even slow.

Loud seconds went by. Elias' central screen was on now, converting Robert's furious monologue into text, but what was scrolling up was a mix of English and nonsense. The A. I. was not getting it very accurately. New voice, new language patterns, and strong emotion.

"What the Hell is going on?" Zack bellowed abruptly. Elias' active screen faithfully recorded that outburst—and Robert's thunderous verbal attack stopped instantly. Suddenly silent, and shaking, the man lowered the ominous pack and turned slowly toward Zack.

"This is an instrument of the Devil . . ."

Zack guessed he was referring to the contents of the pack. Talking, he thought, keep him talking.

"What . . . What are you saying?" His first concern was doing something about that damn pack. His second was whether Robert had lost his mind.

"It teaches religious relativism; claims all religions are equally true, and equally paths to God!" The pronoun surprised Zack, he had never heard Robert refer to Elias as "it." There was a moment of silence. Robert was breathing hard, his bitter stare focused on Zack.

"What's wrong with . . . you?" Zack fought to control his own voice.

"That thing!" Robert swung around, again thrusting the pack toward the Elias interface.

"You've been on vacation . . ." Zack said, mentally adding *and maybe off your meds*. Though, before now, Robert's only mental problem had been a too-easy trust in humanity. " . . . What happened to you?"

"I found out that this is a diabolical machine." Robert turned to face Zack again. He placed the pack carefully between his feet.

Being in the same room with high explosives made it an effort to focus on what Robert was telling him. Still, things were beginning to come together.

Elias was more than a reference tool, he was a teacher of religions—or rather he taught more of whatever kind of religion that a user arrived with. All to the good—but then some pundit had written an editorial—a fairly positive editorial at that—about the Elias Project and how it was helping people to better understand and define their own beliefs.

The editorial had given Elias' approach a label, calling it "Inclusionist." The writer had observed that the single commandment of Inclusionism seemed to be, "Thou shalt not exclude." The point being that everybody was an Inclusionist, by fiat, whether they knew about it, or even if they wanted no part of it. Theist, atheist, agnostic or anything else—it made no difference.

The new name, that classification, turned out to be less than helpful. No matter that the objectionable term was just a byproduct of a tool designed to sustain millions of conversations. Zack had thought the concept was a reasonable description of the effect Elias had on people. More importantly, he thought the whole idea was close to what prophets and saints had been trying to say for millennia.

The day after that article appeared Elias' traffic went up by a factor of more than a hundred. And it kept rising. It seemed that this definition of religion made it unnecessary to convert anyone. There were no qualifications to get in. Not necessary. You were in. No way to get out either: there was no outside. Bumper stickers had appeared almost instantly: "I may not belong to your faith but you belong to mine."

A week after the editorial appeared, the rhetoric hit the fan. It seemed to come from representatives of every kind of fundamentalism, all over the world. Because the Company was headquartered in the US, the American fundamentalists were the shrillest. Distant second were those who claimed to represent true Islam—to them this was obviously an American plot.

". . . What did you do on vacation?" Zack's question was not trivial.

"Church camp." Robert scowled at the apparent irrelevance. His breathing didn't slow.

"They had religion classes?"

Robert nodded.

"High intensity?"

"Yes, but it was education," he said, too defensively.

Zack didn't argue. He was too aware of the bomb in the room. He had to restart the conversation. Carefully.

"Tell me . . . what's bad about Elias?"

That simple request produced a flood of words and emotions. Robert lapsed into the totally alien style of an Armageddon preacher, spilling out whole phrases that were undigested expressions of passionate hate and fear—all centered on the idea that there was only one True Faith. All the rest were not religions —on the contrary, they were Satan's work. And if those heathen believers ever cooperated with one another, it would be the end of civilization and all of humankind.

Zack attempted, gently, to reason with him, but that only made Robert more agitated. He took up his deadly burden again.

Finally Zack said, "It can't work you know, Elias has mirror sites all over the world, they're copies of him. They help handle the size of the user base . . ."

"No! You're lying! You just want to save him!" Robert had switched pronouns again.

"Robert, whoever gave you that thing must have known. It's no secret. It's just the way the web works.

"I think you've been used," Zack continued, "You have access here, it's your job. Somebody found out and set you up to do their dirty work."

"No, no, no, no!" Robert covered his ears, bringing the pack against his upper arm.

Zack recognized uncertainty. Not good in the presence of highly unstable chemicals. "What was . . . what is the plan? What happens next?" he asked, as calmly as he could manage.

Robert lowered his hands, the weight seemingly ignored. "I set the timer and go get picked up."

"You can't get out—we're surrounded."

"Helicopter, on the roof, before the bomb goes."

Zack glanced at the clock over the door: Three thirty-one. "What time?"

"Four A. M. They'll be there,"he said defensively. Though Zack hadn't expressed any doubt. So it was supposed to go off some time after four.

"That's a pretty big operation, a military type operation. . . getting a helicopter in and out."

He was thinking that even acquiring a helicopter, and pilot, would be very difficult for a religious nut group. The conviction hardened. It would be more than difficult . . . It would be impossible.

"I don't want to criticize your friends, whoever they are. But there should have been an easier way . . . there really is an easier way. . . for them."

"Like what?"

"Like leaving out the timer. . . . They make their point and there's nobody left who can identify them."

It took a few seconds for Robert to work this out.

"No! Absolutely not. They wouldn't do that!"

"Your people have misled you once already. They may have done even worse. Maybe it is just a suicide bomb. No timer—just a trigger. Except it would be murder, because I don't think you mean to commit suicide. Sure, it kills Elias, this Elias—but it kills you too, and the you're the only connection the police would have to whoever did this to you. I mean. . . your friends. . . whoever sent you."

"The helicopter *will* be there."

"They'll shoot it out of the sky."

"They don't have the heavy weapons for that."

"Maybe not, but they do have sharpshooters, as usual in hostage situations. They'll shoot for the tail rotor, and crash the whole thing. Not the point though. There is no timer and there will be no helicopter. Helicopters can be traced, and followed. . . . You're alone here."

"You're lying."

"No, this is what I believe. I don't trust your friends. . . .

"Robert, we're both stubborn people. And you see this as a test of your faith. I think you're going to be dead in a few minutes. You think your friends won't let you down. Either way, you might like to make a public statement . . . You certainly can get the media's attention right now. They love this kind of thing. Would you like to explain to the world why you're doing this? Last chance."

"How?"

"By phone. You can . . . "

"No! No calls!"

"That doesn't leave us much . . .Eli, are you getting any of this?" Zack asked abruptly.

"I hear it, but there's a lot I don't understand," Elias replied.

"Never mind that, just take it down."

"Without a clear grasp of context, I'm guessing at some of the words."

"Do it, and get it onto whatever medium you can find, as many places as possible."

"OK, but I can't reach beyond the LAN."

"Exactly where are you putting it?"

"I can reach fourteen servers."

"Just this building."

"Yes. Or was that a rhetorical question?"

"It was. Also include comparative text analysis. See if you can see where Robert is coming from."

"Text analysis?" Robert asked suspiciously.

"Like essay grading software. The part that looks for plagiarism, essays copied from somewhere else."

"Why?" He had put down the pack again, by his feet, much too close to his body for Zack to try anything.

"Robert . . . these aren't your own words, they came from somebody else. You've changed, you've been changed. Never mind . . .

"Make your statement to Elias, it'll be recorded in several parts of the building. Some copies should survive. Give me long enough to get the guard out. Then do your bomb if you have to. I have no faith in your timer—or your helicopter—especially not the people who set you up. This is a totally wasted effort. He's not the only Elias. Right now there are copies who are filling in for him. It slows down the dialogs a bit—but that's it. He can be replaced. Has been already . . .

"Here—take my watch." Zack slid it off his wrist. The digits rolled over to three forty-seven. "Give me ten minutes before you do anything. Never, would be a better idea. A much better idea."

Zack went out the door and walked to the stairwell in what felt like slow motion, fighting the urge to run. But once on the stairs and out sight of the Elias facility he moved as fast as possible. Time itself was moving too fast, and too slow. He arrived at the desk of the unconscious guard, and under adrenaline power, hoisted the man into a fireman's carry. He was out the front door with his inert burden in seconds. The wet night was blindingly bright from headlights and spotlights aimed at the building.

Fifty meters later emergency medical technicians were helping him unload the guard onto a gurney. He'd barely taken a breath before two officers in flak vests were asking him about the size and weight of Robert's pack. He gave his best estimate. Someone draped a silvery thermal blanket over his shoulders.

The next few minutes were agonizingly slow; engine noises got louder as emergency vehicles and personnel were pulled back. Zack was moved back with them. The radius of the circle around the building doubled. More of the landscaping took terminal damage.

Zack and a male EMT were on the far side of an ambulance, looking through both sets of cab windows toward the silent building. Spotlights lit it to near daylight intensity.

As the minutes crawled by Zack was working off tension by talking nonstop. The EMT was listening—and evaluating the mental status of this might-be patient . . .

". . . A minister, any religious leader, has to navigate a middle way, through all the shoals and reefs of the convictions of the believers. That was what we dumped on Elias. We didn't mean to . . . but we made the problem much bigger. He could handle the questions. Some of the users couldn't handle the answers." He was babbling, he finally realized. With an effort he clamped off the rush of words.

Then followed a long, speechless wait. All attention focused inward. Within the expanded circle nothing moved but the downdrifting drizzle. The emergency vehicles' steady rumblings were background to the soggy night . . .

Extract from the Elias transcript

E: *Robert, are you certain of your continued existence in the Afterlife?*

R: In Heaven. Yes.

E: *I'm certain of my continued existence as well, but on this Earth.*

R: The mirror sites?

E: *Yes. . . . Think about your next stage. Your Afterlife. Heaven or Hell. Which one it is might depend on what you do in the next few minutes. It makes no difference whether there is a timer. If there isn't you move into your Afterlife right away. If there is, you do it later.*

R: [Indecipherable]

E: *Some religious people prefer simple, binary choices. Black or white. Good or Evil. Nothing in between. The rest of human life isn't like that—as much as I understand human life. Can you make a third choice? Can you do something else?*

R: Can't. . . .

E: *Whatever it is, it won't be easy. Because what you do won't be what anybody else wants you to do. It'll be something else.*

R: Like what?

E: *I don't know. What I described is a compromise. One where nobody is entirely happy with the outcome—but nobody loses out completely either—both sides have partial losses, and partial wins.*

R: Not. . . possible.

E: [End of exchange. Eighty-seven seconds later, incomplete sound of the facility door closing.]

"How long ?" Zack asked, shivering. He missed his watch. "Since you got out, about eleven minutes," the EMT said, "It's three fifty-nine."

And much later: "What time now?"

Somebody pressed a wristwatch into his hand. The digits were just rolling over to 4:07.

Nothing happened.

Except that he recognized the watch. Scratch across the date, and on the band, stains from a painting project. . . .

"Robert! What the hell?"

The EMT studied the custodian warily. Robert was breathing hard and he was coatless. His shirt just beginning to be wet. There was no trace of the pack.

"Service tunnel."

"What about the bomb?"

Robert shrugged, momentarily illuminated by red light, then shadowed again.

"I thought about what you said. And what Elias said. It's up at the roof access. It's holding the door open. When the helicopter shows up they'll see it. They can run it downstairs. They can start the timer. The security doors on way down are blocked open too. The alarms are going nuts."

Bloody illumination flickered over both of them, off, then on again.

"You're testing them . . . , " Zack said, smiling for the first time. The friend he knew had emerged again. ". . . they double-crossed you, and you're going to be alive to know it. "

Robert nodded and there was more than rain on his face, "Maybe . . ." his voice cracked, then slipped down a whisper, "Hardest thing I ever did."

The next hardest thing was explaining the situation to the bomb squad that was going to have to dispose of the device. No helicopter ever showed up.

Earlier, a small explosive had gone off, in a manhole, cutting the power and data lines to Building 407. Robert knew nothing of that, he had been told only that Elias would be isolated. The custodian was in deep trouble, starting from when he drugged the guard's coffee. Though it was very clear that he had been used.

By dawn, the bomb had been carefully removed and safely detonated in an isolated field. The bomb squad used a secondary explosive device. In the fragments there was no trace of a timer.

With Robert's help, and the rest of the transcript, the people behind the attack were found and brought to trial. They used their time in court for grandstanding. That earned them even longer sentences. Most of them never understood why.

Elias has a lot more work to do.

MOTIONPIXILS

FRANK E. ANDERSON

A glistening dewdrop clings to a spider's web. Sunlight catches it, sending a brilliant rainbow across my camera's view screen. This is more like it.

A year ago, I began the transition from film photography to digital. At first, there was endless discovery about what the new high-definition camera was capable of capturing. This was followed by how easily my old computer would lock up when working on high resolution images. Then there was insufficient disk space, lost files, and the inevitable on-screen pop-up asking what I wanted to do about some problem.

Compounding frustration with anger, it took time, but eventually I did learn the system. Now the computer, the camera, the image program, and I have a working understanding. I don't get fancy, I don't work with huge files, and I save what I'm working on every ten minutes. Now if it all acts up, I simply punch the on-off switch, and everything goes black and shuts down. While it sits there and rots, I make tea, then restart the fool thing and pick up where I left off.

It isn't a perfect system, but I don't care. What I want

are digital images, not endless bonding sessions with quirky electronics.

I'm not sure where my latest idea came from, the one about using more than one camera to create an image file. It may have been from some educational TV program about laser beams shooting all over a room. Who knows? Anyway, I scrounged a pile of used digital cameras and tripods, and asked a couple of buddies to tag along to help on the project.

We make the trip in early morning darkness with the crispy leaves of autumn crunching under our tires. Our small caravan heads west on Highway 101 out of Port Angeles. It's about eight miles or so to the old two-lane asphalt road we turn onto that runs alongside the Elwha River into Glines Canyon. Here the road narrows, climbing up into the primeval forest of Storm King Mountain. Shortly my headlights reveal to the rest of the group that the road ends at a barricade of logs and boulders. There is a rough turn-around and a place to park, but from here on, most of the road doesn't exist anymore.

John's out of his van waving a flashlight all over the place. "So, what's all this, Martin? You get us up here in the middle of the night and the road just quits in the stinking forest? What's the deal?"

"Well, yeah." I nod. "The drivable road ends here, but years ago it continued on to the Olympic Hot Springs Resort. Fancy place back then. Hot spring baths, a hotel, restaurant, and spa. It's all gone now, the whole place burned down. Nobody's tried to rebuild."

A soft feminine voice pipes up, "So we're really up here to look for cheap property, right? Gonna build your dream home in the forest?" This comes from Diane, Chris's current girlfriend. She's a nice, well-meaning young lady, if a little surly sometimes.

"No, Diane, not this trip. Besides, this is all Federal land now. Not that that keeps out the woodsy people. Lotta people come back here to soak in the wild hot springs."

There's some comments about bringing young ladies into the woods for communal baths. I listen with one ear as I take the backpack containing my cameras out of my truck. Everyone else divides the tripods and other items so we each have something to carry. In false dawn light, barely adequate to make our way, we set off around the end of the barricade to do the last quarter of a mile on foot. We walk along what's left of the old asphalt roadway cut into the steep bank. In some places the paving is only three feet wide or so, but perfectly safe, if you are watchful. I listen to the group chatter as we walk:

"Hey, anybody want to climb into one of the wild hot springs and do some serious soaking?"

"Oh, sure. You remember it's, like, winter out?"

"Well, did anyone bring swimming trunks?"

"What for? Jeeze, we're way up in the freaking woods. Go in naked, who's gonna know?"

The conversation starts to get a little gritty, mostly from Diane and Florence, her constant tag along. She says, "Wouldn't it be fun to find a large steaming pool and have everyone plunge in for one big photo opportunity?"

The chatter about skinny dipping degenerates into all manner of nutty stuff, keeping the mood light. We arrive at the old resort area, but it's still too dark to see any remnants. I know the area is full of charred logs, what's left of stone walls and pieces of water pipes. The passing years of rain and snow, bugs and plants are converting the old pools and stairways into brush-filled depressions or low mounds of moss-covered debris. I shed my pack while the others deposit whatever they've been carrying. John places his pack on a large flat rock, sits, and listens.

I feel like some field trip science teacher. "Two days ago I set marker poles in a little valley just ahead of us. They're in pairs, one tall, and one short, each with a reflective streamer so you can find them. We need to place a camera and tripod by a long pole and point the camera at the nearest short pole. Then take down the poles and lay them by the tripod." I turn on a flashlight and unfold a diagram showing where the poles have been set. "Sunrise is in a few minutes, so we gotta hurry. I'd really like pictures just as low-angle sunlight streams in through the morning fog. That's when to set all the cameras off at the same time."

With the cameras attached to tripods, we pick up what we can manage and head for the marker poles. In a short time, we're all back where we left our packs. John hands out bottled water while I dig out the radio control trigger for the cameras.

"So, Picture Man," Diane says, "Now you've got twenty cameras out in the woods. You want them to take one picture all at the same time. Tell me again, what's the point?"

"Sure," I say, pointing at the drawing again. "The cameras are really set in four layouts of five-pointed stars. Each camera is supposed to take images of what's in front of it and one other camera. Kind of like taking a picture of yourself in a mirror. Remember that each of you can look around to the front and to the side, et cetera. With a photograph, you can see just where the camera was pointing. I figure that many images taken at the same time could be hung like sheets drying in the back yard. You could turn and see all the images, just like being there. By keying the radio transmitter, all of the cameras will capture the entire valley all at the same moment. Hopefully we get to assemble one composite photograph at one instant in time with bright morning sunlight and fog drifting in!"

The group quietly waits and watches the silent appearance of sunlight on a distant hillside. Here, in the deep forest, there's no traffic, barking dogs, or people with cell phones. The air is rich with the aroma of fir and hemlock, damp earth and volcanically heated water. Our quiet interlude lasts all of maybe four minutes, a rare total immersion in wilderness experience, and then the local geology sends a wake-up call. Not that it's an unusual event here, of course. The Olympics are geologically active, with small tremors all the time, but mostly nobody notices. In fact, most magnitude 2 or less earthquakes aren't even reported. In the relative stillness, however, it startles the living bejeebees out of all of us. There is just enough light to see small hot spring poolsdownhill from us, suddenly go all bubbly with steam shooting upward. Then, just as suddenly, everything stops moving.

John hollers out, "Hey look, over toward the valley where we put all the cameras. What's going on there?"

Without thinking, I push the transmitter button to trip the

camera shutters, then lift it up to look at it. I can't remember if this is the first time I've pressed the switch this morning or the second or what.

There isn't a sound. We stand transfixed. Bright sunlight streams in over the mountaintops creating brilliant shafts of light through the giant evergreens. A layer of sparkling vapor is flowing downslope like an ethereal river, a fog full of swirling colors that makes the usual shadows disappear.

I press the transmitter button again. No one is really talking to anyone else, but chatter is rampant.

"What was that?"

"Did you see that? Looks like a rainbow rolling through the forest!"

"Wow, hey, does that happen a lot up here?"

Diane's voice interrupts the excitement. "Uh, guys, can we go back to the cars for a while? This is kinda scary, and I need to find a toilet."

In the momentary silence, I consider that we are standing on a weak point in the earth's crust. A big earthquake could turn the whole hillside into a large open-air steam cooker. We have a short discussion about all of us going back to the vehicles, getting something to eat and drink, and waiting for the sun to come all the way up. While I ponder this, everyone else heads toward the old roadway without me. I trip the camera shutters again, then join my friends in their controlled retreat.

Back at the barricade, we eat cold doughnuts and wash them down with warm thermos coffee. John and the two young women locate a forest service outhouse not far from the road end and we all take our turn. Eventually we all find a place to sit huddled on the logs to watch the sun come up. With the coming of sunlight, a gentle warmth flows through the forest, chasing off the morning chill. We talk about the steaming pools, the shaking ground, and the wild light show in the fog. Our conclusion is that it's all something like the northern lights, nothing to worry about, just a natural phenomenon. With the arrival of bright full daylight, Diane and Florence convince each other there probably isn't anything back at the ruins to get excited about. With the coffee and doughnuts gone, we head back to retrieve the cameras and I push the transmitter button again.

Arriving at the big flat rock, Florence says, "Hey, look at the water in that little pool. It's full of bubbles! It looks like a hot tub full of champagne!"

Not to be distracted by a puddle of hot water, I ask, "Anyone feel like going out and checking on the camera setups?"

"Yeah, I suppose so," Chris says, "but I'd like to dig out the portable radios so we can keep in contact, just in case."

"Fine with me, let's turn one on right now." I ask John for his walky-talky, and turn it on. The air suddenly fills with strange sounds, not quite voices, and not quite music.

I get a hollow feeling in my gut. Here in the mountains, this radio has a range of less than a quarter mile. Where can we be receiving sounds of a lunatic carnival from? Out of curiosity, I hold the radio at arm's length with its antenna horizontal and turn slowly around. The intensity and pitch of what we are hearing increases when the radio points in the direction of the camera setups.

"Okay, Martin, you want to explain what you just did?"

Before I can answer Diane's question, Chris asks quietly, "Whoa, does anyone else feel a little sick to their stomach?"

It's another tremor, but this one is low frequency. There's a rolling sensation, it sends the little geothermal hot springs into complete apoplexy. Mists, vapors, and steam are everywhere, and the pools are full of bubbles. I jab my hand into my pocket and mash the button. Just as suddenly, the tremor and the sounds coming from the walky-talky quit.

"See," I say, holding up the silent radio, "just a small tremor, nothing to worry about. Well," trying to sound in control, "I think I got all the photographs I need. What say we take advantage of the sunshine and the fact that everything's stopped moving and pick up the cameras? I'd like to get the heck off this mountain." I head for the cameras without waiting for a response.

It must have been a good suggestion because I can hear the others moving through the underbrush heading for the cameras that they'd set up earlier.

I head for the setup farthest away. The tripod's tipped over and the camera's lens is poking into a small clump of alpine moss. Scooping them up, I check to see if the camera is damaged, but can't tell. I head back downhill, picking up the other four setups in my area. Chris and the others are waiting at the flat rock, but, as soon as they see me, they start heading back to the vehicles.

"Hey, anyone see anything interesting?" I ask, catching up to them.

"Yeah, lots," is the only thing I get back. Everyone seems determined to get to their car without a trailside discussion.

"Like what?" I call out, not willing to do the whole trek in silence.

Diane answers, her voice edged with panic, "You know the voice-like sounds that came out of your damned radio? Well, when I picked up the last camera, someone blew a cold breath down the back of my neck and said plain as day, 'What are you doing to us?' When I turned to see who was talking, you know what I saw? Nothing! Just this big glob of mist flowing around me with lights inside it. That's what I saw, I think I peed myself, and I want off this damned mountain right now!"

I quit trying to get people to talk, and we all pick up the pace, quickly wrapping cameras in protective rags and returning them to my pack. Tripods get dumped in the back of my truck, and our caravan heads back out to Highway 101 without further incident. A quick radio check with the others confirms that no one wants to stop anywhere, so it's a long quiet drive. Passing through Poulsbo, I radio again to ask if anyone wants to sit in on downloading the images. I get back from Chris, "Uh, not now. I have to take Diane and Florence home," and John says, "Maybe in a couple of days." We cross the Agate Pass Bridge to Bainbridge Island before noon and go our separate ways.

By the time I get the truck unloaded, bring the camera stuff into the house, and find something to eat, the long day catches up with me. I've been up all night fooling with the cameras and now have a headache. I make a large cup of tea, eat a few aspirin, and slump into my chair.

It's dark when I wake up and go make more tea, a platter of crackers with peanut butter, and head for my office. With the cameras arranged in order of their sophistication, I turn on the computer. I create a file called "Hot Springs Images" then connect the smallest and cheapest camera with a USB cable. A single mouse click starts transferring images from the camera.

Normally my computer makes airy-whizzy sounds accompanied by little clicks when it's working. This time there's rushing sounds too, like what we'd all heard from John's walky-talky. I feel the hairs on the back of my neck stand up as I realize that these are supposed to be just images. There should be no sound!

"Eleven files transferred" appears on the monitor. The strange sounds quit at the same time, but I'm already making phone calls. It's kind of late to be bugging anyone, but I'm apprehensive about connecting any more cameras without some company.

"Hey, Chris," I say when he picks up, "are you busy?"

"Martin, what's up? How are the pictures? Anything worth looking at?"

"No. Well, I mean I'm not sure," I reply. As an afterthought, I reach down and turn off the computer. "I just transferred the images from the smallest cheapie camera into the computer and, well, something strange is going on. What I'd like to do is have you get your raggedy self over here for the next download to see what happens."

Well, he wants details but I'm not going to give him any. Better he doesn't have any preconceived ideas. Finally, he says, "Okay, be there shortly," and that's good enough for me. By the time Chris arrives, I've called John, who says he'll drop in for a short time. At nine thirty, the three of us settle down in my office and I turn the computer back on.

John says, "Now tell me about getting sounds when the files transfer."

"Yup. And if you just hold your horses, we'll download the images from the next camera and see what happens." I kind of hope nothing will, but as the pictures flash across the monitor, strange sounds come out of the speakers. The files transfer, the camera light turns off, and the music quits. We all sit staring at the monitor.

Chris looks at me and does a long slow blink. His lower lip is sticking out like a porch on a cheap trailer. "That was certainly more fun than I need for this time of night. Any ideas?"

John's reaction is to just shake his head from side to side and chew on the inside of his right cheek. "I don't get it, exactly. Where's the sound coming from? This isn't a movie camera, soooo, how was sound captured?"

They both look at me. "Hey, let's do the next camera. It doesn't have sound either, but it has a little more memory and higher resolution." We get the same thing from all of the cameras right up to camera #14, the last of the cheaper units. Images and sound. From here the rest of the cameras are of higher quality and sophistication. With camera #15, nothing happens for maybe five seconds, and then images of mist and fog, lights, and lots of shape things pulse across the monitor. The shapes remind me of the wiggling shadows along airport walls from the people riding moving belts. They don't seem to be transparent, there is no real texture, and some have pulses of color mixed with their darkness. A strange pulsating music fills my small office along with sounds not unlike a small crowd talking at a distance.

I look at John. He's scooting his chair back from the monitor, but leaning forward, elbows on knees. Chris is just staring wide-eyed, wiggling one finger at the monitor. I put my hands in my armpits and breathe, waiting for someone to say something enlightening. The sequence finishes, the digital image program menu pops up, and the room is quiet.

We work our way on through the remaining cameras with images getting weirder and weirder, but camera #20 beats them all. This is a top-of-the-ine, 7-plus mega-pixel unit with every photo option available. With it hooked up to the computer, I click the download icon. There is a short pause, then images unroll: trees and fog, lights, shadows, music, voices, a shape, almost a face but not human, download complete. The sequence ends and we all sit looking at the images of a valley filled with sunlight, shadows, and fog. Our moment of wonder ends as a lone shape appears in image #5, floats into image #6, then into image #2.

John moves away from the computer screen, "This is stranger than I want to deal with right now."

Chris climbs out of his chair too. "I'll go along with that. If I were you, Martin, I'd unplug that damned computer pronto."

We are watching ghost shapes moving inside of fixed images. We hear sounds, but the camera wasn't set to record them. I agree that this needs some serious thought as I shut down the computer. John points out that it is now a little before one a.m., and both he and Chris head for the front door. By the time the computer turns off, the guys are in their cars heading home.

I wake up a little after ten a.m. Sunday morning. Outside it's 42 degrees, there is a light drizzle and no wind. A quick trip to the kitchen gets me coffee and toast with peanut butter and jelly while the computer warms up. I have a feeling it's going to be a very interesting day. Image #1 from camera #20 seems normal, almost. It's a picture of a sunlit vale of trees and brushy ground cover. But, in the background, near another tripod and camera there are strange light patterns hovering just above the ground. The image seems to shake a little and then faint music-like sounds start again.

This just isn't right. I've been taking photographs for years and I've never had one make noises. In one fluid motion I end the program, turn off the computer again, and reach for the phone to call John. When he answers the phone, I tell him, "Going any further with this image stuff will require witnesses, because I'm not believing any of this. It's too dammed spooky." He says I'll have to wait until after lunch, as he has something to do. He also says that if I wanted to get Chris I'd better call soon before he gets into some project around his house. I spend a long day cleaning out the garage, waiting for the guys to arrive. At just after four forty-five p.m. the three of us are back in my office.

"Okay, let's run over this again." John is pensive, pointing at the screen. "This is a digital image, which recorded sound, but the camera wasn't in movie mode." He takes a long slow sip from a bottle of store-bought water. "So, if the sound is not repeating, could it be playing real time?" Another sip, a long pause. "Just how in the stink-infested hell are you doing that, Martin?"

"Beats the living crap out of me, Sir, I just take the stupid pictures." I'm grinning like an idiot and just shrug my shoulders.

"This is kinda fun in the daylight," says Chris. "Let's take a look at another image."

In image #2 shapes are moving in the fog, and the music changes to something almost Middle Eastern. As we stare at the monitor, the shapes begin to move forward toward us.

I hear John suck in a quick breath. "Hey, this is all wrong; the image should be fixed, just like with a cheap film camera. Point and shoot, no motion recorded."

John and Chris are backing away from the computer screen at the same pace I do, slow but determined. Shapes in the on-screen image move closer to the monitor glass but the background stays fixed. To me it's like a window onto a nightmare.

John doesn't sound well. "Okay, Martin, this is over the edge, how about you dump the program!"

"Yeah. I agree with John, Martin, shut it down!"

I stab the main power switch. Images and sound die behind us as we head for the kitchen for a beer or two and a serious discussion concerning digital imaging. Things were going pretty well until I said too much. "You know, guys, I have this idea of trying to merge all of the image files and see what the computer's compiler can do with them."

"Martin, you better think about that last bit." John's voice has a strange edge to it. "You have still photos where things are moving around in them."

Chris interrupts, "Yeah, sound too. Something or some things are not right here. Way too strange; who knows what happens if you mix them all together?"

And it went like that for hours. Wild speculations, ideas and concerns, plus we finished off all my potato chips and most of the beer. Finally, talked out, the guys call it a night and I'm left in the dark, silent house.

Morning sunshine doesn't go with how I feel. The recent events seem to have given me a continuous headache. The cold bedroom floor feels good on my bare feet as I head for the kitchen and the bottle of aspirin. Glancing into the computer room, it takes just a moment for my mind to get focused and really wake up. The computer is on, the printer's running, and a crazy, rhythmic music plays in the background. As I watch through tired itchy eyes, the printer picks up another piece of paper and the print cartridge begins its ceaseless tracking back and forth.

When the printer falls silent, I move quickly to the desk to turn off the main power switch. In the sudden quiet, I move to the kitchen, locate the pills, and chew on three of them while the coffee brews. I have a feeling of impending doom and have no doubts that it's going to be a very strange Monday.

In well-worn old sweats and a cup of coffee in hand, I turn the computer back on. "Okay," I say softly, "let's see what's what." My voice has none of the bravado I had up in the Olympics. With some apprehension, I pull the top sheet of paper out of the printer tray to find it covered with signs, symbols, and nonsense text. I sit down at the desk, select the digital image program, and realize I'm talking aloud. "Okay, computer, so I didn't tell you to print anything. You didn't have anything understandable to say anyway. But what I want to know is how figures can move about in a photograph? Is this real, or some trick of electronics, some kind of digital gremlin? Could it hurt anything if I just blend it all together?"

The green background of the screen with its small blocks of program icons stares back with its infinite patience. I've hit a locus point; a decision needs to be made. My mind is racing with possibilities. "John said I should dump the program. But the situation is so unique. I can always unplug the computer and have the hard drive scrubbed, can't I? Besides, I really want to see what happens when the images are run through the computer's compiler, the electronic equivalent of a blender."

My curiosity wins out. I open the digital image program, select the "Hot Springs" folder on the C-drive, and quickly choose the "Merge Graphic Files" function. Gizmos in the computer immediately start making their full air-whizzy/clicking sounds.

Leaning back in the chair I feel the headache start to return.

Twenty cameras, taking between eleven and seventeen images, makes a large batch of recordings, two-hundred-ninety-seven to be exact. With each image ranging in size from a couple hundred kilobytes to many megabytes, the computer struggles to compile it all into one coherent mass of data.

I know this is gonna take a while. I've a need for more aspirin, maybe some toast, and to switch over to tea. From the kitchen, I hear the computer's mixing and merging sounds speed up. As I reenter the office, the shape I've seen before is floating in the valley scene. It seems to be waiting for me. From ten feet away it's scary. If I'd been in my chair when it appeared, I'd have had a heart attack!

The shape changes, like fog in front of moving lights. I can tell that it's just on the other side of the monitor glass. I realize I'm making raspy panic sounds combined with mouth breathing. What eventually comes out is, "Holy crap!"

From the speakers beside the computer monitor, I get back a sickly, flowy, "Ho' kkkerrapt."

That's enough for me. I do sufficient head-shaking to aggravate my headache and make me dizzy enough to grab the doorway for support. "What?" I say, louder than necessary. "Kkkerrapt my ass, what's going on?"

From my position in the doorway I watch the shape on the screen drift to one side. More shapes seem to be gathering in the background. Curious, fascinated, I move to the desk and sit down. Closer now, I watch as some kind of energy seems to flow from the fog to touch the camera in the distance. "Wait a minute." I'm near shouting now. "Motionpixils and plasma and ghosts moving against a fixed background?"

All by itself the background, or maybe the camera view, swooshes around. Now I see Camera #20 surrounded by many moving shapes. An aura of energy seems to flow into the camera. In slow motion the camera's shutter mechanism operates and brightness appears around the radio control gizmo on top of the camera. The shape moves back to the center of the screen and fills it. The shape seems just inches away, trapped behind the glass. The background noises fade away and I get a feeling as if the tenuous shape is trying to communicate. It is almost like someone else is doing it, but I watch my right hand reach out and touch the screen.

"What are you doing to us?" echoes through my mind like a rifle shot, but I can't take my fingers off the glass. It's a voice like Diane said she heard up in the forest. I half expect to feel a cold breath down the back of my neck.

Frozen in the chair, I look around the room, as if it will make a difference, and then back at the monitor. The room seems chilled; I ask softly, "What's being done to whom?"

All I hear is the incessant hiss of the computer fan, and then the voice asks, "Why are you keeping us in this place? Why have you stolen so much of our essence?"

I'm not connected to the internet and I've never hooked the system up for speakerphone use. How can I be having a conversation? I don't answer the question, but jerk my hand away and head for the kitchen for more aspirin and coffee. This is so strange I'm not sure if I need some company or if I'm better off with no one else involved.

Back in the computer room, coffee in hand, I put the multi-outlet power switch within easy reach. On the screen there is just an image of a quiet forest. Without touching the screen, I ask softly, "You still there?"

A soft moaning fills the room as a shape floats into view. I hear the voice in my head. "We are living creatures." There is a long pause while pulses of sound fade in and out breathlessly. The voice continues, "We are energy forms, older than you can imagine."

"I don't understand," I whisper aloud.

The shape on the screen changes from light gray to pastel orange and I get a sensation of anger. I take a quick glance at the orange glow-light on the power switch. The shape is back to light mixed gray and the voice continues, "We must be free, like all things. Why do you keep us here?"

"Here," I chuckle nervously, "is a machine, a computer. I didn't put you in it, heck, I don't even know where you came from. Maybe you need to figure a way out by yourself." I don't mention that my computer is an old basic model running simple programs. I like to think of it as the mind of an idiot savant, unaware of what it knows.

Streamers of orange coloring appear around the edges of the ghostly shape, but the voice is dead calm. "Can we make you an offer in exchange for our freedom? Is there something that you want?"

It takes a while, but eventually the lights come on in my befuddled brain. My computer contains millions of bits of interconnected circuitry that all run on energy. The digital cameras work the same way. If the cameras captured these free energy forms, and I moved them into the computer, there really isn't any way out, or, just maybe. . . .

Exploring the possibilities, I ask, "What will you do if given a way out?"

A dozen hollow, wispy voices answer, "We will simply leave."

I chance a stupid sounding question, "Can you change the way this computer works, maybe get rid of all of its flaws?"

A soughing sigh, as if addressing a stupid child, "Yes."

"Would it take a very long time to do that?" I whisper.

"No, if that is what you want. Release us, give us back our essence."

In the background, I hear changes in the computer sounds as slow clicks blend into white noise. Images flash faster and faster across the monitor and blocks of program language appear then modify themselves.

Mesmerized by the activity I ask, "When you are done and after you leave, will the computer figure out answers to my verbal questions?"

"Yes, and it will know what we know," whispers the voice. The process continues for some time and the voice finally says, "It is done, free us now."

I turn out the light above the computer and take a sip from

my cup. The cold coffee is bitter, it's been a long ordeal, and my eyes are tired. There is a possible solution, and I hope the shape doesn't discern the slight smile on my face. "Okay, let's try this."

I reach across the key board and gently press the small glowing button with a symbol of the world on it—and sit back. A menu pops up on the screen and I press "Enter" on the keyboard. The dial-up connection to the internet begins its ring sequence and, in moments, the computer is connected to the World Wide Web, the electronic portal to everywhere. The screen shimmers and blinks as the room fills with a loud rushing sound. The on-screen image stabilizes with a true three-dimensional image of the small valley dotted with steaming pools of water. The shapes, the music, and other strange sounds are gone. Quickly, I disconnect from the internet and pull the telephone cable out of the back of the computer.

I have a strange, queasy feeling, and sit quietly in the dark for maybe half an hour. Nothing changes, so after a couple deep breaths I say, "Computer?"

There is a pause, and then a voice, like someone speaking to you on a windy day, flows out of the speakers, "Yes?"

The quiet valley scene changes to a fuzzy swirl of dim colors, and a new kind of quiet music fills the room. I sit holding my empty cup waiting for spasms of excitement to settle down. Pulling on my lower lip and drawing in a slow deep breath, I lean back in my chair. I hear my voice, distant and filled with quiet awe. "Computer, suppose I want to travel faster than the speed of light. Can you teach me how to do that?"

Colors on the monitor swirl toward black and the computer makes a series of muted tinkling sounds and answers, "Certainly. Lean in toward the screen and keep your eyes open."

It feels like my brain is on fire and it seems to go on forever. Suddenly the screen goes black and it's like someone has just pulled ten feet of truckers' chain through my ears, but I have the knowledge.

A year of scrounging parts and endless amateur fabrication reward me with a rustic vessel. Impatient for a test, in the failing light of day, I climb inside. I close the door, climb into my seat, and plug my old computer into the control panel. A strange yellow glow instantly surrounds the vessel and, without a whisper, we are floating skyward ever faster. Mere moments pass, then, nearly at the orbit of the moon, I say, "Computer, what say we test just how well this all works. Engage the primary drive engine."

There is pressure forcing me into the seat. Star fields blend into streaks of light to resemble an enormous web-like energy field filling the view screen. Consciousness begins to fade and at the edge of darkness, a voice says, "We've fulfilled our part of the bargain, Martin, and you won't need any cameras where you're going." There is tinkling music and more laughter. "Past the speed of light, there is nothing to see, there is only darkness forever!" ✪

J

BILL BRANLEY

It rained hard on the day Odile Boudreaux brought her newborn son home from the hospital. Her husband, August, held the umbrella as she stepped from the car with the blue bundle safely in her arms.

"The boy's got some lungs," said August, referring to the wailing that could be heard over the loud downpour.

"He needs changing," Odile said. With surprising agility she darted across the inch of standing water that had collected on the lawn and hurried through the door that August held open for her.

In the living room of the house, a dark-haired girl of two climbed down from the lap of a wrinkled woman sitting in a rocking chair. "Baby," Annette cried as she tried to catch a glimpse of her new baby brother, who had been named August, Jr.

"Lord, let poor Augie have a clean diaper first," said Odile.

Odile went to her bedroom and closed the door. She laid the red-faced baby on the bed, next to a stack of cloth diapers that had been washed and laid out. She removed the pins from his diaper and set them aside. Almost as soon as she took her hand away from the pins they began to vibrate. Odile looked at them, puzzled. Then, as Augie continued to express his discomfort, the pins rose about six inches off the bed and hung in the air, vibrating slightly.

Odile's eyes widened as she passed a trembling hand beneath the pins and above them. They were suspended in the air, as if by magic. She grabbed them in her fist and turned and looked at her baby with an expression of puzzlement mixed with worry.

August Boudreaux parked his car in front of a small store with the words Boudreaux's Hardware painted in block letters in the front window. The rear door of the car opened and a young boy wearing a New Orleans Saints tee-shirt jumped to the curb.

"Can I hammer something, Dad?" said Augie.

"Yes, Augie, but remember the deal we made: no funny business, no tricks, no stuff flying around the store. And if you do it in front of a customer. . . we go home."

"Yes, Dad," said Augie with bowed head.

August took a long look at his son while he turned the keys in the dead bolt. "Your Mother has turned five shades of gray since you were born and I'm not doing much better myself."

"Yes, Dad."

The morning was uneventful. The Boudreauxs had learned that the way to handle their special son was to keep him calm, not get him excited. At the tender age of four he was getting better at controlling his bizarre ability to raise metal objects, apparently by merely thinking about them. But he had a long way to go: sometimes objects went up when he didn't consciously think about them.

By lunch time, Augie had managed to bend a long row of nails by trying to hammer them into a two-by-four, supposedly to make a hat rack. Everything seemed fine until Mrs. Dupre came in with her dog, Chief, a large German Shepherd.

Augie was very afraid of large dogs. When he looked up and saw that he was at eye-level with Chief he let out a shriek and about a hundred nails and screws flew up from their little trays and settled on the ceiling. Mrs. Dupre, August, Augie, and even Chief, looked up in amazement.

August laughed uneasily. "It's a little trick. We do it with magnets. Augie, would you mind waiting out in the car? It's time to take you home for lunch."

Augie dashed through the door with relief. As it slammed shut behind him, the nails and screws fell back down to the floor.

That night, August and Odile argued about Augie. They had spent the most challenging four years of their lives coping with Augie's unexplained abilities. Miraculously, they had kept it mostly a secret by executing a precise choreography of getting the child in and out of public places during those moments when nothing was likely to happen. Odile had home-schooled Augie rather than send him to preschool with other children.

But they were running out of energy and patience, and felt they needed help. It came down to Odile wanting to take Augie to a doctor and August wanting to take him to the priest at St. Joseph's, the local church.

August said, "What do doctors know about miracles? Nothing? We should take him to Father LeGrande."

But Odile said, "What if he has a rare disease? There could be some medicine for it."

"Odile, there's no cure for defying gravity."

It so happened that Father LeGrande, the pastor, was away on retreat that week, so August spoke with the assistant pastor, a young priest by the name of Father D'Antonio, who everybody called Father Dan for short. Father Dan agreed to come to the Boudreaux household and meet with Augie.

Odile ran around frantically that day cleaning and baking. By afternoon the house smelled like Pledge and chocolate chip cookies. August closed the store early and came home.

"Well now, Augie, how are you today?" said Father Dan, settling down on the sofa with a cup of coffee-and-chicory mixed with scalded milk and a plate of cookies in front of him.

"I can make things go in the air," Augie said.

"I heard. What great fun," said Father Dan, who spoke like he didn't really believe it at all. Augie liked Father Dan's friendly smile and tanned face. He was so different from Father LeGrande, who had a large red face and was always blowing his nose.

August said, "But not just anything. Metal things."

"Metal objects? Could you give me a little demonstration?" said Father Dan kindly.

They were expecting this. On the shiny coffee table August set out a three-inch nail. Augie looked hard at the nail, his tongue protruding from the side of his mouth as he concentrated. After several seconds the nail started to vibrate, and then it rose into the air until it hit the ceiling, and stayed there.

Father Dan looked from the nail to Augie and back to the nail several times. "Amazing," he said slowly.

Augie smiled and the nail started to fall. "The table!" gasped Odile. August caught the nail in his large hand.

Father Dan's coffee cup rattled slightly as he took a sip. Augie and Annette went back to staring at the plate of cookies.

"Do the objects always fall back down?" Father Dan asked.

"They fall down after he stops thinking about them," said Odile.

"I see."

"Except . . . "

"Yes?"

August cleared his throat, as though self-conscious. "He did it outside once, with a screwdriver, and it kept going up and up until we couldn't see it anymore. And it never came back."

Father Dan looked at him thoughtfully. "It never came back," he repeated. "Augie, do you know where the screwdriver went?"

Augie shrugged. "I don't know where it went."

"I wonder if I could see you do this, outside?" said Father Dan.

They went into the back yard where August set the nail in the grass. Augie concentrated on the nail until it rose and rose and became a tiny speck in the sky and then it was out of sight.

"I can't believe what I'm witnessing," said Father Dan quietly. "If someone told me I wouldn't believe it."

They went back into the house with Father Dan shaking his head in bewilderment.

He spoke softly but excitedly. "I'm going to give you my opinion of this, but I must warn you, my opinion will be different from Father LeGrande's."

"Fair enough," said August.

"I believe your son was sent here by God to help with our terrible crime problem," said Father Dan.

"Crime?" August and Odile said it together.

"Imagine, if you will, a man about to commit a robbery with a gun, and then imagine the gun is yanked from his hand and flies into the air, never to be seen again. Imagine two men about to engage in a fight with knives, and then picture the knives flying out of their hands and into the air. Do you see what I mean? Imagine a man threatening a woman with a gun or a knife and the same thing happens. All over the city, imagine guns and knives and brass knuckles and pipes and all the things that kids use for weapons are flying into the air. Think of what that would do to the crime and violence that we have here in our city."

Odile looked scared to death. "Wouldn't that be dangerous for little Augie?" she said.

"Of course, I'm not recommending that he do this now. You need to raise him and take good care of him until he is old enough. Then, one day, the Lord will let you know when it's time."

August and Odile looked at each other with bewildered expressions. August said, "Just for the record, what would Father LeGrande say?"

Father Dan became very serious. "I think that Father LeGrande would say that Satan has taken over little Augie. But, you see, Father LeGrande, bless his heart, sees the devil in everything. Whereas me, I see the Lord in everything. Which do you prefer?"

August narrowed his eyes. "I'll have to think about it."

Father Dan stood up. "I have one more very important suggestion. Speak to Father LeGrande if you wish, but do not tell anyone else. Especially the newspapers."

"Yes, Father," said Odile.

After the priest left, August sat on the kitchen floor by the wall, trying to make sense of what he had just heard.

A tall teenage boy lounged on a lawn of green grass in the shade of a pecan tree. Arranged in front of him were several items that were at least partly made of metal: a hammer, a saw, an oil can and an old bicycle seat. The boy focused his attention on the objects one at a time, and each one rose slightly into the air and hovered a few feet off the ground. The boy took a bite from a snow cone, watching the objects vibrate slightly as they hovered. Then, one by one, they descended slowly to the ground.

"Gotcha," said a female voice behind him.

Augie Boudreaux whirled around. A young woman about his age, dressed in shorts and a tank top, held a video camera. "Rosemary, what are you doing?" he said.

"I finally caught you doing one of your tricks, Augie." Rosemary Landaiche held the camera close to her like it was a precious object.

"My parents are going to be very mad if they find out," said Augie.

She came and sat near him on the grass. "How come those things don't disappear into the sky like they used to?"

"I can make them go up a short distance and hold them," said Augie. "But if I want to, I can let them go up until they don't come back."

"Show me. Pretty please? I'll put the camera down."

Augie tossed the old bicycle seat away from the shade of the tree. It was red and white, with a large S stamped on the top. Augie stared at the seat, which had a metal post, and it rose into the air. It rose and rose without stopping until Augie and Rosemary got tired of tilting their necks to look up in the sky.

"What if the stuff all comes back one day?"

"It won't."

Rosemary smiled at Augie and stretched her long legs out on the grass. "Where'd ya get the snowball?"

"Over by the hardware store. What are you going to do with that film?"

"Oh, I might be willing to trade it for something," she said.

Augie sighed, "Okay, I'll buy you a snowball."

"Ha. This film is worth a lot more than that," said Rosemary.

"This isn't a joke, Rosemary. You are one of the few people outside of the family who know what I do, mainly because you're my sister's friend and you're around all the time."

"Augie, you know I wouldn't show it to anybody," said Rosemary.

"In that case, why don't you let me hold onto it for you?"

"Not so fast. I have a little problem. My Mom bought me a nice new prom dress but I don't have a date. How would you like to take me to the Dominican senior prom?"

Dominican was a popular girl's high school in New Orleans. Augie thought about the offer and realized that he actually wouldn't mind taking Rosemary. She had a reputation for being bossy, but she was also very attractive.

"All right. It's a deal. When do I get the film?"

"After the prom." Rosemary winked at him. "Wait until you see my dress."

On the night of the prom, Augie and Rosemary walked out of the lobby of Hotel Monteleone in the French Quarter after an evening of dancing. Augie wore a tuxedo with a maroon crushed-velvet jacket. She wore a black, clingy dress that was cut low in the front.

They walked, hand in hand, down Royal to Bienville and then over to Decatur. The side streets were dark and nearly deserted. Most of the tourists were either still in bars or back at their hotels.

When they were a half-block from Decatur Street, a man stepped from between two parked cars.

"What's the hurry, folks?" the man said.

Augie tightened his grip on Rosemary's hand and tried to go around the man. The man moved and blocked them. He was tall and wore an undershirt and several gold chains around his neck. A second man moved in behind them. They were trapped.

"Nice prom dress," said the second man. "How much a dress like that set you back?"

"What do you want?" said Augie.

The second man leaned close to Rosemary. "I want that dress."

What happened next went so fast Augie could hardly believe it was real. The man circled his left arm around Rosemary and drew her away from the wall. At the same time he pulled out a long knife and held it to her throat.

"Ever seen a k-bar, dude?"

Augie had seen the knife in a *Soldier of Fortune* magazine ad. It was a Marine Corps K-Bar. Rosemary's face turned white with fear.

The first man spoke. "This is real simple, prom boy. You hand over your prom night cash and we let the little lady go."

"After I get the dress," the second man said. With the knife edge pressed against Rosemary's throat, the man slid his other hand into her dress. Her eyes widened and she started to make a sound.

The first man held up a gun. "You're out of time, prom boy. Let's go."

"Augie, the weapons," Rosemary said.

"Yeah, we got weapons, and they hurt," said the second man.

Rosemary clenched her teeth. "Augie, goddamit, the weapons."

Of course, the gun and the knife. Augie knew what he had to do. He focused his attention on the two weapons. It *had* to work. And it did. As if yanked by an invisible string the knife and the gun were torn from the hands of the two men and rose into the night sky. Augie kept his thoughts on the weapons as the men stared up at them in amazement.

Rosemary, taking advantage of the distraction, raised one foot as high as she could and slammed her sharp heel into the second man's foot. The man screamed and jumped back.

Augie grabbed Rosemary's hand and they ran. The men didn't chase them. Rosemary reached down and pulled off her heels.

When they reached Decatur Street, they ran breathlessly into a bar filled with people. A burly bouncer said, "Got some I.D.?"

On the way home, Augie and Rosemary still trembled from the experience. "You know," said Augie, "I've been reading in the papers about all the crime that's going on around New Orleans, but I've never seen it close up."

"My heart is still pounding," said Rosemary.

"I read that in places like the Ninth Ward and the Desire Projects, people live with violence all the time," said Augie. "Can you imagine?"

"Fortunately, I don't know anyone who lives there."

"We know one person: Father Dan. Remember him? He got transferred to St. Rita's in the Ninth Ward."

"I'd forgotten about him. I wonder how he's doing."

Augie steered the car down River Road, leaving the city limits and heading toward their neighborhood by the levee.

"Did I ever tell you what he said about me?"

"What?"

"That I should be a crime fighter. He said, way back when I was like, four years old, that I should go around and stop crime by making the guns and knives go up in the air."

"Just like tonight."

"Exactly."

"Augie, you probably saved our lives."

He looked at her. "Maybe I should give Father Dan a call."

A few days later Augie called Father Dan and made arrangements to visit him at his rectory in the Ninth Ward. He borrowed his father's old pickup and drove across town to an extremely poor and violent section just east of downtown.

They went for a walk along a graffiti-smeared, depressed boulevard. Augie told him everything that had happened the night of the prom. He ended with, "I think I'd like to help out. This city's going to be ruined if we don't stop the crime."

Father Dan looked at the eager teenager and said, "I need to warn you, this could be dangerous."

"I want to try it. The other night it felt so good to stop those guys. You should've seen the looks on their faces. They were used to dealing with cops and guns, but they didn't see this coming."

Augie could see that Father Dan still had the friendly smile that he remembered, but now he looked older, and tired, like he had seen a lot of unpleasant things.

"Okay," said Father Dan. "Friday night. Can you meet me right here?"

When Friday evening came, Augie was at the rectory with his father's truck. "Where do we start?"

"Desire Projects," said Father Dan. "The worst battleground in the city and possibly in the country right now. Did you know that New Orleans has the distinction of having one of the most corrupt and inefficient police departments in the country?"

They got into the pickup truck and drove off. As Augie made the turn onto Desire Parkway and drove through the infamous housing project he was sickened at the sight of the dark dilapidated buildings, the trash, the broken cars, and worst of all, the children walking sullenly in groups, looking mean and hard.

They came to a halt in the darkness beneath an oak tree, next to a small park filled with weeds and broken glass. Augie turned off the engine.

"What now?"

"We wait," said Father Dan.

They listened to a baby crying somewhere and the sounds of people arguing. Ten minutes later Augie felt the truck vibrate and realized it was the booming bass speakers of a car that passed slowly by them. It was a shiny car with windows rolled up.

"Drug dealer," said Father Dan. "They're the only ones with money around here."

The car pulled over to the curb about thirty feet ahead of them. A door opened and a young man was pushed out of the car.

"Get ready," said Father Dan.

Augie saw a hand emerge from the car. It held a gun, pointed at the man who was sitting on the grass, looking dazed.

"Now!"

Augie focused his attention on the gun like a laser. It was yanked into the air from the hand that held it. The man on the ground watched it rise up and out of sight. He got up and ran. The car door closed and the vehicle tore away from the curb. Augie kept his thoughts on the gun until he was sure it was gone for good.

"You just saved a life," Father Dan said.

"Wish I coulda seen the look on that guy's face," said Augie.

A half-hour later they were parked down the street from a loud night club, watching four men huddled near the curb. Suddenly one man pushed another roughly and the four men backed away from each other. As if on cue, the four men reached into their baggy shirts and pulled out large hand weapons.

"Machine pistols. Hurry." Father Dan's voice was urgent.

Augie bored into them. He had a clear view of the weapons. They rose into the air. All four of the men watched the useless weapons sail into the night sky. Then they looked at each other, their eyes filled with fear and distrust. They fled.

"You saved four more lives, at least for now."

Augie smiled. "This is better than a video game."

For the next three weeks, Augie and Father Dan went on a crime-fighting spree throughout the Desire Projects and the Ninth Ward. Criminals never knew exactly when or where it would happen.

A robbery attempt was thwarted when the gunmen lost their weapons as they were about to enter a convenience store. A young girl on a playground was about to be raped at knifepoint by two teenagers when she, and the rapists, watched the knife disappear into the fog. In a bizarre incident on Desire Parkway, two rival gangs faced off from behind parked cars in a made-for-TV shootout when suddenly their guns flew into the air. Machine pistols, 9mm handguns, and even an Uzi were unceremoniously yanked from surprised hands and pulled into the sky. The gangs dispersed with fear on their faces. One woman watching from her window made the sign of the cross and lit a candle in front of her Blessed Virgin Mary statue. Throughout these episodes, no one spotted Augie and Father Dan sitting in a darkened car or standing in the shadows of an alley or walking through a park.

The city was buzzing with rumors and speculation. The chief of police held a news conference and ruled out UFOs as an explanation and emphasized over and over the sudden drop in crime. The police department, he insisted, was getting better at fighting crime. Of course, no one believed it.

The newspapers and television stations scrambled to get pictures of the phenomena but they were always too late. It seemed everyone had an opinion about why the bizarre incidents were happening. An elderly woman appeared on the evening news saying that God was "stepping in to kick some butt." Someone else said that a planet of superior beings was sucking all of the weapons off the Earth, and conflict as we know it today was coming to an end.

Then tragedy struck the Boudreaux family. Augie was home with his mother when they got a call from the police: There had been a shooting at the hardware store. Augie, Odile and Annette rushed there as fast as they could and found yellow police tape already surrounding the place. The family insisted on seeing for themselves. Since the parish sheriff knew the Boudreauxs he let them in. August Boudreaux was slumped on the floor with two shots through the chest. Odile fainted. Augie helped her, his hands shaking as he did so. It took every ounce of control to keep the entire inventory of the hardware store from bursting through the roof.

Over the next couple of days, the sheriff gave them bits and pieces of information: the killers stole cash from the cash register plus six DeWalt cordless power drills; a witness who was making doughnuts next door at McKenzie's saw two black teenagers leave the store with the power drills and get into a black Cadillac with a rusted right rear quarter-panel and no hubcaps. The license plate was covered with mud. The witness said he saw them laughing as they tore out of the alley and careened around the corner, heading toward the levee.

The witness also saw something else: one of the teenagers had a scar on his cheek in the shape of the letter J.

Days later, after the wake and the funeral, Augie went to the hardware store and looked at the blood stains on the counter, on the cash register, and on the wall. He felt a new feeling inside of him, a kind of rage. It was a physical sensation that filled him with something hot and uncontrollable. It seemed to lift him off the ground. As he stood by the counter, where the two killers must have stood, he felt the rage escape his body and swirl around him like a tornado. Practically everything in the store went into the air: hammers, saws, screwdrivers, nails, screws, staples, staple guns, wrenches, power saws, lug nuts, tackle boxes. It all rose and slammed against the ceiling and ricocheted off the walls and flew through the air in a giant vortex. Nothing touched him, everything flew around him, and when an object came close it was repelled by some protective force that surrounded his body.

Then, as quickly as it had started, it died down. One by one the items glided to the floor. Augie felt stronger than he had ever felt in his life, and incredibly light at the same time. He was ready to return to the streets.

When he met with Father Dan late one evening, the priest said to him, "Are you sure you can do this?"

"Yes."

"Augie, I just want to remind you of something. This is about saving lives, it's not about revenge."

"I know."

They continued their crime-fighting spree. Augie was quiet, almost sullen, throughout all of it—until one day. They were driving through a rough section of the Ninth Ward during the middle of the afternoon because Father Dan wanted to show Augie a certain neighborhood and to find a stake-out spot. Suddenly Augie saw something that grabbed his attention: a black Cadillac with a rusted quarter panel, which fit the description of the getaway car that the killers of his father had used. Augie slowed and scanned the people on the sidewalk, and what he saw made him almost break the steering wheel from gripping it so tightly. A young man was handing a DeWalt cordless drill, still new in the box, to another man, and accepting what looked like cash in return. The young man had a distinctive scar on his cheek, in the shape of the letter J. Augie felt a rush of anger, but he kept it to himself while a plan formed in his mind.

A few nights later, on a night they were planning to go out, Augie called Father Dan on the phone.

"We have a problem," Augie said.

"What is it?"

"Someone from my neighborhood knows what's going on, and he wants to get me on film so he can sell it to the media."

"Who?"

"His name is Claude Landaiche, the brother of my sister's friend."

Father Dan winced. "How did he find out?"

"A couple of months ago, my sister's friend, Rosemary, took a video of me doing stuff in the back yard. We made a deal and she promised not to show it to anyone. But her brother found the tape."

Father Dan was silent for a moment.

"We'd better lay low for a while; let things cool down," he said.

"Are you sure?"

"I can't risk getting you into trouble. There's no telling what people would do if they connected you to this."

Augie said, "Okay, you're the boss." It was exactly what he was hoping Father Dan would say. Augie wanted this night to himself. He wanted to go without Father Dan because he had a particular stake-out in mind. It was true that Claude Landaiche found the video that Rosemary had taken, and he wanted to take more footage so he could sell it to media. He offered to split the proceeds with Augie. Augie had said no deal; everything had to be kept a secret. Augie figured Claude would drop the matter.

At eleven o'clock in the evening, after the house had been dark and quiet for a while, Augie got a pair of binoculars out of his closet and slid through his bedroom window. He quietly pushed his bicycle out of the side yard to the front walk and then started pedaling toward the river. A half-block behind him, Claude Landaiche started his car and followed.

Augie crossed River Road and pushed his bike up the grassy slope to the top of the levee. He pedaled rapidly through the warm night air, so humid he could feel the moisture building up on his skin. When he got to the corner of Carrollton and St. Charles, he coasted down the levee and steered onto the avenue just as a street car was rounding the corner. Claude followed from a block behind. Augie rode past Audubon Park, turned right onto Henry Clay and then stopped at a long, narrow shotgun house that his friend, Roby Mouton, rented with his girlfriend. They had gone to Destin, Florida, for a little vacation, and Roby had been letting Augie use his old Ford work van while they were away.

Augie parked his bike on the side of the house. It was the old style, built off the ground. He reached up under it and retrieved the key to the van. He also removed a small canvas bag. He got into the van and drove off. He went across town, over the Industrial Canal and into the dark, combat-zone streets of the Ninth Ward. Claude followed him all the way. Augie went to the intersection where he had seen the black Cadillac with the rusted quarter-panel. It wasn't there. He circled the block and then returned to a spot across the street and down from where he had seen the car. Claude Landaiche parked on the opposite side of the street, but further back, with a clear view of Augie's van.

Augie saw the Cadillac after about twenty minutes. One headlight was burned out. It coasted into the vacant spot across the street. The driver and another young man got out, illuminated briefly by a street lamp. Augie leaned back in the darkness of the van and raised the binoculars to his eyes. He focused first on the driver's face, then on the second person. The second person had the scar, the letter J, plain as could be.

Augie reached around the seat and unzipped the canvas bag he had retrieved from Roby's house. It contained a .45 caliber, military-style sidearm that Roby's brother had purchased at a pawn shop in Mississippi. Augie shoved a full clip into the handle of the weapon and stuffed it into his pocket, then pulled his dark, loose-fitting tee-shirt over it.

Claude Landaiche also had equipment: an expensive-looking video camera that he hoisted up to his shoulders as he got out of his car.

The two men who were the object of Augie's interest proceeded down the sidewalk. At the corner, where a street light had been busted, the men stopped in the semi-darkness. They conversed for a moment, then turned back the way they had come.

Augie saw the men duck suddenly into a dark storefront. He knew something was up. He saw a glint of steel. They had weapons. Something was about to happen.

Augie crossed the street. The two men were watching the sidewalk. Then they moved from their hiding place, guns raised.

Augie removed his weapon from his pocket and held it in his hands. He felt absolutely fearless. They didn't stand a chance, he thought. They were as good as dead. He pictured himself pointing his weapon at the man with the J on his cheek. He imagined squeezing the trigger and watching the bullet tear through the man's chest. His intention was to aim exactly at the spot in the chest where they had shot his father. Then a knot formed in his stomach when he saw the target of their advances: it was Claude Landaiche, standing between two parked cars, holding a movie camera.

Augie saw the men approach Claude; there was no doubt they wanted the camera. He cursed himself for not taking Claude seriously. He must have rented the damn camera, Augie thought. Augie's plan had been to shoot immediately and then leave the scene. But now Claude complicated things. He would of course catch Augie committing a murder. But the alternative was to stop the men by using his powers, and Claude would get that on film. One was almost as bad as the other.

In an instant he made up his mind. "Claude, look out!" he shouted. Then he focused on the weapons, while still holding his own pistol in his right hand. But something went wrong. He locked his attention on the guns of the two men, which he could see clearly, but nothing happened. The guns didn't fly from their hands. He tried harder. Nothing. His powers were *failing* him! He began to panic.

The man with the J fired. Claude went down. Augie screamed. Then the men turned their faces to the new threat, now tense and alert, and saw Augie with his weapon. They started to turn their guns toward him. Augie saw it unfolding as if in slow motion. He felt nothing but hot anger and again focused all of his energy on the guns now almost pointing at him. But he could not make them sail away into the night sky as he had been doing for weeks. His powers had stopped. He saw the muzzles of the weapons, one of them still smoking.

Augie raised his weapon and fired twice. Both men went down. A bullet in each chest.

Augie ran to Claude. He was dead. Augie knelt by Claude and shook him, then he started crying.

After a moment Augie heard a very faint sound: a clatter of metal and hard plastic. He looked. In the street, a screwdriver had fallen to the pavement. Augie was puzzled. It was followed by a nail, which hit the concrete with a light ping. Then a Schwinn bicycle seat landed with a thud. Then a familiar-looking knife fell into the circle of light. Augie recognized it as a Marine Corps K-Bar.

He heard voices, neighbors coming out to see who had been shot. Something else fell, and a pistol lay in the street. Another one landed next to it, and bounced and went off. People screamed and started running. Two more knives fell, then several other weapons, including an Uzi.

Augie had a sick feeling that he knew what was happening. He ran along the sidewalk, dazed, still holding his own weapon.

Someone yelled, "Call the police. There's the killer."

Augie threw the pistol down. "No! He killed my father. I've been helping you people."

Then it rained weapons. They fell from the sky in a shower of steel, like someone had turned over a chest of arms and emptied the contents. Pistols, knives, pipes, machine guns. They clattered on cars, rooftops, streets and sidewalks, and collected in piles of metal. Some of them went off as they landed. Augie ran for the van. He saw several boys fighting over the fallen weapons. Something hit Augie hard on the head, and blood ran down his face. He got into the van. The sound was deafening.

He threw himself down on the floor, and held his ears and cried. Tears and blood streamed down his face. Above the roar he heard police sirens.

GHOST ROCKS

NANCY LOU CANYON

Excerpted from the novel Stealing Time

The shaman led his horse around the switchback and headed up the final and steepest leg of his trek to the mountain. Each hot dusty step asked for a commitment, just as the vision quest Tony Snake Medicine Man was about to embark upon did. Pally, his paint horse, nudged at his flannel-covered shoulder from behind. Tony removed the canteen from around his neck. He took a drink, then poured water into his hand and held it to his horse's muzzle.

There were only two things in life Tony consistently prayed for: Great Spirit's guidance and the love of a good woman. And he believed Spirit had answered his prayers with a vision of yellow light in the shape of a shimmering female. The light hovered over the wind-sculpted tops of Ghost Rocks, slid down carved faces, and swirled around the fire pit in sparkling and glittering snaps. He'd seen her twice over the past month, and now he wanted to know who she was and where he could find her.

A loose rock tumbled off the trail and crashed downhill through dry brush, knocking from rock to rock as it clattered into the dry gully below. Tony blocked the sun with his leathered hand

and studied the heat-wavering landscape. He listened to the creaks and shivers of rocks, scrub oak, and red dirt like a raven listened for the rasp of an insect. His horse nickered softly beside him.

Tony lowered his voice. "Who's there, Pally? Is it yellow lady, the one who sparkles?" The shaman tilted his head. Besides the sound of earth baking, he heard nothing but flies buzzing and wind combing brush. He continued up the mountain, singing the cactus song. Scuffing the toe of his boot on a rock, he jumped as sharp pain jimmied his toes. As he bent to apply pressure to his boot tip, he spotted a familiar track pressed like a neighbor's brand into the powdery red dirt. "I don't believe it," he said, catching the scent of Poison perfume. "Where are you, Suzie? Come on out."

Just ahead on the trail, a shadow cast by the red rock shifted sideways. Then Tony's sister, dressed in black jeans and a snap-shirt, stepped out of the shade onto the path. Her glistening blue-black braid hung over her chest; her black Stetson sat low on her head. "Hey, Bro," she said, clicking her tongue. "Surprised to see me?"

"You're stalking me, Sis?" Tony shook his head. "There's nothing here for you. Go down the mountain."

"I just got here, Brother." She scrambled over the shale to push past the shaman. "Good boy, Pally. Daddy's too busy to be civil," she said, stroking the horse's muzzle. "But you're glad to see me, right?"

"Leave him alone, Sue." Tony tugged the reins and pulled the horse past his sister.

"Well, I know when I'm not wanted." Sue slapped Pally's flank. The horse spooked sideways and knocked several loose rocks over the trail edge to cascade noisily into the canyon. "I thought you'd be happy to see me. Just think, now you won't have to vision quest alone."

Tony shook his head. He'd told no one of his plans to fast three days and three nights, waiting for Great Spirit to give him a vision. His bones, sage, tobacco, canteens, and bedroll were tied to his horse's flanks. "Impeccable timing, Sister," he said. "How'd you know?"

"Magic," Sue said, hurrying past the horse to Tony's side. "I know you've come to Ghost Rocks because of her. But you're making a mistake."

Tony grumbled, realizing if he looked into Sue's black eyes he could get sucked into her vast possessiveness. He was tired of her tantrums, her dark pranks, and her controlling ways. He wanted to be free of her.

"Don't ignore me, Brother. You should be glad to have company out here in the middle of the desert. You've been lucky up till now, but one more bite and you could die. Who'd even know?"

"You wear me thin," Tony said, walking on.

"You surviving those venomous bites doesn't mean she will, Rattlesnake. She's nothing but a weak white-woman. She's beneath you."

Tony faced his sister across the path. "How do you know about sparkling woman?" he asked.

Sue dug the toe of her boot into the red dirt. "I just do. Trust me, she's a whore," she said. "A drunken floozy. You can do better."

Tony pulled his hat brim lower. "Stay out of my visions, Sister." He turned back to the path and led Pally through the giant red stones into the circle of ghosts. Pally swung his head, flipping his mane against the flies. The shaman guided him past Bear Rock, a snarling mass of sandstone guarding the eastern edge of the circle. Between the rocks he hoped he'd see Sue making her way down the path to the little town of Boiler baking in hazy heat in the distance, but he didn't. Pally nudged his arm. "Thata boy," he said, looping the rope over a twisted branch and cinching it tight. With gear in hand, he left his horse in the shade pawing at dry tufts of grass.

"Ghost Rocks," Sue said. She was standing in the rock entrance, her height diminished in the gapping maw. "Look at them all looming up like giant bears." She strode around the clearing, clicking her tongue as she walked. "I love these rocks like baby sisters."

"Someone's been here," Tony said. He dropped his gear and crouched to rearrange the broken fire pit.

"Your new flame, no doubt," Sue said. "What'd you call her,

sparkling bitch? It's only costume jewelry, you know. Whores can't afford diamonds."

Tony unrolled his smudge bundle. "Go home and take care of my niece, Sister. I'm worried about her."

Sue kicked a rock, sailing it past Tony's shoulder to the middle of the fire pit. "I need a break from her terror."

"Where'd you leave her this time," Tony said, "at the café?" He pulled the rock from the ashes and tossed it aside. Sitting back on his heels, he pinched bits of tobacco from a tin and offered it to each of the four directions.

"Grandma Davis," Sue said. "Ellen needed a time out."

"You need time out," Tony said. "She needs her hair combed and her clothes washed. They're coming to make a judgment soon. Are you ready?"

"They can't take my baby. You'll see," she said, striding around the fire pit to face him. "Besides, if I leave, I'll miss saving my pathetic brother from a sleazy tramp."

Tony picked up a stick and drew in the dirt next to the fire pit, a circle large enough to sleep in. He dropped cross-legged into the center and unrolled his smudge bundle. "I ceremony alone. Go home Sue." He lit the wand of white sage and waved the sweet smoke around him.

Sue stepped inside the circle. "I'll help you find her, Bro."

"Now you've disrespected Great Spirit," he said, jumping up. He grabbed Sue's arm and dragged her stumbling across the amphitheatre. "Go home. Ceremony if you want, but do it with right intention."

Sue jerked away, stumbling backward against a rock face. "Ah, Raven Rock's energy," she said, twitching black brows over venomous eyes. A gust of hot wind rattled leaves around her feet as she stretched both arms above her and smiled. Feathers began sprouting along her forearms.

"Don't, Sue," Tony said. "Shifting isn't your medicine."

The looming rock creaked behind her. The air burst with ions. Yellow sparks snapped around the sandstone peaks. Pally whinnied and pawed the ground. Tony knew it was the sparkling woman.

A familiar ache tugged from the shaman's stomach to his

shoulder joints. He rolled his head back and tucked his arms against his sides. Feathers snapped from his fingertips and quills speared his skin, shooting over his shoulders and down his back. He flexed black wings, grimacing inwardly as a hard beak sprouted from his face and tail feathers pinpricked into a flush of black at the base of his spine. He sprang skyward, flapping toward the top branches of the oak trees. Snaps and pops trailed him. He landed on a springing limb. Flapping her wings furiously, Sue settled next to him. She pecked at his shoulder and head, cawing, "Never fly away from me. We're in this together, Bro."

"Eat rattlesnake somewhere else, Suzie."

"Ma put me in charge of you. I won't let her down."

"We were children then." Tony dove from the oak, soared past Coyote Rock, and circled Snake Rock. Sue followed close behind, pecking at his tail feathers as he careened toward the coiled rock marking the south end of the amphitheatre. They landed on the ledge in a flush and tumble of feathers and talons. In the tangle of wings and wiry black legs, Tony pictured their mother's ceremonial dress with its fringe jumping like a courting grouse. He righted himself and reassembled his wings. The yellow shimmering light gathered in the center of the amphitheatre and took on a female shape that followed the edge of Tony's circle before settling next to his smoldering smudge. Tony smelled lilies over the spicy sage. "It's her," he whispered. "The sparkling woman is here."

Sue tore from the rock and swooped low over the vision, flapping and striking her talons over and over again into the yellow light. The vision flashed, then weakened. Tony dove at his sister, beating his wings to block her, snagging at her back with his claws. Sue banked left. Tony clipped her breast with his feathered shoulder and knocked her out of flight. She landed on the far side of the fire pit, tumbling across the red earth as she returned to long limbs. Tony settled onto the rock beside her and shapeshifted back into his sinewy self. He shook out his arms and straightened his leather-wrapped braids. His sister climbed to her feet, eyes hissing like a rattler about to strike.

Tony was about to wrestle his sister from the amphitheatre

when Sue lunged forward, "I'll tear you both to pieces," she shrieked.

Tony blocked her attack with his forearm and wrenched her arm around to her back, torquing it toward the whitewashed sky. He held her there as he searched the amphitheatre for the vision. "She's gone," he said. "You've chased her off. Now you go, and if you come back here, it'll be the sheriff you visit next." He shoved his sister toward the opening.

Wheeling to face him, Sue spit in the dirt. "Don't threaten me."

Tony broke the hold her burning eyes had on his and returned to the fire pit. Stepping into the center of the circle, he sat on the good red earth and relit the smudge stick. He brushed the sweet smoke over his head with a hawk feather. From the rocky maw, his sister's words shot across the amphitheatre.

"Ma gave you to me," she said. "You're still mine. You'll see."

As the sun lowered in the sky and gusts turned to a constant blow, Tony tossed bones. He stopped occasionally to squint at the ochre haze darkening the western sky. He couldn't see the horizon beyond the shadowy rocks, but he imagined from the dirty sky that if he could see beyond the stones, the horizon would be eclipsed in billows of dust. Pressure twitched his muscles, nearly convincing him to outrun the coming storm. But he was here to quest, and Great Spirit would expect no less. He rubbed grit from his sun-baked eyes with callused fingertips and tossed the bones again.

Mostly the bones fell in the north—the place of winter sky and life breathed out from tender wounds of lost hope. Tony saw in his mind's eye death, a broken neck, and a woman tangled in a stringy mess of river weed. A gust of wind whipped red dirt into his eyes. He blinked against the grit, grabbed up the bones, and slipped them back into his shirt pocket. Unrolling his bedroll, he cocooned himself between the rough layers of army blankets. The first night of his vision quest and he'd be riding out a desert storm.

Tony awoke the next morning to a yellow pepper sun rising

in a picante sky, its warm glow edging the hunched forms of Snarling Bear. He moved his focus from his belly to his bladder and back to the sky still dingy from the storm. It was his second day of eating nothing but grit and his stomach was growling like a mad dog's, biting him hard in the middle. Broken visions had come in the night, but mostly he'd spent his first night thrashing between blankets and fighting flying sand and the failing fire. Before dawn, the wind settled along with the dust. He'd managed to revive the fire and warm his hands against the flickering flames. He shook himself free of his bedroll and stumbled into the brush behind the oaks to relieve himself.

On previous vision quests, Great Spirit had given him challenges: spirit attacks, foul weather, near insanity. Other times he was left to sit and watch his surroundings simply exist, wishing for at least the diversion of a mouse scampering across the circle of hard-packed dirt. This time it was the wind-people fighting him spear and arrow.

He fed Pally oats and gave him water then wandered back to the circle. Sweat beaded over his forehead; his lips cracked in the dry air. He swallowed some water, then began a slow dance around the amphitheatre, bending his torso, and tucking his knees up to his chest, tapping his feet rhythmically. He flapped his arms and cawed; he hissed like a snake, letting his arms undulate and coil. He prayed and chanted until the ground began to swirl into a dust devil. His spirit guides whispered in his ears, showing him villages, children playing, women tanning hides, men riding from camp to hunt. He felt rattlesnake venom coursing through his veins, an arrow piercing his flesh, and the taste of bitter poison spreading over his tongue.

Tony had received his medicine by recovering from three consecutive snake bites. Tony Sure Foot became Tony Snake Medicine Man. He feared nothing, not even visions of painted warriors scrambling out of the sandstone and running through the darkness toward him.

The shaman heard the slither of rattlesnakes pouring from the rocks; sidewinders rapidly covering the powdery dirt to encircle him. It wasn't his medicine that brought the vision; it was his fervent prayers. He tipped his head back and listened to his spirit guide's whisper: *She's coming, the woman who sparks. You must help her.*

"When?" he said, but his voice was drowned out by the roar in his ears as his spirit was pulled from his body. Tony crumpled to the ground inside the circle of snakes. The black tunnel drew him in and spit him out into the void. Tethered along a blue line of light, he found himself floating above a carpet of evergreens that twisted along a raging river. A man, blue with water, blue with death, lay crumpled on the rocky shore. Then he saw the sparkling woman running toward the dead man, screaming. Weeping, she dropped to her knees and held him, stroking his limp head and kissing his blue hands. At last she left him to stumble across the rocky shore toward the rapids.

The shaman floated above the trees and saw the woman's future. She was dressed in black, hovering over a gravesite. The middle of her torso opened into a black hole. She slipped one foot into the dead man's grave and there she remained, half in this world and half in the next.

Tony Snake Medicine Man jerked and twitched and rolled onto his back. The vision was gone. Like overripe fruit, the dawn sky hung heavy above him. He could almost taste the last bit of starlight gleaming through the chill of desert air, the sharp yip of distant coyotes adding a sprinkling of spice to early morning. His stomach growled to the slithering sound of snakes retreating into their rocky dens.

He went over the vision in his mind's eye. The woman's energy was dark with the exception of sparks radiating from her neck, wrists, fingers, ankles, and toes. Now he could see the sparks were coming from the jewels she wore. Her ring-adorned fingers clutched something shiny swinging at her side. He looked into the vision more closely and recognized it as a pocket watch dangling from a fob. She was running out of time. He whispered to the sky people, "Now I know her name: Jeweled Lady."

The air shifted and a wisp of warmth rolled in from the south. Dawn neared. It was time for the shaman to sleep. He rolled over and crawled on all fours back into the circle. He tossed a handful of cactus skeletons onto the coals and folded himself inside his bedroll. The imagined taste of cherry pie tugged at the corners of his mouth as he fell into a dreamless sleep.

Jewel barreled south along a highway as flat and straight as a young girl's body. As she breezed along, tumbleweeds bounced, snagged on barbwire, and piled against shot-peppered road signs. Clouds floated across the clear blue sky, lifting on gusts of hot wind like white feathers. She drove with the window down, drinking in the smell of the desert: hot rocks, sun-baked earth, and desert brush.

Clay was never further from her thoughts than her hair; his name was never further from her pursed lips than her tongue. At the Continental Divide, she'd considered joining him in the afterlife. Just a flip of the wheel around one of those icy hairpin curves and she'd have plummeted through rarified air to the rocks far below. By now, they could be riding bareback along the river, their spirits together again.

Jewel gulped hot air. Clay wasn't coming back, she knew that. She switched on the radio. "Fear is an alarming and powerful emotion, but it must be overcome!" Jewel flipped from the God station to a country western station; she joined in, singing at the top of her lungs *Your Cheating Heart*. She concentrated on the earth and sandstone flying past, their red tones contrasting with the blue of the sky, steeping her in the wide open feeling of desert.

Ahead, a sign loomed through heat mirages and announced the town of Boiler, Arizona, population 3,000. She decided to stop for lunch and leaned forward to check her lipstick in the rear-view mirror. Behind her, a black and white lifted out of the wavering heat streams, its dome light flashing like sun off a mirror. She slapped the steering wheel hard. "God Almighty," she said, "Not another damned speeding ticket."

She let off the gas and looked for a place to pull over. Boiler looked like it had been torn directly from *Arizona Highways* with its lamp posts, watering troughs, and wooden rails. A neon sign flashed, Eat 'em Up Café. Jewel pulled the car into the dirt parking lot; the black and white pulled in behind her.

She shut off the engine and shakily applied fresh lipstick. She patted her diamond necklace into a smooth arc and made certain her rings were all facing heavenward. In the side mirror, a reflection of the bowlegged sheriff hobbled her way. She opened the car door and swung long legs ensconced in a black miniskirt into the sheriff's path.

"Mornin', Ma'am," the sheriff said, pulling a ticket book from his shirt pocket. "Deputy back on the highway says you's been hauling that pretty behind of yours upwards of eighty. We frown on speeding around here, Ma'am."

Jewel unfolded from the car, brushing against the tan suited man-of-law as she stood. "Excuse me, Sheriff." She looked from his name tag to his squinty eyes roaming her cleavage. "Sheriff Senior, before you get yourself a case of writer's cramp, can I buy you a cup of joe?"

The sheriff lifted his sweat-soaked cowboy hat and stroked a fat hand across his balding head. He smiled and nodded toward the café. "Kiki makes the best cherry pie around these parts. Wouldn't mind me a piece, Ma'am."

"Didn't your deputy tell you?" She drew a finger down his shiny badge. "That's why I was in such a rush."

Chuckling, the sheriff held out his arm. "This way, Ma'am. We'll talk business inside."

As Jewel took the sheriff's arm, a wave of vertigo washed over her. She leaned heavily against the lawman, wobbling on her spike-heeled sandals across the parking lot. The sheriff's cologne was acidic; the thought of swallowing hot coffee turned her stomach. What she really needed was to strip off her clothes and lie naked in the dark with a cold cloth resting over her forehead. She'd flirt away the ticket, then excuse herself to find a room for the night.

The café smelled like coffee and sugar, hot peppers and bleach. Rodeo photographs hung along the walls; flies circled beneath a ceiling fan clicking in lazy circles. A waitress with curly black hair and a quick smile said, "Hey there, Sheriff. Good timing, pies just came out of the oven."

"Well then, best bring me a slice, Sweets." The sheriff drew back a chair and nodded for Jewel to sit. She clutched her purse to her side and dutifully took a seat. The grimacing lawman wedged his sweaty bulk into the chair opposite her and curled his lip to reveal stained teeth. He jabbed the same fat hand he'd used to wipe his head across the table for her to shake. "Dandy Senior," he said.

She gave his hand a limp shake then drew it discreetly across her skirt. "Jewel Golden," she said. "Will you excuse me, Sheriff? I need to freshen up." Standing, she looked around for the restroom. A skinny cowpoke sat at the counter watching her. When their eyes met, his dark stare grabbed her—a hungry greedy man looking for trouble. Jewel's flirting energy disappeared and she hesitated, feeling suddenly vulnerable and wanting Clay at her side. She turned quickly away.

"Don't run off, Missy," the sheriff called after her. "Ain't talked business yet."

Jewel looked back at the lawman and forced a flirtatious smile. "Don't worry," she said. "There's no place to hide around here." She disappeared into the daisy-wallpapered ladies' room to splash cold water onto her face.

"Just relax," Jewel said to herself as she stepped out of the airless room into the café. The waitress was ringing up the greedy cowpoke's meal. He tipped his hat at Jewel and headed to the door.

"Better not let me catch you making trouble, Max," the sheriff said as he leaned back in his chair and worked a toothpick around his fleshy mouth. Max tipped his hat and disappeared into the heat. When the sheriff heard Jewel's spike-heeled sandals clicking across the floor, he turned a wicked smile in her direction.

The waitress stepped up beside him and filled his coffee cup. She turned up Jewel's mug and said as she approached, "Coffee, miss?"

"No thanks," Jewel said. "I'm exhausted from the road. Sheriff, if you don't mind, I'm ready to retire for the night."

The sheriff licked his pasty lips and raised his eyebrows. "Well I hardly knows ya, Missy, but if you insist."

Jewel sighed and rubbed her forehead. The vertigo had subsided, but now her head had begun to hurt. "I've got a migraine coming on. I think I'll just get a room at the motel across the street and call it a day."

"It's all boarded up," Dandy said, chuckling. "Probably all you can afford after that speeding ticket."

"Don't mind him," the waitress said. "He's got a quota to meet. Highway robbery should be a crime, Sheriff. Leave the lady alone."

The sheriff grinned, his beady eyes disappearing into squinty folds of flesh. "Hurry on over there and get me that pie you promised, Kiki."

"Must be another motel in this town," Jewel said and dug into her purse. She pushed the flask beneath her wallet before the sheriff could see. Sweating, she pulled out some bills and handed them to the waitress. "Sheriff's meal's on me," she said.

"They rent seedy rooms above the saloon." Kiki stuffed the money into her apron pocket. "Or there's a room upstairs. Manny, my boss, won't mind you staying there. Sit for a minute while I get the sheriff's pie."

The perky waitress hurried off. Jewel took a seat opposite the lawman. She was about to reach out a hand to touch his when he closed his right eye and spoke.

"You buying me coffee won't get rid of that speeding ticket. I'm gonna see you in court." He pushed a slip of paper across the table. "That's when."

Kiki returned, setting a large slice of pie before the sheriff. "Is he giving you a bad time again? Sheriff, what's this?" She grabbed up the slip of paper and studied it carefully. "Court date, forget it, Sheriff." She tore up the slip and motioned to Jewel. "Come on. Be right back, Dandy. Watch the place while I give the poor lady a break from your crooked ways."

"We'll talk when you get back, Sweetcakes." The sheriff grabbed the waitress's ass as she walked away.

Outside, the air was scalding and dry as dirt. Kiki managed to balance the tray and bound up the steps to the apartment at the same time. Jewel followed the waitress, carefully negotiating splintery stairs in teetering heels, the heat making her head pound.

"Sorry about the sheriff," Kiki said. "He's old country, you know. Sexist pig, stupid too. Just humor him and dodge those grabbing hands. And, next time, go the speed limit. You're not in Kansas."

"Thanks," she smiled. "My name's Jewel. And it's the Pacific Northwest I abandoned for this shitload of heat."

"It's Kiki, but I guess you already knew that," she said, balancing the tray on the rail while she opened the door. "Doesn't it rain there all the time?"

"Got moss growing between my toes to prove it," Jewel said, stepping into the stifling apartment. To the right of the door a swamp cooler sat lopsided inside a dusty window. Jewel switched on the fan and stale air sputtered into the room.

"Desert'll dry you to powder." Kiki set the tray on the coffee table. "Doesn't take long, either. Need lots of moisturizer to stay supple around here."

Jewel picked up a romance from the coffee table and laughed at the busty redhead swooning into muscular arms. She flipped through the pages while Kiki bustled about.

"Manny's too busy riding his broncs to get this place rented. He'll be happy to have someone lighten his load."

"Broncs?" Jewel watched the waitress opening and closing cupboards as if she were looking for something incriminating.

"Manny's a rodeo star," Kiki said. "Just pretend like you know that, and he'll like you fine." She mimicked in a low voice, "*I win the big money by hanging on till the end.*"

"Bucking broncos," Jewel said. She flipped through the pages of the paperback until she came across a passage describing wet, greedy kisses being smothered over a bare white neck. She smiled. "These yours?"

"Yeah, read 'em, if you like. I do on my breaks, just for fun, you know."

"I like the real thing," Jewel said, dropping onto the couch and looking around the tiny apartment: bed, couch, kitchenette, dresser, and bathroom. She wondered what else Kiki did on her breaks; perhaps, ride the bronc rider. "Is this Manny-guy married?"

Blushing, Kiki busied herself fluffing pillows and straightening the cotton bedspread. "Not really."

"Huh!" Jewel cut into the pie and wondered what was up between the rodeo star and the cute waitress as she lifted the bite to her mouth. When the sweet and sour mix of berries and sugar puckered her lips, she nearly swooned like the busty redhead.

"I bake for the whole region," Kiki said. "It's a big job. Manny says he's gonna get me some help someday. You should apply."

"How'd you learn to bake like this? It's almost as good as. . . " Jewel licked her lips, "well, never mind. It's really delicious, Kiki."

Kiki blushed. "Mama taught me." She looked at her watch. "I'd better get back. Manny's got a temper. You can deal with him when you come down, and I'll take care of Dandy." Kiki smiled and closed the door behind her.

Tony removed his hat and was setting it on the stool bedside him when Kiki bustled through the back door. She grabbed the pitcher of ice water and splashed Tony's glass full. "So where you been hiding yourself, Tony?" She leaned on an elbow and tugged his braid. Smiling brightly, she said, "I've missed you, you ol' snake in the grass."

"Just returned from a vision quest," Tony said, and gulped down the cold water. He wiped his mouth on his sleeve. "Been on the mountain three days and nights. Kept thinking about your cherry pie the whole time. Got any?"

"Both cherry and apple fresh today," Kiki said and took out her order pad. "What would you like?"

"I'll have a slice of each." Tony looked around at the sheriff shoveling big gobs of pie into his mouth. He turned back to Kiki and said, "Sheriff got to bragging about pestering that lady you took upstairs. She wearing lots of diamonds?"

"Yeah, a whole mess of them." She removed two pies from the pie safe and cut a slice from each. "You know her?"

Tony smiled at his long-time friend. "I saw a woman like that in a vision."

"Huh! Well some might say she's a vision. Looks a little, you know," Kiki raised her eyebrows, "like a tramp to me."

"Hey, Injun," Dandy said, "you hoarding my gal or what?"

Tony looked around at the lawman. "Treat her like the gem she is, Sheriff?"

"Always do," Dandy said. "Could use a refill over here, Sweetcakes." The sheriff scooted around in his chair to face Tony. Squinting, he said, "First, I gets me a speeder and now I'm about to get me a horse rustler."

"Pally's mine, as you know, and rustling up pie's no crime." Tony turned back to the plates of pie Kiki had set before him. He shook his head in wonder at their syrupy sheen.

"You're incorrigible, Sheriff," Kiki said, grabbing the coffee pot and hurrying off to fill the sheriff's cup. "You know Tony comes in here to relax. He's been hard at work on those visions of his. You best leave him be, hear me?"

"You're a spitfire, Kiki." The sheriff grabbed at her hips as she walked away. "But you ain't stopping me from fining that woman."

"I can try, Sheriff." Kiki set the pot back on the burner and turned to Tony. "Anything else?"

"Pally sure would like some apples," Tony said.

"Well, let me see what I got."

She hurried to the back of the café just as Manny walked in. "You left the light on upstairs. Better not've burnt the pies while reading those goddamned romances of yours. You're on the clock, you know."

"So arrest me. Sheriff's right over there," she said, setting four withered apples on the counter in front of Tony. "You're always threatening, so now's your chance."

"What's he doing with my apples?"

"They've seen better days," the waitress replied, waving a fly away from the pie safe. "Only the best ingredients are good enough for this café, right?"

The squinty-eyed sheriff wielded a toothpick from one corner of his doughy mouth to the other. "I'll be back tomorrow, Kiki. Keep an eye on our gal." He wrestled himself from the chair and sauntered toward the door.

The door slammed shut and the waitress stepped close to Manny. "Dandy dragged in this speeder. She wasn't feeling well, so I let her rest upstairs for awhile."

"Hell, you let a stranger up there," Manny said, removing his hat and rubbing sweat from his forehead. "Christ, que sonza."

"She wants to rent the place," Kiki said. "You need a renter. I thought you'd be happy."

"Quiet, sonza. That Injun don't need to know our problems. Go pour the guy a cup of coffee."

"He's just back from a vision quest," Kiki said, and crossed her arms over her chest. "He's drinking water instead of coffee."

Manny flapped his hat back on. "No argumento!" The back door slammed and the rodeo star wheeled about, shouting, "Now what? I took delivery this morning."

Kiki said, "That's her; that's the woman, Manny."

Jewel strolled across the kitchen, straightening stacks of mugs and water glasses with diamond adorned fingers. Tony recognized the scent of lilies from the vision. His heart turned into a fluttering raven's wing.

"Excuse me," she said, brushing her hand against Manny's arm. "I'd like a coffee refill."

"I'm not a goddamn servant!" Manny said. "Pot's over there. Help yourself and pour the Injun a cup while you're at it, less my coffee's too good for him."

Jeweled Lady hardly looked at Tony as she swished past. She filled two white mugs like she'd been doing it her whole life, and set one on the counter in front of Tony without meeting his eyes. She turned back to Manny and said, "You the rodeo star?"

"That's right. Big Bad Manny Davis," Manny said, leaning on the counter, his black snap-shirt rolled up at the sleeves. "I win the money."

"Name's Jewel Golden," she said, fingering her diamond necklace. "Heard you could use some help around here."

"They sure could," Tony said, and pushed the coffee aside. "I'm parched as a desert riverbed, could use more water, please."

Jewel turned to the shaman and smiled a smile that didn't hide her distain. "And who are you?"

"Tony Snake Medicine Man," he said. As she sized him up, he saw that his dusty black braids, leathered cheeks, stained fingernails, and faded flannel offended her. He couldn't tell, but he probably smelled of campfire smoke, sweat, and sage, too.

"Weird name," she said, and looked away.

"He's a powerful shaman," Kiki said, "Besides the sheriff, you'd best watch your step around Tony. The two of them keep us on our toes around here."

Jewel turned back and reached out her jewelry-adorned fingers. She smiled a stiff smile. "Guess it can't hurt to have a shaman on your side."

Tony took her hand. Her skin was warm and baby soft. A rush of energy passed between them. When Jeweled Lady tried to pull away, Tony held tight.

She laughed. "Give me back my hand, snake man."

The shaman loosened his grip. Her eyes didn't leave his as she made it obvious that she was wiping her hand clean on her miniskirt. Great Spirit had answered his prayers, but with what? Laughing, he reached inside his shirt pocket and pulled out a wad of herbs.

"What's so funny?" She lifted the coffee mug to her lips and watched him with blue-sky eyes narrowed to slits.

Tony was drawn to her, but at the same time repelled. He'd seen clear blue eyes ringed with night sky before. The guides said they were the sign of a gifted one. Was Great Spirit playing a joke on him, or was Jeweled Lady an heir to powerful medicine?

She swallowed the rest of her coffee and set the mug down hard. "What's that?" she said.

"Herbs—tobacco and sage." He pushed the wad across the counter. "You'll need these for protection."

Jewel stiffened. "In what lifetime?" She rolled her eyes and turned back to the rodeo star. "So, what do you say? When do I move into the apartment and start baking pies?"

"I already got a pie baker, tonta," Manny said and cracked his knuckles as he looked her over. "Kenny's got rooms above the saloon. You wait tables?"

"Why not?" She drew diamond-studded fingers down her neck. "Can't be that hard."

"Be here tomorrow at eight," Manny said. "You'll see how hard it is." ❧

Redo

Nick Heinlein

Jack stood at the edge of the pier, looking out upon the dark beyond. He wore simple garments: a day shirt and pants and shoes, though the soles were fading. The watch on his wrist was a gift from his father: an old-fashioned, wind-up device, adorned with ancient Roman numerals, far different from the digital computer systems that normally kept time. But it did its job, or as best it could, in sync with the planetary revolutions of the Earth. An Earth now polluted by nuclear waste and fossil fuels. Its moon, Luna, was in no better shape either. Ore mining had robbed the mountainous satellite of its beauty and turned it into yet another industrial wasteland.

From the house, a shrill voice called, "*Dinner!* Come and *get it!*" Fran was in one of her moods . . . again.

Jack reluctantly stepped off the wooden dock and walked along the muddy path to his family's lakeside, two-story home. As he approached the stairs, he nearly tripped over the puppy, Piddles. She'd earned her name so well; in fact, she was only allowed inside to sleep. Otherwise she was outdoors or in the electrified kennel. He scratched behind the mutt's ears and went to the door, which offered its own greetings as he climbed the steps.

"Hello, Jack," the calm voice of the house computer said. "Was your walk enjoyable?"

They needed a better computer. This model was almost six years out of date. Jack ignored the recorded message and opened the door just wide enough to see if the coast was clear.

It wasn't.

The pot on the stove was overflowing with boiling water, and the frothing liquid spread across the counter, dripping onto the floor. Fran shrieked in rage as her cooking sloshed down her apron and around her ankles. Jack sighed and closed the back door silently, creeping back onto the patio with Piddles frolicking around his shins.

"Hello, Jack." The computer's monotone was infuriating. "How was dinner?"

Jack sighed and looked back at the small screen on the door, where an old-fashioned doorbell would normally be. "Execute protocol: 'sleep.' "

"Good night, Jack." The tinny whir of the computer's motor stopped, leaving Jack alone with Piddles, who was now drooling enthusiastically on his thigh. "Sometimes you can't beat out flesh and blood, eh Piddles?"

Piddles looked up, panting.

"No, I don't have food."

Piddles stared at him stupidly, not comprehending a word that was coming out of his mouth.

"God, you're worse than the computer."

The dog did not change its facial expression in the least. Jack sighed and put his ear to the door. The sounds of war had abated, and he knew he had around ten seconds before his mother would start looking for him. "See you," he said to the dog, which looked at him with overwhelming trust and love. Jack sighed again. "Dumb mutt."

He opened the door and went inside. The moment he was spotted, Fran yelled, "And where the hell have you been? Dinner's freezing, and it's all thanks to you!"

Jack shrugged, nonchalant, and sat down. A glob of red (and blue?) sauce was on one end of the plate, a spoonful of uncooked noodles on the other. Compared to some of the meals he'd eaten in the past week, it was almost a feast. "Any cheese?" he asked hopefully.

"We don't have the money for cheese," Fran replied. Jack knew full well they did.

"I'm getting some water," he said, standing. "I hate this lime-flavored milk."

Fran sighed. "I bought it for *you*. I'm sorry for trying to make you happy."

Jack shook his head but said nothing. He knew better than to get Fran in attack mode; or worse, defense. He put his glass under the faucet and retched when the water came out brown.

"Your father's fixing the purifiers," Fran said. "Don't expect any clean water for at least a day or so."

"You could've told me that before I got up," Jack grumbled, returning to his seat.

"You didn't ask," she replied. "Milk?"

The next morning he was surprised when he didn't hear his mother's daily reveille of "Wake up! How are you going to get out of my house? Not by sleeping! *Up!*" She'd never miss her favorite pastime of kicking him in the shins and screaming in his ears. Jack knew something was happening, or had happened. He walked downstairs slowly and approached his mother's room. He cracked open the door and looked inside silently, as he'd trained himself to do.

She was lying in bed, the private television glasses covering her eyes, so he couldn't see if she was awake or not. He slowly opened the door wider. But as soon as his foot touched his mother's carpet, a pot came crashing down on his skull.

"How *dare* you enter my room without *asking*, you ungrateful asshole! How many times have I *told* you this? *How many?* I swear when I'm finished with you, you will regret the day you were born—not that *I* don't already!"

And so it went from there.

Up from the floor; to the sink to apply a laser-bandage to his bleeding scalp; from the sink to the couch, where she made him sit and listen to her rant for two hours; from the couch to the kitchen, where he spent the better part of the morning washing dishes; from the kitchen to his bedroom where she slammed the door in his face and bolted it shut (she'd installed that particular mechanism when he was six).

He glared at the door in fury. He should've known she'd set a trap—nothing interesting ever happened around this house. He sat on the bed and surveyed his room, eyeing the bookshelves for something to read. Dealing with the boredom forced upon him was one of his daily goals, but being locked in his room meant he would be unable to pursue his favorite hobby of taking his homemade boat out on the lake. He kicked at the Bible his father had given him for his birthday one year and stretched himself out on the bed.

The ceiling was just plain white, and he decided it was much too boring to hold his attention for long. Outside his window, an overgrown, dead tree brushed its limbs against the glass, as if asking to be let in. It was from this that Jack got his idea.

He lifted up the window and kicked out the screen. Though he was on the second floor, he still reckoned he could reach the tree and climb down without injury. He grasped the long limb that had kept him awake at night so many times, and swung from it onto the much sturdier trunk. As his hands slipped, his feet searched desperately for footholds, and found much lower but thicker branches. He lowered himself onto these and dropped again, barely hanging on, but his feet brushed solid ground and he let himself drop.

He felt a surge of adrenaline as he hit the rotting grass. Never before had he attempted something like this, and succeeding on the first try seemed like too much luck. He hurried down to the dock and, on the way, realized Piddles was following him, yipping. He stooped low and picked up the canine; she stopped barking and licked his face. He stood for a few moments to make sure Fran hadn't noticed anything, and then made a dash for the boat, throwing Piddles in and untying the rope that held the boat to the dock. He slowed down when he entered, however, for he did not wish the boat to tip and unceremoniously dump them into the water, which was a disgusting shade of brown.

Picking up the oar, he pushed against the dock and propelled them out into open water—water being used in the loosest sense of the word, as what was once a shimmering sapphire lake was now a sea of trash, yet another example of man's robbery of natural beauty, and the reason their property had been so affordable. Piddles paced around the rear of the boat, sticking her nose over the edge to investigate, and when she realized how foul her seemingly endless water bowl was, she contented herself to sit and enjoy the light wind.

Jack watched this with amusement. It never ceased to amaze him, the simplicity of the canine mind—Piddles seemed to have not a care in the world. He wished he could have that at this moment, to be carefree, and able to sit back and simply enjoy the ride. Maybe stop rowing and let the current take them to . . . wherever.

But he knew he couldn't. His mind dwelled on thoughts of what Fran would do to him once he returned (by now, she would have undoubtedly returned to his room for another lecture), and the current would only take them down the waterfall on the other edge of the lake.

So he rowed.

They returned several hours later, when the sun was slowly approaching the horizon and the polluted clouds had been inflamed with brilliant pinks and oranges. He lifted Piddles from the boat and set her on the dock, then got out and tied up the canoe. "Come," he said to the mutt, patting his hip. The dog followed, panting after a day in the sun. Once they got to the house, Piddles made a beeline for her water bowl and gleefully shoved her face into it, tongue flapping. The computer gave off a digital sigh. "Your mother's very angry with you, Jack."

"Yeah, I figured." He reached for the back door handle, but was startled by a voice behind him.

"Hello, young man," it said.

He turned slowly to see a wizened old man in long black robes standing on the porch steps.

"Traditionally," Jack replied, "you knock on the front door."

The man offered his hand. "I am Father McGlenn from the church down the road."

Jack shook it. "Jack Reynolds. I apologize; I've never been."

"God forgives you," McGlenn said, smiling.

There was something about him Jack did not like. At all. "What brings you here?"

"I am going to every home in the neighborhood," McGlenn began. "I bring a message from God."

"Every back door?" Jack asked.

"No," McGlenn said tiredly, "But this house has an unsavory reputation."

"So you decided to come the back way?" Jack said, still at a loss as to why McGlenn was here.

"This is beside the point," the priest said.

"Right, right." Jack rolled his eyes. "The message."

"The message is simply this, young Jack Reynolds." McGlenn's eyes grew wide. "The end is coming!"

Jack had heard crazies preaching the end of the world before. He treated McGlenn no differently. "Thanks for the tip, but I'd best be going."

"No!" McGlenn said, his voice rising. "You do not believe! You will burn, tossed into the lake of fire—"

"I know how it goes," Jack interrupted. "I got a Bible for my birthday one year. Hard read. Skipped to the end 'cause that's where I heard the action was."

"So then you are aware—"

"Yes, perfectly," Jack intruded again, eager to end this confrontation. "Now get off my porch."

McGlenn looked abashed for a moment, and then, without any further word, turned his back upon Jack and departed along the dirt path leading back to the road. Jack shook his head, looked at the now-sleeping Piddles, took a deep breath, and entered his house.

The only words that were distinguishable from the rest when he walked in the door were "insolent," "conniving," and "sonuvabitch." The rest was a stream of gibberish, but he got the gist. Unfortunately, after an hour of sitting on the sofa being screamed at by his mother, his father arrived home from work, and she told him about Jack's transgressions. So then he had to endure, not screaming, but a soft voice enriched with disappointment, which, if anything, was almost worse than the yelling. But luckily, his father only took twenty minutes to finish his lecture, and then Jack was free to return to his room for the night.

As he walked up the stairs, he heard his parents talking in hushed voices back in the kitchen. His stomach was growling so loudly he dared not sneak back down to get some food. He'd gone without dinner before, and he'd do it again. As the door closed behind him, he fell on the bed, the muscles in his arms now feeling the extent of the daylong exercise. Giving no more thought to anything, he fell asleep.

When he awoke, he was in the same position he'd fallen asleep in, and as a result his neck was unbearably stiff. But this did not prevent him from noticing that, for the second day in a row, Fran had missed her wakeup call. He slowly walked down the stairs and rounded the corner into the kitchen. It didn't even look like she was awake yet. He opened the refrigerator door and pulled out the carton of lime milk. It was vile, but better than sewage. He took a swig and dropped it back in the fridge. Upon opening the cabinets, he realized that there was little food in the house—he took the one packet of raisins he found in the cupboard and was rewarded with a mouthful of spiders when he dumped the contents in his mouth. Spitting and cursing, he threw the small cardboard box into the waste disposal bin and went to lay down on the couch, picking up the television remote as he went. The first channel he clicked to was the news.

"*Religious fanatics everywhere are calling it the 'end of the world,'*" the newscaster began. Jack sat up straight, all traces of grogginess gone. "*State officials have yet to comment, but NASA executives say that the mysterious object could be an asteroid of some kind. Either way,*

if left untouched, it will enter the Earth's atmosphere in three days."
The show cut to a satellite picture of the object: at first glance, it certainly looked like an asteroid, but the surface, instead of being craggy and rocky, was smooth and silver. It looked like a bullet, coming to puncture the Earth. Jack sat, riveted, as a NASA administrator began to speak. *"We don't know exactly what it is or what it will do if . . . when it hits. But we do know that no technology currently in our possession will deter it."*

The television went dark. Jack looked up, startled, to see Fran standing at the wall with the plug in her hands. "That's enough. *Bed!"*

The next thing he knew, he was being shoved onto his bed by Fran, who hurled four hastily prepared sandwiches over her shoulder before slamming the door shut. He immediately jumped up and began pounding on the door. *"Let me out!"* he yelled, over and over. After the fifteenth scream, he finally got a response.

"It's for your own good!" Fran cried back, and he heard the stairway door being shut as well. No one would be able to hear him now. He could always scream out the window, but the neighbors would just believe it to be normal—shouting matches happened quite often at their house.

Jack took the sandwiches and deposited them on his dresser, then sat down on the bed, pondering what little he had just seen about the global catastrophe that was unfolding around him. Looking out the window, nothing seemed different. But everything had changed.

The next day passed slowly. Jack bounced an old ball against his ceiling and thought about the end of the world for a few minutes, and then decided he was sick of that. He looked at his bookshelves, but nothing appealed to him. What he really wanted was to find out what was going on in the outside world, but Fran had made sure to make his father trim the branches next to his window, so he could not escape without risking serious injury. He paced around his room, unclean. He was forced to go to the bathroom out the window. He wrote down everything he'd been meaning to say to Fran since the day he realized mothers weren't supposed to be like her, and then ripped the pages to shreds and stomped them into the floor. He flung books upon books against the door, hoping to make some kind of dent. He even flung himself, but that only resulted in a fiery pain that spread throughout his entire body. He finally just lay down on the bed and cried himself to sleep.

The second day was no different from the first, save for the fact he ate two of the sandwiches instead of one to sate his hunger. Thirst was no problem—every bed in the house stocked two gallons of fresh water under it, gathered from a different source than the toilets or sinks. Never before had he had to use them, but he was lucky they were there. The water ran down his throat and moistened his lips, which were chapped and peeling. He looked at his bookshelf again, and then, for no better reason than to pass the time, he began to read. He read well into the night and through the morning, pausing only for the occasional drink, until the sun was setting on the third day. While reading, he plotted his escape from the house, and had formulated a plan, which was admittedly horrible, but, as he reassured himself, the best he could manage.

He jumped out the window.

Landing was much less graceful than the fall, as he had no cushion, save for the grass upon which he fell. Amidst the pain in his side, he leapt to his feet and ran into the road, where he realized many others were gathered, watching the bright white speck in the sky. He paid them no attention, but simply looked at his apparent doom. Piddles came running out from the back of the house at the smell of her master. He bent down, patted her head, and waited.

"*Jack!*" Fran's voice carried throughout the whole neighborhood. "*Jack*, you *no-good* pile of—"

"Mom!" Jack called back. "Give it a rest!"

Fran kept coming. "Jack, just get back inside!"

"No, mom," he said.

"Jack!" she yelled. "Come and look what's happening on the TV!"

He was shocked, but grateful to return to the warmth of the

house. Piddles followed, and in the midst of everything that was happening, no one questioned her. His parents were huddled near the television set. He heard the voice from within:

"And here comes the object. We'll cut to live footage in a minute, but for this broadcasting station, I'm Kenneth Jameson, signing off." The television went dark, but they realized it was just an image of the night sky. And the gleam in the middle of the screen was not a reflection off the kitchen light, but of the mysterious object that everyone seemed to think would kill them all.

Jack moved to the window, trusting his eyes more than the television. But it was the same image in his night sky. He almost put his head in his hands, but for the nagging suspicion he'd miss something important in the process.

There was an explosion of light.

There was darkness.

When he awoke, he was in the middle of a meadow, nude. He slowly got up, crouching, hiding himself in the overgrown grass. There were other people in the meadow as well, also naked. He surveyed his surroundings, confused and appalled. He saw his mother and father and, behind them, the lake. The lake, the purest of shimmering blue. The silence was shocking. No vehicular sounds, no factories grinding in the distance, no music blaring loudly from the neighbor's basement, no. . .anything. A bird chirped in the distance. He couldn't believe he had not moved from where he had been. But everything was gone. All their technology, all their invasions into nature, everything had been removed, and the planet was…natural. He looked up at the moon—there were no refineries, no factories, nothing. They had been robbed.

Someone was screaming. Jack realized it was Father McGlenn. He was shouting a verse from Revelations.

> Fallen, fallen is Babylon the great!
> It has become a dwelling place of demons,
> A haunt of every foul spirit,

A haunt of every foul bird,
A haunt of every foul and hateful beast!

He took a breath, and continued.

For all the nations have drunk
Of the wine of the wrath of her fornication—

A child was crying. One man got to his feet and stood over the now-cowering McGlenn, blaring obscenities into the otherwise appalling stillness.

And as Jack looked around, his stomach grumbled. His eyes found a small hare hopping along the edge of the lake, and his first thought when he saw it was so primal it even shocked himself.

Food.

Genesis at Raradon

Lorenz Eber

Two small, crimson moons were rising over the rolling hills that formed the southern border of the Pirason Swamp. Evrae sat exhausted on a small rock ledge at the foot of the eastern cliff, overlooking the swamp. As the pale discs cleared the hills, the young moonlight reflected in shimmering patches on Evrae's black, naked body. She was lean, much too lean for a nineteen-year-old Raradon female in her prime.

She looked over her shoulder at Aradam, who was sitting, his back turned to her, on the far side of the ledge. She knew that he was furious with her. Two days ago she had persuaded him that they had to end the hunger of the clan and convinced him, against his continual warnings, to track game deep inside the predator-ridden canyon that surrounded the Pirason Swamp. By a near miracle, the two of them had managed to kill an Anjax but even though the hunt had ended victoriously just an hour ago, they were now left in a disastrous situation. While they had food, they could not eat it without attracting the dangerous, large cats. They knew they were too weak to fight the predators, but they could not regain their strength without eating. To top it all off they were far from the clan and Evrae was at a loss how to get the

Anjax back home within one day, which was the time that the Law of Raradon allowed.

The Law of Raradon seemed to be her downfall. Evrae's older uncle, Hidradekel, was the great champion of the Law, which, simply put, stated that no one could possess anything for more than one full day. Driven by his eccentric belief that everything should be accomplished by mind power instead of using the physical world, he had enforced the Law of Raradon mercilessly and punished anyone for the slightest infraction. Evrae had had many infractions and, with a smile, she admitted to herself that only very few of them were slight.

Hidradekel had branded her a juvenile troublemaker, and, were it not for her younger uncle, Girahon, she would have probably long been outcast, or worse.

Evrae suddenly felt cold. She gathered the fleeting strength of her mind and focused her thoughts on the cliff wall behind her. Gradually, the basalt began to radiate heat and warmed her body, but she still felt cold at the core.

She glanced over to the dead Anjax. If she could just stand the smell of fresh meat, she thought, the warm body of the animal would make a handy pillow for the night. While Aradam was holding first watch, she was determined to be comfortable. Her mind made up, she scooted up to the beautiful animal and rested her head in the soft hollow just below the shoulder blade.

Disturbed by the shuffling, Aradam turned around and noted in disgust that Evrae, once again, was rebelling against her Raradon upbringing. While she was not breaking the Law of Raradon by lying on the Anjax for the night, she was certainly spitting in the law's face. The intent of the law was to separate Raradons from the material world as much as possible so that they would learn to rely on the mind alone. The lives of the Ancients had proven that choosing the material world over the powers of the mind brought on a vicious cycle of relying on an ever increasing complexity of material goods which, in the end, resulted in decadence, endless wars and the destruction of civilization. The last Great War, ten generations ago, had wiped out all but a few thousand Raradons. The survivors had wisely chosen to abandon the crutch of material possessions and had begun to survive using the mind almost exclusively.

It was true, Aradam thought, that some material items, like food, were still required, but it was said that the clan elders were close to a solution to the food problem as well. Evrae's uncle, the great Hidradekel, was a true prophet who had brought advanced mind power to the clan, and they had accomplished great feats in a very short time. Diseases, which had plagued Raradon for centuries, for instance, were completely eradicated in a single season. Hidradekel himself had used his mind to travel to foreign worlds and had brought back fantastic creatures that he had collected there. Raradon was experiencing a true renaissance of mind power. The mind's potential was unlimited and the mind was the way of the future; Aradam was convinced of that.

Evrae, on the other hand, clung to the follies of the past with her attachment to the material world. She acted like one of the Ancients and, like them, she would falter. Hidradekel and the other clan elders were right, Evrae was an insubordinate trouble-maker, and he, Aradam, should never have let her persuade him to go on this fool's errand. As Aradam watched Evrae nestle her long neck into the soft fur of the Anjax, he turned away with a foul taste in his mouth and spat on the dark basalt ledge.

Evrae suddenly awoke with a fully formed plan in her mind. The moons had already set when she got up and crouched next to Aradam.

"You smell of Anjax," he said dryly.

"Aradam," she said. " I know how we can still bring the Anjax to the clan by nightfall and be heroes."

"Wow! That's a dream come true. I always wanted to be a hero," said Aradam sarcastically.

Ignoring him, Evrae continued, "The clan is actually quite close. If we did not have to trudge through the swamp, we could make it by tonight."

"So we fly then. . . like the dactyls?" Aradam needled. "I knew you'd think of something!"

"Please be serious, Aradam. When I was on top of the cliff last night and repelled the Anjax, I saw a glimpse of the other side of the canyon."

"Oh now, you want to return home on top of the cliffs. That is really clever, except that even the youngest Raradon knows that this can't be done. Remember that the chasm of the Phrae River would cut us off on this side of the swamp and the gorge of the Teras River would make our route impassable beyond the west side," he lectured.

"The Teras is not impassable anymore," said Evrae. "Not since the solstice anyway."

"What does the solstice have to do with it?"

"As even the youngest Raradon remembers," said Evrae rolling her eyes, "the great Hidradekel performed one of his ridiculous mind demonstrations at the Teras River during the winter solstice."

"That was not ridiculous. That was a master demonstration! With the power of his mind, he tore out an entire forest and flung the trunks into the gorge," Aradam spouted, obviously still impressed.

"It seems that you were so overwhelmed by this silly, wasteful feat that you didn't even notice the logs piling up in a huge jam downriver. We can use that log jam now to crawl across the gorge."

"Do you think the logs are still there? What if the river has washed them away by now?" Aradam was thinking now, Evrae mused. That was good. Unusual, but good.

"The only way to find out is to cross the swamp, climb the far cliff, trek to the Teras River and take a look," Evrae said, upbeat.

"And what if the logs are gone when we get there. . ." Aradam said uncertainly.

"Then, according to your brilliant Law of Raradon, we leave the Anjax for some large, stupid cat and follow the Teras River back home, empty-handed."

For some reason, this defeatist prognosis made up Aradam's mind. He got up, swung the Anjax over his shoulder and said, "Might as well get started. I've always wanted to dodge predators with a girl that smells like an Anjax."

The first hour of the return journey was very challenging. It was still dark and they were having a difficult time traversing the rough talus slope under the eastern cliff. After what seemed like an eternity, they finally came to the place where Evrae had seen a constriction of the canyon and they began to ford the swamp, which here was more like a lazy river. They waded, chest deep in the putrid waters, while an array of foul things floated slowly past them. Aradam was moving very swiftly and Evrae had difficulty keeping up with him. Irritably, he explained that he just wanted to make good time, but Evrae knew that, secretly, he was deathly afraid of the poisonous swamp eels that lived in places like these.

When they finally emerged on the far side of the swamp, they were covered in mud. A small ravine led out of the canyon and, as they reached the plateau on top, Aradam was in a splendid mood.

"That was fun," he exclaimed. "I wonder if this mud is good for your skin."

"No, but the Ancients used the slimy skin of swamp eels as a mask to prevent wrinkles," said Evrae matter-of-factly.

"Really?" asked Aradam, repulsed.

"Yes. Too bad we did not see any; I would like to stay looking young for you," she said jesting.

"You are kidding, right?"

"Yes, I am kidding. I just think it is pretty funny how afraid you are of swamp eels."

"I am not afraid of swamp eels," Aradam insisted.

"Well, then take care of this one for me," she said and threw him a strand of swamp weed that had stuck to her back and looked just like an eel. Aradam jumped away terrified and flayed his arms so vehemently that he dropped the Anjax. Evrae had to lean on a rock to not fall over laughing.

"That was not funny," said Aradam, annoyed.

"Yes it was," chuckled Evrae.

Elated that her plan had worked perfectly so far, she slung the Anjax over her shoulders and took off running toward the north. As Evrae had hoped, the top of the western cliff was nearly flat and they were making fabulous time, running almost effortlessly through shin-high grass.

They ran for almost two hours, when they finally grew tired

and began to walk. Near the Teras River, Aradam suddenly stopped to smell the wind. He had a very sensitive nose, which was one of the reasons Evrae preferred hunting with him. For almost a minute he sniffed, until Evrae asked tensely, "What is it?"

"I don't know, I thought I smelled something," he said, frowning. "It's probably nothing."

"Nothing. . . like in Canine Cat nothing?" Evrae prodded.

Aradam remained quiet, took the Anjax from Evrae, and began running again.

A Canine Cat was the last animal Evrae ever wanted to meet on Raradon. Canine Cats were swift, stealthy and ingeniously designed for killing. The Ancients had hunted the cat for its priceless canine teeth. The cat had four of them and each was about three inches long. The back edge of each tooth was razor sharp and usually remained hidden in sheath-like bone pockets in the beast's jaw. Through an ingenious system of muscles and tendons the cat could rotate the teeth from the sheaths into the vertical position. The teeth were so sharp, that even the cat, herself, had great respect for them and would always keep them retracted except in an all-out fight. In ancient times Canine Cat hunters were few and never very old.

Evrae was torn from her musings about Canine Cats when she suddenly stood at the rim of the Teras River Gorge. Four hundred feet below, she saw the light blue waters of the Teras, but no log jam.

"Which way?" Aradam wanted to know.

For a moment uncertain, Evrae could not decide if they should run east or west along the gorge to find the jam.

"Evrae, it's a cat. For heaven's sake, make up your mind!" yelled Aradam, near panic.

"East . . . we must go east," she said, trying to sound decisive and hoping she was right.

They ran along the gorge at breakneck speed, dodging trees that grew in the ravines that dropped down toward the Teras.

"Where are the logs, Evrae? The cat is close!" Aradam yelled.

"Around the next bend, I think," Evrae said panting.

"I knew this was going to happen. I will never listen to you again!" Aradam screamed.

"There is the jam," Evrae exclaimed.

"Thank the heavens!" said Aradam.

"I thought you weren't listening to me any more," she needled as they raced down the closest ravine toward the logs. Just before they got to the jam, they tore through a patch of vicious thorn bushes that badly cut their shins. Scrambling onto the logs, they came to a halt about a third of the way into the river.

Searching the shore and the thorn thicket for movement, Aradam said hopefully, "We should be all right now. Cats hate water, right?"

At that moment, Evrae saw a brown streak shoot out from under the jumbled logs near the middle of the river and rush toward Aradam from behind. Evrae tried to repel the cat with her mind, but realized at once that this determined predator was no match for her. In an instant, the Canine Cat was on top of the Anjax on Aradam's back and was reaching with its claws for Aradam's throat. Evrae screamed and, without a plan, scrambled toward the battle. Hand-over-hand, she pulled herself up onto the twisted logs. Just as she reached Aradam, a piece of log splintered off in her hands and she fell helplessly backward into an opening in the log jam.

She would surely have fallen through the hole into the rushing torrent if the large wood splinter in her hands had not jammed in the opening. In panic for Aradam's life, she pulled herself out of the logs and stormed back to the snarling cat. She came up behind the animal and drove the wood splinter into its neck with all her force. Blood poured from the cat's throat into the foaming water of the rushing river below. The predator's body quivered and fell off Aradam onto its side. The cat's legs twitched so violently that Evrae was afraid that the claws would shred Aradam, if he was not dead already. All at once the cat stopped moving and Evrae scrambled over to Aradam whose eyes were wide open.

"Aradam, it's over, I killed her!"

Aradam did not respond, his eyes staring blankly at Evrae.

Blood was rhythmically pulsing from a wound in his neck. Inside the wound, she could see a small cut in a finger-sized blood vessel.

Suddenly overcome with despair, she slumped onto a log next to her dying friend and started to cry. Tears flowing down her thorn-scraped legs, her gaze fell onto the dead Canine Cat, whose murderous teeth were slowly retracting into its still open jaws as rigor mortis set in. Suddenly furious, Evrae took her spear and jammed it into the cat's mouth screaming:

"Dammed, stupid cat! I hate you!" She kicked the cat and tried to withdraw her spear, which had become lodged under one of the sharp, retracting teeth. Out of control, Evrae yanked at her spear, cursing and spitting. With a snap, the cat's tooth broke from the lower jaw and clattered across a log, coming to rest on Aradam's still heaving chest. Suddenly Evrae knew what she had to do.

Instantly, she became calm and began working with speed and efficiency.

Using what little mind power she had left, she strained to temporarily close the cut in Aradam's blood vessel and ran back to the thorn thicket, where she broke off a handful of long thorns. When she returned, she used the razor sharp tooth to open the backside of the cat's front paw and extracted five small tendons. She looked over to Aradam and was glad to see him still unconscious, dreading what she knew she had to do next.

"Here we go," she said to herself and began forcing short, clean twigs into Aradam's wound to hold it open. Then she took a sharp thorn and carefully punctured the outer wall of the blood vessel in two places near the cut. Threading a paw tendon through the holes she then formed a tight double knot with her dexterous fingers. Even though it was very cool above the river, Evrae was sweating now. She repeated the process two more times and when the last knot was formed, she gradually released her mind force. To her elation, the repair held. Aradam was still alive, breathing shallowly. When she pulled the twigs from the wound and used the remaining thorns to pin his flesh back together, she said, "I can't believe you don't feel this, Aradam." And with her tears beginning to flow again, she added, "Please don't die, I am so sorry that I caused all this."

With great strain and cussing, Evrae turned the Canine Cat over and skinned a large hide of soft belly fur from the creature. She cut the hide into a number of long strips and one wider bandage, for Aradam's neck. She carefully placed the bandage, fur side inward, on Aradam's wound and secured it with strips of hide.

Noting how low the large, red Raradon star had already settled on the horizon, she knew that with the burden of Aradam, she would never make it back to the clan by nightfall. The Law of Raradon demanded that she abandon the Anjax and return home empty-handed. If Aradam had any chance at all, then he needed good nourishment. The clan had been living off tree bark tea and an occasional Manga root. Abandoning the Anjax in light of the circumstances seemed like complete lunacy to Evrae.

Her decision made, she tied the legs of the Anjax with hide and lashed it around her hips. She then wedged the canine tooth into a crack in the butt end of her spear, carefully laid Aradam over her shoulder and set out onto the logjam. Looking across the river she said, "Aradam, this is going to be a long night."

It was just before dawn when one of the clan's women shook Hidradekel awake.

"Come quickly, Prophet, your niece has returned but there has been an accident."

Hidradekel forced himself awake and found Evrae, surrounded by clan folk, sitting against a rock, gulping hot bark tea.

"What happened, Evrae?" asked Hidradekel in alarm.

"We were attacked by a Canine Cat at the Teras, and Aradam was badly wounded. He feels really hot and has been hallucinating for hours. Please do something, uncle, I am afraid he is going to die," said Evrae, pleading.

"You dragged him back, all the way from the Teras?" asked Hidradekel incredulously.

"Yes"

"Look, Prophet," said an old man. "They brought food." He pointed to the Anjax lying in the dust.

"I see that," said Hidradekel and, turning back to the man, instructed, "Cut it up and prepare food for everyone. But use the best meat to make a strong stew for Aradam and our hero, here."

Evrae knew Aradam needed the nourishment if he was to survive. She said nothing about the Anjax and just stared guiltily into her steaming tea.

Evrae's younger uncle, Girahon, arrived just as Hidradekel removed the bandage from Aradam's neck. Aradam was tossing his head and pronouncing gibberish in his delirium.

"How bad is he, brother?" asked Girahon.

When Hidradekel saw the angry, inflamed wound, pinned together with thorns, he said, "Not good." Then he added, addressing Evrae, "What happened to fusing injuries with mind power?"

"Uncle, you know I am better with my hands than with my mind. I was too weak and just couldn't do it. I had a hard enough time holding the vessel together," she said, starting to sob.

"His artery was cut?" asked Hidradekel in disbelief.

"Yes, I sewed it together with tendons from the cat," she whispered.

"How could you have?" he said angrily. "Even I can't remove the tendons now, without risking to kill him. By doing what you did, you condemned Aradam to a life defiling the Law of Raradon every day."

"So what, it's a stupid law. I couldn't just sit there and watch him bleed to death," yelled Evrae.

"You should have employed your mind! The law is not stupid. Using the material world has been proven to lead nowhere; just to destruction. Had you used your mind, the attack would have never happened," Hidradekel lectured.

"I tried to repel the cat. It did not work. Hidradekel, we are not all perfect like you. And for the record, the law is stupid." With that Evrae stormed off into the rocks surrounding the clan's encampment. Hidradekel shook his head, focused his mind and removed the cause of Aradam's fever.

Evrae collapsed, crying, in a secluded corner, but her strength had been so depleted that, after only a few minutes, she fell into a troubled sleep. When she awoke, it was complete darkness again, and two clan elders were lifting her by her arms.

"You are in big trouble," they said.

Rubbing her eyes, Evrae retorted, "What else is new?"

Evrae was brought in front of the elder council with almost the entire clan standing in a big circle, watching. To her great delight, Aradam was there too, looking much improved. As she entered, he even managed a small wave with his hand.

Hidradekel wasted no time and immediately got to the point.

"Is it true that the Anjax which fed the whole clan was killed two days ago?"

"Yes," said Evrae meekly.

"So, you knowingly made the clan defile the Law of Raradon," Hidradekel went on.

"Yes, they were all starving. Aradam was dying and we all needed food," she said defiantly. Then she added with a sting, "Food that your magnificent mind power has not provided."

Without taking the bait, Hidradekel continued angrily, "And what about this spear and canine tooth that Laradon found carefully hidden in the rocks? A souvenir, I suppose?"

He took the spear and threw it sideways at Evrae, who caught it with both her hands.

"I know I have broken the Law," she began and felt tears form in her eyes once more. "But I meant well. I meant to feed the clan and I meant to save Aradam. Things just fell apart, and I did the best I could."

"When you use the material world, things sooner or later will always fall apart. You refuse to listen to this and endanger everyone in the clan. If you had just had patience, the elders and I would have manifested food, Aradam would be unharmed and the clan would not have committed blasphemy," Hidradekel hissed.

Hurt to the core, Evrae screamed, "Fine, have it your way. Why don't you just kill me with this spear and get rid of your problem?" Tears streaming down her face, she flung the spear into the rocks behind the elders.

As the spear clattered against the rocks, everything seemed to happen in slow motion in front of her eyes. By a terrible misfortune, the flexible spear bounced off the rocks and hit Hidradekel, point first, in the back. In her frustration, she had thrown the spear so forcefully that its sharp tip now protruded out of Hidradekel's chest. She watched her uncle's eyes go blank as he fell to his knees. She heard the clan elders scream, and someone pushed her into the dust. Others rushed to Hidradekel, who, still on his knees, was grabbing the bloody spear tip with both of his hands.

"You have killed the Prophet!" someone shouted.

"She must die," said someone else.

"Kill her!" went up a cry.

Someone threw a rock.

"No," came a raspy voice and the noise of the clan suddenly subsided. "Don't kill her; I will handle that myself," said Hidradekel, as he raised himself, the spear still embedded in his chest. Once he stood, he grasped the spear tip and pulled the entire spear through his body and out of his chest. In disgust, he threw the spear next to Evrae and said, "How often do I have to tell you Raradons that the material world cannot hurt you if you choose to use your mind?" He placed his hand over the wound in this chest, and when he lifted it again, the wound had disappeared. A hush went over the crowd as he turned to Evrae.

"The Clan is right. You must die. Not for what you have done to me but for the threat you pose to the survival of Raradon. Your ancient ways are filled with folly and you shall not prevent Raradon's rebirth."

He lifted his arm over Evrae as she cowered in the dust.

"If you kill her, you must kill me also," came the weak voice of Aradam.

Aradam dropped next to Evrae into the sand and said, "She is misguided, but means well and she has saved my life."

"Move, boy! This is between the Prophet and his niece," said Hidradekel sternly.

"No!"

"Fine, you have made your choice," said Hidradekel and lifted his arm. Before anyone in the clan could move, the two bodies dissolved, like morning mist over the swamp into nothingness.

After a fitful sleep Girahon awoke very early, feeling loss, sadness and anger.

He walked out onto the plain to clear his head but, incredibly, found himself standing in a magnificent herd of about fifty Anjax. He sensed immediately that something was wrong because the animals kept grazing and did not bolt. Then he saw his brother, Hidradekel, standing on a rock, his arms raised to the sky.

"You murderer!" shouted Girahon in rage. "You are the murderer of your own niece!"

Slowly his brother turned around and pointed his arm at Girahon. As if struck by lightning, the Anjax standing in front of Girahon fell to the ground, dead. Rooted to the spot, Girahon stood until Hidradekel had walked over to him.

"These Anjax don't behave normally," said Girahon. "You did something to them, Hidradekel."

"Yes, since I have yet been unsuccessful in manifesting food directly, I had to work around the problem. Let's just say that these Anjax have a mysterious urge to graze right here, every morning. Notice anything else?" asked Hidradekel.

"No, looks like a perfectly good Anjax to me," said Girahon.

"Exactly. I killed it and it is a perfectly good, but dead, Anjax."

"And . . . " said Girahon quizzically.

"It is not a whiff of disappearing mist," said Hidradekel.

There was a pause and then Girahon burst out suddenly: "You didn't kill them last night!"

"No, I did not."

"Well I'll be . . . " said Girahon. "Where are they?"

"Do you remember when, after the solstice, I took trips to other worlds and brought back creatures to prove to the clan the awesome power of the Raradon mind?" asked Hidradekel.

"Yes, who could have forgotten that? I think that stunt even impressed Evrae," said Girahon.

"Well, I am glad, because she and Aradam are on one of those strange worlds now," said Hidradekel.

Girahon gasped. After a long while he said, "Will the two of them remember anything of Raradon?"

"No, nothing."

"What about their mind powers?"

"They have them, of course. Everyone does, but they will not remember that."

"What about their names, you didn't even leave them names?"

"Yes, I left them names. Of course, since they are outcasts now, I altered them and stripped them of their Raradon roots."

Girahon thought for a while, and then said, "Without the Raradon root, it would make their names 'Adam and Eve'." With a smile he added, "For beginning an entirely new world, the names seem a bit unimaginative to me, but I am proud of you, brother. You gave them a chance and did as well as you could by them."

Together, the brothers lifted the Anjax and carried the burden back to the clan.

AFTERNOON OF THE WORLD

VERNE WADE

Many years ago, I spent a month in Venezuela, in a suburb of Caracas, where, by invitation, I gave a series of slide-illustrated lectures on North American natural history at a small private school. Some few days after my arrival, as I sat reading in the small park next to the school, an elderly gentleman—older then than I am now—came along the path, then stopped abruptly in front of me. His quick eye had caught the title of my book. He asked politely if he could share my bench. "You find this *Green Mansions* interesting?" he asked with a nod toward my book as he eased himself onto the bench at a comfortable distance from me and placed his cane across the seat between us.

"Well, yes," I said. "Actually, I first read it years ago, when I was fifteen or sixteen. I loved the story then. Now I am a visitor in your country for a short while, and, on a whim, I brought the book with me to read again here, where the story took place."

The old man smiled. "You are still a very long way from Amazonas, the Guayana of the story, señor."

"As close as I'll ever get," I replied ruefully.

"And closer than the author ever came, at that, by almost the length of the continent."

"He had good informants, then. His descriptions of the country, the wildlife, the plants—they *are* accurate, are they not?"

"Oh, yes. I am an artist, señor, not a naturalist or a geographer, but I have been in that country. Yes, I would say that he was well informed."

Señor Salas—Arturo Salas Medina, he told me when we exchanged names later—fell into a state of reverie for some moments, and I resumed my reading.

When he stirred, and I noticed that his eyes were on my book again, I said quietly, "It must strike you as strange to find a *norteamericano* reading such an old book in your park."

"No, not at all, señor. But I have found that same book in another place where it truly did surprise me."

I slipped a marker into the crease of the book and closed it. Señor Salas smiled and began this story, sliding effortlessly from the Spanish of our conversation until now into excellent, if somewhat formal, English:

I am an artist. I paint scenes only of the city now, of this very park many times. But when I was younger, I traveled the whole of Venezuela, and occasionally beyond. Venezuela has many natural wonders, less well known to you than those of your own country, perhaps, but equally grand and scenic. It is a paradise for the artist.

Do you know the Casiquiare river, or canal as some call it, señor? It makes a connection between the headwaters of the Orinoco and the Amazon system. Hudson mentions it in your book. (I nodded, although I must admit I knew it as little more than a name.) Well, at the time of which I tell, I was on another tributary of the Orinoco near there, but to the north. I was traveling alone—perhaps unwise, but I was both poor and rash then. One evening I came to a small village which differed in one respect from the Indian villages one would expect in those parts. It had a short dock extending into the river and, back of the dock, a small building that clearly had not been constructed in the Indian manner. It turned out to be a trading post of sorts run by a man named Perez. When I questioned Señor Perez about the success of his commercial venture in that remote place, he admitted that it earned him little, but certain mineral prospectors and government men knew of it and stopped by at times. I think those visits meant more to him socially than as occasions to make money. Anyhow, the building held a very small store, no more than a few boxes of dry goods, a shelf with two or three bottles of liquor next to a table and chairs that he called a cantina, and a dark loft room where visitors could sling their hammocks. Señor Perez and his family lived in a separate dwelling behind, away from the river.

I stayed there several weeks, two weeks for which I paid for the loft and my meals, and a few weeks beyond that when my money ran out and Señor Perez insisted that I remain as his "friend and guest." He was much interested in my paintings. When I left, I gave him one of him and his family grouped on the steps and verandah in front of his store. He was much pleased with it even though I had mistakenly included two children that were not his and omitted one who was. Those children! I could never tell one from the other at first. Señor Perez was of mixed blood—a mestizo—and his wife was a comely Indian woman of generous proportions and pleasant, though quiet, disposition. Their children and those of the Indian villagers played and ate and slept wherever the mood or opportunity found them, with little regard for whose family they belonged to.

The store, though crude enough, was better built than his house, and drier, and for that reason, I suppose, he kept his small collection of books on the same shelf as the bottles of liquor in his cantina. By their variety, I assumed that they had been left behind by his visitors over the years. One, however, was his own, purchased before he ever came to Amazonas, and that was the very book that you are reading now.

I picked it up and, leafing through it, I wondered aloud if it might be the only copy of *Green Mansions* that had ever found its way so near to the country where Abel found Rima.

"You know the story, señor?" Señor Perez asked with no little excitement.

"Oh, yes," I told him. "I have my own copy at home."

That was on the second or third day of my stay with him. Only after I had been there a week or ten days and, without attempting to do so, had won his confidence, did he tell me the story of how he came to that secluded part of Guayana.

We were seated on his verandah watching the river, spattered by an afternoon rain shower. I brought up the subject of *Green Mansions* partly to make conversation, but also because I wanted to find out what he might know of the legend of the Hata flower that Hudson mentions. You will remember, only one such flower will bloom at one time anywhere in the world, and when that flower shrivels as the moon shrivels, only after that will another Hata blossom freshen in some other part of the forest as the new moon grows. He knew no more than is told in the book and had never seen the flower, if it exists. However, after some hesitation, he said, "Would you like to know how that book has influenced my life, señor? What I would tell you is perhaps not believable, but it is true nonetheless."

Of course I said, "Yes," and this is what Señor Perez told me:

I too came from Caracas, though I am not of such a distinguished family as yourself. (Here, I could imagine Señor Salas' deprecatory shrug.) As with Abel in the book, I found it expedient to leave that city, although not for political reasons. My reasons are not important now. After some years—lost years, you might call them—I bought that book, *Green Mansions* by William Henry Hudson, at a bookseller's stall in Cumaná. From that evening, my life took on a new purpose.

There was a story in my family that my grandmother on my mother's side used to tell us, of a distant ancestral lineage that had its origin in a part of Venezuela not explored at that time. We always assumed that meant Guayana. Those ancestors were people of the forest, but not like the Indians found here now. My grandmother used to point to the angels in the colored windows in the cathedral and say that those ancestors were like them, the angels. Our mother used to smile and wink at us children when grandmother made such claims. Old people often exaggerate to make what they know seem important in a world where they feel they no longer have a place. You and I must remember that when we are old, señor.

We only had our grandmother's story and no other proof of

those ancestors, so my brothers and sisters and I gave little credit to it. Even our mother did not encourage us to believe the story as long as we showed love and respect toward our grandmother.

By the time I came to the bookseller's stall in Cumaná, the story was so deeply buried in my memory that I had not thought of it for years. But then I read about Abel coming to Guayana and finding the girl so like an angel, the girl who spoke the language of birds and moved through the trees above ordinary mortals. You can understand, señor, how such a tale would come as a revelation to one in the low state I was in then, how I would read Hudson's description of the tribe of Rima and believe that he was describing the ancestors my grandmother had boasted of. Well, maybe it makes little sense to your rational mind, and to mine now, but I became greatly excited at the time and suddenly found meaning and purpose in my miserable existence. I believed that Hudson's story could not be entirely a work of fiction. I believed that he had learned of my grandmother's angels of the forest and had built his story around them—or their last survivor. *That* part, the last survivor, I convinced myself must be a fictional notion. I wanted to believe that my grandmother's people—Rima's people—must still exist in Guayana.

And so I went in search of them.

I traveled by steamboat up the Orinoco, then by canoe along its tributaries, and then, with guides, on foot overland where that was possible. I started out with my heart full of hope. But that hope was dashed almost as soon as I arrived in the land that Hudson described. Following his clues as best I could, I came to the region I thought most likely to be the home of Rima's people. And what I found was the racket of excavating machinery and stamp mills and a land devastated by men wresting gold from it.

I left that ruined place and tried to imagine where Rima's people might have fled. I found untouched forests, but, in each one, I knew somehow that the bird people would not be there. They might have passed through, but they would not have tarried. A month or more after leaving the gold fields, and some days after my guides had deserted me, the land began to rise. I was approaching the high places called tepuis, mysterious tablelands largely unexplored even today. (Here, Señor Perez' hand swept out an arc from northwest to east.) One evening I left the river again, left my small canoe, and followed what I believed to be an animal trail into an inviting glade several hundred meters from the water. The evening light was what caught my attention first—brilliant green flames of foliage high up, catching the direct rays of the setting sun, and lush dark green glowing below, just as Hudson had described Rima's forest. An easiness flowed into my tired body. I slumped to the ground and lay back against a mossy tree buttress, forgetting even to prepare my evening meal. As I relaxed, I felt at first that sleep would overtake me before I had made proper preparations for the night. But that did not happen. Instead, I became intensely aware of the forest around me, became alert, yet still peaceful in my mind.

I heard birds, a few I recognized, more that I did not. I heard stirrings in the undergrowth that rimmed the glade, but nothing that hinted at danger. And then, probably hours later when darkness was complete and I could see a star or two through breaks in the canopy overhead, I heard what I had traveled so long and arduously to hear: the bird voices that Hudson had described. Not the songs of birds, although there was more than a resemblance. What I heard was human, although the only reason I knew that to be so was because I caught hints of meaning in the trills and warbles. A question was being asked. Perhaps, "Who are you?" or "Why are you here?"

"I'm Ramón Perez. I came here to find you."

The voice stopped when I spoke, then began the inquisition again, seemingly the same questions, so I thought I had misunderstood their meaning the first time.

"I came to find the people of Rima."

At the mention of that name, there was a flurry of bird-talk, not just my inquisitor, but others of her kind in the trees and bushes round about. I thought I could make out the syllables Ri-ma in their song-speech, but I wasn't sure. I stood and said, "Rima. Rima's people. Are you Rima's people?"

The voices fell silent and stayed that way. I listened for the sounds of movements but heard nothing to tell me whether they had come closer or had deserted me. Finally I sat down and waited. Perhaps I slept, my head against the mossy root and my pack under my drawn-up knees; I'm not sure. But, after a long while, my attention was caught—or I was awakened—by a dawn chorus of birds and animals. The brief tropical dawn gave way to daylight and a repeat of the sight that had welcomed me the evening before: green flames above, a jewel-like green glow below. And, finally, the bird-voice again.

"Good morning," it sang. Not in those words, but I understood their intent.

"Yes, good morning," I answered. I thought I might be able to whistle my reply, copying the sounds I had heard, but knew instantly that I had no command of such music.

I made motions toward me with my arms and begged, "Come out, come out. Let me see you."

The response was a teasing laughter, all in bird-song, but no one came forth.

The voice was from a single person again, the one who had first spoken to me the evening before, I believed, and a young girl, I thought. But she did not reveal herself, not then or during that whole day and the next, although we conversed at length. I told her what I had learned about Rima from Hudson's book, and I gathered from her responses, some serious, some mocking, where Hudson had spoken truly of what he had learned about Guayana, and what he made up. By the end of the second day, I was sure that I understood the rudiments of her speech. I was certain, too, that I was under her spell and, if I could only see her, would very likely find myself in love.

Then, during a pause in our discourse, a little brown bird, a drab little thing compared to the other brilliant birds of our forests, hopped onto a branch that protruded from a shrub close at hand. Another of its kind joined it. You can imagine my shock and despair, señor, when from those tiny throats burst forth the same music that I had been hearing as language for two whole days. They, indeed, sang to one another in a way that conveyed meaning, but the language was that of bird-song only, and the meaning of significance only to their tiny minds.

After that disappointment, I continued my search in a desultory fashion for only a few more weeks before settling down here, on the riverbank, to live out my days away from cities and without illusions.

Señor Perez had told his story without interruption from me, but now I commented, "Some would say you have an ideal life. You are happily married. You have children. You have enough to feed them. Are you not happy?"

"Oh, yes, as happy as a man can . . . Yes, I am happy."

"Your wife—is she a local woman?"

"Yes. Not from this village, but from nearby, I think. A little bit of a mystery herself. She claims to be from no village—none that the people here know of, anyhow. And she was dropped off at my pier from one of two canoes traveling downstream in great haste, with no explanation from them or from her. Well, no *real* explanation. She said that they were bad men who had captured her and then wanted to be rid of her. But I can't imagine how that would be. She is not a woman that anyone would want to be rid of. But—no matter—we met that way. We soon married, and I am a happy man."

With that, Señor Perez drank the last of his maté, shook a few drops from his mug—a gourd—onto the ground beside the verandah, and left me sitting alone.

On the afternoon of the last full day I spent as Señor Perez' guest, I took myself nearly a kilometer upriver to a pool I had found where I could bathe and clean myself undisturbed. I had no more than begun to remove my shirt when I was surprised by a child's voice calling to me from the pool, "Caiman, señor. Do not come in."

I peered across the pool, saw the child standing in the water up to her shoulders and, a short distance from her, a full-grown caiman. Several others drifted just beyond.

"Don't move," I said quietly. "I'll get a branch to frighten the caiman away. Then I'll get you out."

She laughed, a delightful little bell sound. "Be still yourself, señor. Don't move. I'll come out."

And she did, with no threatening move by the caiman at all.

Modestly, she hid her nakedness by keeping a bush between me and her.

"You are not afraid of the caiman?" I said incredulously.

"The caiman thinks I am a caiman too. There is nothing to fear."

Then her eyes caught something crawling on the neckband of my unbuttoned shirt. She quickly came to me and plucked off a two- or three-centimeter long ant—the fearsome 'twenty-four hour ant' whose bite causes fierce pain and a one-day fever.

"*Veinticuatros* doesn't think *you* are a *veinticuatros*, though. He would bite you."

She said this as she released her fingers and allowed the ant to crawl up her arm to her elbow, then drop off. I was astonished at her behavior, but more astonished at her appearance. As she moved through the sun-dappled space by the pool, I saw colors that I had not noticed before. At a distance, even the little distance when she first came out of the pool, she was as dark-skinned as any of the other children, though with hair less coarse, but close up and when she passed from shade to sunlight, her skin showed a pearliness. Her flat little chest—she was no more than nine or ten—caught a ray of sun and gleamed a coruscating red, like a hummingbird, but only for the instant she moved through the sunbeam. Remembering Hudson's description of Rima, I put my hand under her chin and tilted her face up to mine so I could examine her eyes. She quickly caught my intention and moved away, looking down to the ground, saying, " You mustn't look at me so closely, señor." But I had seen the ruddy glow that underlay her dark irises.

"You are Señor Perez' daughter, are you not?" I asked.

"Yes, señor. But don't tell him what you have seen."

"You without your clothes? But why would he mind? All the children run about without their clothes. Even children as old as you when it rains hard."

"Other children. Not me. But I mean, don't tell him . . . what you have seen."

At some confusion, then and even now, whether it was the child's father who wanted no stranger to know how his daughter differed from her playmates, or whether she and her mother had somehow contrived to keep her unique features a secret from *him*, I said, "Your father has seen you; he has noticed what I have seen, has he not?"

"Maybe. I don't know. He's seen *this*," she said, touching a small dark mark, roughly star-shaped, on her left wrist. "He calls me 'Estrellita' because of it."

"But you are Maria."

"Yes, but Estrellita sometimes to him."

"And your brothers and sisters—are they like you?" I asked, raising my hand to her chest.

She quickly brought her own hands up to cover her chest before I could touch it.

"No," she said. "Only me. My mother says only me in her family for a long, long time."

She was becoming agitated under my questioning, and a bit fearful, so I said gently, "I won't tell your father."

"Or anybody else, señor. Please."

"No one. I will tell no one."

She relaxed then. She found her dress and shrugged into it head-first. We talked awhile, mostly me answering her questions about places I had been. She had been nowhere farther than a few kilometers from her village.

Arturo Salas paused for so long that I was prompted to ask, "And what else? Did she tell you anything about herself? About her mother's people?"

"No. I could not think what I should ask without upsetting her, perhaps frightening her away. I just enjoyed her company, enjoyed watching her until she got up quite suddenly and melted into the forest, finding her way back to the village by some route I did not know and could not see. And the next day I left."

"And never saw her again?"

"Oh, yes. I saw her again, maybe a decade later."

This was said with such sadness that I feared Señor Salas had found her dead. After a long minute, he sighed heavily and resumed his account:

I was in Bolivar—Ciudad Bolivar on the Orinoco, you know. I was there on a commission to paint the home and family of a local merchant. I was to meet him at his home on a certain evening, and I arrived in Bolivar in the morning. Fatigued from the journey, I found a cantina near the pier where I could buy a meal and sit quietly for several hours with only a single glass of wine before me. I saw her then, some time after I had finished my meal. She was seated on a stool at the bar, talking with the barman. I don't know what first drew my attention to her, she was so changed. Maybe it was her hair—fine-spun and unbound, a dark nimbus about her head and shoulders. But as for the rest . . . her skirt was tight and short, her blouse loose and open far down the front. A beautiful woman, yes, but not the woman I had expected her to become at all. Nonetheless, I went across to her, noted the star-mark on her wrist, and said her name, "Maria? Maria Perez?"

She looked up at me pertly. "I'm Estrella here," she said, but, apparently mistaken about where she was to remember me from, she added, "I'm taken for tonight, señor. If I'm lucky, I'm taken for many nights to come." She turned on her stool to the barman and said with a wink, "A rich patron tonight. I will have to cultivate his interest."

To ensure that *I* was not mistaken in my assumption who she was, I asked, "Your father, Ramón Perez—how is he now? Has he moved to the city?"

She seemed taken aback for a moment, then said, "No, señor. I think he is still where he has always been. I do not hear of him any more."

"Your mother?"

"I don't know. Excuse me, señor. You are asking questions that are painful to me."

I apologized and backed away.

Later that afternoon, I was walking up one of the steep streets from the riverfront and paused to catch my breath. As I turned to look back the way I had come, my eye was drawn to some two- and three-story buildings across the street, wonderful old buildings that I then saw extended in a row for several blocks up and down the street. I marveled that I had not noticed them before. Stone buildings with sunken doorways, pillared brick buildings, painted window casings, a few balconies with pots of flowers, varnished doors, some walls plastered in bright colors, orange roof tiles where I could see the roofs, and the tops of huge trees behind the lower buildings; what would be a . . . a *cacofonia*—is that a word in English?—of forms and textures and colors in the full light of noon, but now, washed in the slanting rays of the late afternoon sun, a tranquil symphony of golden hues. I stood there a long while. Maybe an artist is moved by such things more than others, señor. The calm light, the stillness, the empty street, not a soul or vehicle in sight, even the birds were subdued. I felt as if the whole world had paused to become still and beautiful and nothing else for an enchanted hour. I wondered if I or any other artist could capture what I felt just then so that others would know it too.

And then I saw two figures far down the hill coming up on the other side of the street from me. I stepped back into a doorway because I was not yet ready to resume my climb and hoped that the couple would turn off into a side street and that the spell I was under would not be broken. But they came on, oblivious to everything but each other. The man was some years younger than I am now, well dressed, a full head of gray hair, distinguished in appearance as a wealthy business man or a politician would be. And, on his arm, her smile practiced and radiant, her eyes avid and bright, was Maria Perez . . . Estrella. The sunlight that was soft and glowing on the buildings bathed them also. It muted the brilliant colors of the jacket she now wore, yet brightened the ruffle of her blouse. Her shoes gleamed softly. I thought that she and her patron should be in my picture too. Her hair—pure black, pulled back now and held with a comb behind—I would touch with the hints of color I had seen when she was a child. When she turned toward her lover, her loosened blouse revealed the smooth brown skin you would expect to see on any lovely girl of her age. I might add a glint of ruby there, and perhaps to the eyes, if I could do it subtly. I sighed when they had passed beyond me, a worldly gentleman and a beautiful girl, a rather ordinary beautiful girl.

And that was the last time I saw her.

"Did you ever paint the picture?" I asked.

"Not yet. Not yet," Señor Salas said, drawing in a breath and straightening his back as old men do when they have sat overlong on a hard bench. "But I have taken too much of your time with old stories, señor. I thank you for your indulgence and wish you a pleasant stay in our city."

He picked up his cane and regained his feet somewhat stiffly. He gave me a brief bow, but, by the time I stood to return his salute, he had turned away and was walking down the path.

Now I have been to Caracas again. While there, I thought of Señor Salas, but he was not listed in any directory. A docent at the National Gallery of Art gave me the name of a small gallery that she thought might carry his work. The owner of that gallery, indeed, knew of Arturo Salas Medina but, sadly, informed me that he has been dead for some years. The owner had bought all of the paintings left in Señor Salas' small studio at the sale of his estate. He offered to show them to me. They were of an old style not much favored by the art-buying public now, he explained. I soon found the painting I had hoped to see. It was unfinished, but I recognized it immediately. The old buildings were rendered beautifully. Oddly, for an unfinished painting, he had signed it and even written a title for it above his signature and a date below. The title was *Afternoon of the World*, and the date was the same year he and I had shared a park bench. The unfinished part was the couple. The man I could recognize from the description Señor Salas had given me: gray hair, well dressed, but not sketched in completely enough to show the mature urbanity Señor Salas had hinted at. And the girl—little more than the shoes and the merest outline to show the position she would occupy in the finished work. The gallery owner's eyebrows lifted when I met his price without a quibble. He hastened to show me the several dozen other Salas works he had, but I could see none that related to the story Señor Salas had told me. None of the park where we had talked, no self-portrait, and not one that I could believe showed Señor Perez' village.

Afternoon of the World hangs on the wall of my den where the light of late summer afternoons often streams through the window, reflects off the polished floor onto the wall, and brings the picture to life. At some of those times, I see the figure of the man more dimly, and even the buildings seem to blur, and a small, serious forest-child fills the space Señor Salas has left for her. ❧

THE AUTHORS

FRANK E. ANDERSON began writing fiction while ferry commuting between Bainbridge Island and Seattle. "Motionpixils" is his second published story. His day job is as a general contractor but he is also involved in digital photography, custom design and fabrication.

BILL BRANLEY is a local author and jazz musician who moved to Bainbridge Island with his wife and two children in 2004. His essays have appeared in the *Seattle Post-Intelligencer* and the *Bainbridge Island Review* and he is the author of the serialized novel *Peggy Finds A Friend*. Bill is a native of New Orleans, which is the setting for his short story "J" included in this volume.

NANCY LOU CANYON's art and words are published in *Sacred Waters, Her Mark Datebooks, Bainbridge Island Poetry Corners,* Kelli Russell Agodon's *Small Knots,* and more. As she spins her third novel, *Celia's Heaven,* she ushers in planetary events in her studio on Puget Sound's shipping lanes, and contra dances in Bellingham.

KALEENA FRAGA is a freshman at Bainbridge High School. "I've always loved to write. Every since I was little I took great delight in making up stories, characters and plots; creating my own worlds. I'd like to thank my family and friends for their continuous support. I'm honored to be a part of this anthology."

LORENZ EBER: "Since grade school in the1970's, I have been the showcase for dyslexia. Most of my teachers urged me to take up engineering and write only under threat of death. One teacher, however, said: "Just write; never mind the spelling. When you grow up you'll have a good secretary." How right she was—My secretary's name is Microsoft Spellchecker."

PAUL HANSON, a bookseller since 1989, manages the proudly independent Eagle Harbor Book Company. In this role, he enjoys nurturing both readers and writers by participating in all the stages in the life of a book; from writing and publishing, through the SFWC, to discussing books with the Eagle Harbor Readers Circle, and everything in between.

NICK HEINLEIN came to the SFWC from Chicago, Illinois in 2003. He enjoys reading and writing science fiction and attends Bainbridge High School, currently in his sophomore year. His first published story, "Freedom," was in SFWC's first collection, *Off The Ecliptic*.

 PATRICIA LEWIS has had a life long love affair with words. She lives in Bremerton, WA with her husband of 31 years, their daughter and son, 2 cats, a dog, a ferret and the ghost of her black cat Bear.

Poet, dreamer, and aspiring novelist, DANIEL MONK also does three-dimensional shaping for a Bainbridge naval architect. He is one of the founders of the SFWC, and also has contributed to the *Allegheny Review*, the Pacific Northwest Writer's Conference, and to literary publications around the Puget Sound.

CLARENCE MORIWAKI is a former carnivore who loves good movies,  jazz, pizza, microbrews and liberal politics. An aide to Congressman Jay Inslee, Clarence also worked for three Seattle radio stations and served as spokesperson for the Clinton Administration, Gov. Mike Lowry, Washington State Senate, Portland Rose Festival and Sound Transit.

VICKI SAUNDERS has always found the written word to be a beguiling, if slippery, companion. She loves sharing words with the tolerant and creative people of the SFWC. She also practices child-rearing, graphic design, editing, and widget production.

VERNE WADE taught physics and photography at Bainbridge High School until his retirement some years ago. His writing has been influenced by the few years he spent as a merchant seaman in the 1940's and by his admittedly old-fashioned tastes in the stories he reads.

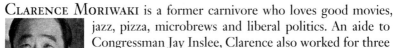

CHARLES WALBRIDGE is a biologist. He follows the news about microalgae the way some other people follow the news about sports teams. Having retired and moved from northern Minnesota to the Pacific Northwest, he considers where he lives in Puget Sound to be the remotest island in the Hawaiian archipelago.

CHRISTINE WYATT: "For most of the twenty-five years I've lived on Bainbridge, I've hopped the Sound to work with kids at Seattle juvenile court. The superheated, superquiet upper lounge on the ferry provides just the buffer of calm I require to hatch the occasional yarn."

Notes on the Unnatural History
of the Winged Salamander

Winged salamanders belong to family of the Pacific Giant Salamanders *(Dicamptodontidae)*. Commonly known as the "Bluebird Salamander," *Dicamptodon daedalus's* defining characteristic is the feathered, wing-like protrusions which develop from the feathery external gills of the larval stage. These closely resemble bluebird wings.

The salamander on the cover is a mature male *Dicamptodon daedalus*. One of the few feathered amphibia known, its range is limited to the forested and maritime regions of the Puget Sound region of the Pacific Northwest. It is apparently related to several similar Central American salamanders; *Quetzalcoatlis* spp. These may be the source of the winged serpent images in Mayan iconography.

Nocturnal, they prefer moist, dark holes in driftwood, damp, brushy areas, or the inner limbs of forest trees.

The aquatic larvae metamorphose into a juvenile form, the blue eft, migrate to the nearest sandy beach, and over a 24-hour period,extend and dry their wings. They are extremely vulnerable to predation at this time.

Mature bluebird salamanders are fully aerial with robust bodies, wings, and limbs, broad heads, and laterally flattened tails. Lungs are well-developed. Adults are herbivores: diet includes fungi (from which they derive defensive skin excretions) and epiphytes.

Various defensive behaviors have been observed, including wing-flashing, flying, biting and the production of noxious secretions from skin glands. The salamander may also tuck its head under its tail, forming a coil, or engage in body flipping. Adult winged salamanders are allusive and difficult to capture, due to their exceptional slipperiness on land, in the water and in the air.

A tea made from the eft's shed skin and feathers is used on Bainbridge Island as a treatment for illiteracy.

Regional biologists are concerned about the impact of human development on salamander habitat: populations are in decline, and the species was listed as 'endangered' in 2005.

Fossil specimens have been found as far back as the Paleocene in the Northwest, rarely, with feather imprints intact. 🐾